D1648893

WE'LL NEVER TELL THEM

Fiorella De Maria

We'll Never Tell Them

A Novel

IGNATIUS PRESS   SAN FRANCISCO

Cover photo from Panoramastock.com

Cover design by Riz Boncan Marsella

© 2015 by Ignatius Press, San Francisco
All rights reserved
ISBN 978-1-62164-061-5
Library of Congress Control Number 2014949940
Printed in the United States of America ∞

This book is dedicated to the staff of Saint Joseph's Hospital, Jerusalem, with my heartfelt thanks, and to the generation of women who lost their sweethearts and then their sons in two of the bloodiest conflicts in human history.

The characters and stories included in this book are fictional. However, I have drawn closely upon the written accounts of those who witnessed events that are now passing out of living memory.

And when they ask us, how dangerous it was,
Oh, we'll never tell them, no, we'll never tell them:
We spent our pay in some café,
And fought wild women night and day,
'Twas the cushiest job we ever had.

And when they ask us, and they're certainly going to ask us,
The reason why we didn't win the Croix de Guerre,
Oh, we'll never tell them, oh, we'll never tell them
There was a front, but damned if we knew where.

—First World War soldier song

PROLOGUE

She had been to this place before. That was why, in her darkest hour, Kristjana had returned; she remembered the city from some far away dream of happier times and had come searching for it as though it were still to be found. She had not felt lost the last time she had stepped through Damascus Gate and walked among the hot, narrow, noisy streets of old Jerusalem, or if she had, she had not cared then. At eighteen years old, everything—even loneliness—had felt like an adventure. The space of a few short years could change everything, and Kristjana told herself that she might as well be an old woman, walking cautiously down the stone steps to a crypt where she felt more at home than among the jostle of the living.

She found the place she had sat on her last journey, partially hidden by a wall of smooth rock. It sheltered her from the gaze of anyone else who might wander round, and it was close to the tabernacle and the glow of the sanctuary lamp. When she had sat there as a gap year traveller, her head had still been full of the literary classics she was cramming for university, and she had thought in a pretentious moment that it would be a good idea to do what Sebastian Flyte had suggested in *Brideshead*: leave something precious in that place so that if life did not turn out as she had so hopefully planned it, she could return again and find the object. That way she could remember for a moment what it had felt like to be young and free and contented.

Kristjana was still young, though she had never been truly contented with life and was certainly not free. She was Scheherazade, a woman with a story to tell or to discover, whose only weapon to evade death was to be found in the weaving of stories. And somewhere in amongst all those mysterious threads of memory and make-believe, she thought she could discover a powerful enough reason to stay alive. Kristjana knew that if she stepped outside into the heat she had so recently escaped, she would find a stone pool where long ago a blind man was sent to wash the mud from his eyes and saw the world for the first time. That was why they all came, the tourists and the pilgrims in their orange baseball caps, visitors by the air-conditioned coach load. They were all explorers of a kind, hoping that in this most sacred and most divided of cities they might find the world and all its meaning in a blaze of overpowering light.

Kristjana was not like them, she was not an explorer by nature. If she was anything, she was a deserter hoping to hide among this forest of humanity—and where better for a refugee than a land of refugees? She was not even sure what she was running from, but in that worst year of her entire life she felt desperately frightened, not of the past, the place from which most people run, but of the future and what might be in store for her.

When I dipt into the future far as human eye could see;
Saw the Vision of the world, and all the wonder that would be.

It was never easy to know where to start any tale. That was why writers and storytellers relied on formulas to get the narrative moving: "Once upon a time", "In the middle of the journey of my life", "Tell me, Muse". Kristjana's story began with the words of Tennyson: "When I dipt into the future far as human eye could see". That was how she had come to find herself hundreds and hundreds of miles away from home, sitting in ponderous silence. That was how it had started, far away in London, the city she called home, when she had looked into the future and seen nothing. *Nothing*, the sum of all human fears. She had convinced herself that she had no future, that there was nothing to look forward to, nothing to work for, and it was in that bleak, bewildered frame of mind that she had committed the craziest act of her entire life.

I

I

There is a little part of every person that dreams of doing this, but most adults are too rational and too anchored by life to contemplate actually going through with it. All Kristjana could say in her defence once she had carried out her plan—if it truly had been a plan—was that she had not been entirely in possession of her mental faculties at the time or she would never have done such a thing. When she had woken up that morning, she had had no intention of doing anything other than going through the same routine followed by millions of others at the start of the day—washing, dressing, making the bed—but instead of donning her black trouser suit and man-frightener high heels, she had found herself dressing in jeans and a T-shirt. Before she knew it, she had walked past her briefcase sitting squat and reliable near the door and began to pack her travel-worn rucksack with changes of clothing and a few bits and pieces she might need if she were away from home for any length of time. She transferred her purse, phone and passport to a small red handbag that was light and easy to carry, then stepped out of her room without a glance over her shoulder. After that, it all seemed so easy. She just walked away.

Earth has not anything to show more fair.

Nothing could touch her anymore. Not the crowds of commuters, not the buses and taxis and the jungle of office blocks. She had told Benedict once that for people like her, to be at home could never be a comforting feeling, but she was not at home any longer. She was back in the hinterland of her childhood, watching the antics of a tribe she did not understand, and she was content to stay there in that in-between, "not quite" world with no identifying marks or familiar places of its own, except for the holes and empty spaces where those landmarks should have been.

Kristjana came to a halt on the crest of a footbridge in the middle of Saint James' Park. She leaned against the railing and watched the river traffic passing below, her mobile phone poised in one hand as she puzzled over what message to send. In the end, she simply wrote: "Have gone 4 a short holiday. Don't worry about me. Need to clear head. Bye." Then she wondered to whom she should send it and realised there was no one. Her landlady would notice eventually that she had not seen her lodger for a few days; her boss would try to contact her when she did not turn up for work; Benedict was thousands of miles away in a lab in Massachusetts. Friends, well they could never be trusted to notice anything when it came to it. So she deleted the text message and wrote instead: "I resign."

Kristjana sent the message to her line manager's mobile number; then—to the astonishment of several passersby—she dropped her phone into the river with barely a ripple breaking the surface of the water, and walked away in the direction of Saint James' Park tube station and the westbound District Line. By the time she had changed trains and was speeding down the Piccadilly Line to Heathrow, she was certain of her destination. She was going to the farthest point from London she had ever ventured, a country to which the citizens of the world are drawn but where no one could be truly at home. It was indeed the perfect destination for Kristjana Falzon.

2

Last night I lay a-sleeping
There came a dream so fair,
I stood in old Jerusalem
Beside the temple there.

Kristjana left her hiding place and made the hot, exhausting journey up the Neblus Road. It was a week now since she had bought
a ticket to Tel Aviv from an airport travel agent—a round-trip to
make it look as though she honestly intended to return after three
months in accordance with the entry requirements—and made her
way in the back of a dilapidated taxi to the convent hospital in East
Jerusalem where she had worked as a gap year student. If the staff
and sisters were astonished to see her, they did not express it, in this
Don't-Ask-Don't-Tell world where minding one's own business
was a most sacred virtue. Hanna, the hospital receptionist, found her
a room in the nurses' accommodation; Maryam in the laundry dug
out a white starched tunic long and narrow enough to fit her; and
she was put to work on the wards.

She knew the hospital well, and none of it had changed in the
four years that had passed: the teeming L-shaped wards, the intensive
care unit, the outpatient clinic on the ground floor and beyond it
the operating theatre, the laboratory and the X-ray department; the
veranda where doctors and patients congregated to smoke; the chapel
with its pink and cream walls like those of an enormous fairy cake.
Everything about the hospital felt a little tired; written into every
corner were clues of the struggle to care for the poorest people, many
of them refugees. Kristjana was in the act of transporting an elderly
woman to her bed, in a wheelchair mended in many places with bits
of sticking plaster, when Sameer came after her, calling her name.

"Bernadette wants to speak to you," he said, slipping ahead to
open the door for her. "Nothing to worry about."

"There's always something to worry about, *habibi*."

Bernadette, the Filipina matron in charge of the long-term patients, sat in the nurses' room wrapping a dressing set. "Look at this," she complained, as soon as Kristjana appeared. "A nurse uses a dressing set and just dumps it for someone else to find, then I have to take it to be sterilised. Next day she'll come running to me moaning that she can't find a sterile dressing set and has to have one this minute."

"Can I help?"

"Won't be a minute. By the way, would you like dinner some time?"

"I'd love that. Thank you." Kristjana was in no mood for company, but she liked Bernadette and her family. Bernadette had lived in Jerusalem since childhood and spoke fluent Arabic, English and Hebrew; the flat she shared with her husband and four children was a glorious meeting of worlds where Palestinian embroidery hung next to crucifixes and icons of the Madonna. From her gap year Kristjana had fond memories of sitting on Bernadette's sofa, resting her feet on a Persian rug, drinking Turkish coffee and listening whilst Bernadette talked on the phone in Hebrew, ordered her children to be quiet in Tagalog and then settled down to watch an American soap opera.

The dressing set was ready. "How would you like a different job?" Bernadette asked.

"Has Munira been complaining about me again?"

"Oh yes," Bernadette chuckled. "Every hour since you arrived. Don't take it personally, she's pathologically depressed."

"Yes, I'd noticed."

"There was an elderly Englishman brought in a couple of days ago for surgery."

"What for?"

"Cancer. Quite advanced. When they opened him up they found the situation worse than they'd thought. He's got weeks at the most."

"Do we do palliative care here?"

"Not normally; he should really go to another hospital but he doesn't want to be moved. We've given him a room on his own and I am arranging his care. That's where you come in."

"I'm not qualified to do anything."

"It's all right, sweetie, I'm not asking you to do anything complicated. I'll be overseeing his medical care with Dr Nasser. He needs help washing and dressing. He needs company. I noticed on his notes that he is half-Maltese, half-English and thought of you. Well, it's rather providential don't you think?"

"Not really, we Maltese pop up everywhere—like weeds."

She giggled. "No way, that's our job. You will do it, won't you? It's not nice to die far away from home."

A cry from the heart. Kristjana was aware of the two of them standing together, a Filipina nurse and a British Maltese misfit, in a country to which neither of them belonged, discussing the care of a patient who, like them, had found himself washed up in an alien land like driftwood. Kristjana looked at his medical notes. Leo Hampton; date of birth, 10 November 1916; place of birth, London; ethnic origin, English/Maltese; previous places of residence, London, Jeddah, Amman, Valletta; religion, Roman Catholic.

The mention of Valletta warmed Kristjana to him immediately. He had lived once in her mother's city, in some house in that jungle of steeply sloping streets; a house with a covered, painted wooden balcony and a front entrance with heavy double doors, one of them always slightly ajar. From just the word "Valletta", she could even imagine herself walking around the house where he might have lived—treading the patterned tiles on the floor, smelling the aroma of coffee percolating early in the morning and of mince and onions frying; seeing the icons and the paintings crowding every white-washed wall.

"I thought you wouldn't mind," said Bernadette, filling a plastic basin with warm, soapy water. "Get a flannel and a towel out of that cupboard, will you?"

Kristjana still felt a certain girlish embarrassment at the idea of undressing a man, and she had stern, silent words with herself on her way into room 37, commanding herself not to blush or to show any awkwardness. They stepped into the stuffy room and saw an elderly man lying in a bed, looking at them with the intense interest that comes from having been alone too long. "Good morning," chirped Bernadette cheerily. "Time for a bath. Look, I've brought you a nice Maltese girl to look after you."

Kristjana gulped with embarrassment, thinking that Bernadette had sounded more like a madam approaching a new client than a matron. She distracted herself by thinking of the poor man watching them, who evidently wished he was almost anywhere else. His sense of mortification was palpable. As Kristjana carefully rubbed the wet flannel across his skeletal body, she felt the muscles beneath his pallid skin tightening with the discomfort of being so exposed before two women. Even the muscles of his face were taut, his teeth clenched together, eyes tight shut.

"I'm so sorry," she said. "Are you in pain?"

"No," came the strangled response, "I'm sorry. I don't mean to make a fuss."

"Please don't apologise. We're nearly finished."

They dried him and dressed him in a clean hospital gown, then Bernadette gathered up the bathing things and slipped out of the room. Kristjana looked over her shoulder at the woman's retreating back and longed to follow her away from this oppressive room and the intense gaze of a man who seemed to be trying to figure her out. She could hear the tick of the wall clock announcing the passing seconds and cleared her throat awkwardly. "My name is Kristjana Falzon, Mr Hampton."

He smiled, continuing to look intently at her. "A good Maltese name for a good Maltese girl."

"Not very good I'm afraid, and I grew up in England."

"Me too, my father was English," he explained in the polished, rounded vowels of 1930s BBC English. "You look a little like my mother did when she was young. She was a good Maltese girl too."

He chuckled, giving Kristjana the sense that there was a mischievous person in that frail body desperate to come out. "She never thought she was very good either. Her name sounded a bit like yours. Liljana."

"That's funny, I have an aunt called Liljana, but I suppose there are lots of women with that name." *I have made my first mistake*, thought Kristjana, *I should have let him continue talking, not interrupted his thoughts by talking rubbish.* "Did ... did she meet her husband in England?"

He laughed again, a tired, wistful laugh that time. "No, there were plenty of Englishmen in Malta back then."

If Kristjana could not have placed his background any other way, the deferential tone he used as he talked about his mother, the fact that she was the first person he thought to tell her about—the veneration of the mother figure—was so quintessentially Maltese. Like any child of that nation of storytellers, he was trying to tell her a story. Kristjana recalled the name she had given herself shortly after her arrival here, Scheherazade, and thought that perhaps it really belonged to Leo, a terminally ill man with nothing to fend off the encroachment of death except his own story, which began with a person called Liljana, who never thought herself a very good girl.

"Why don't you tell me about her?" she asked, settling herself into the easy chair at his side. She had never found it easy to listen, but anything was better than having a stilted conversation with a man who clearly realised that she had been sent to distract his attention.

The corners of Leo's mouth twitched but he said nothing. It was impossible not to notice how lined his face was, not just with age but with the stress of staying alive. Kristjana suspected that he had been seriously ill for months before his diagnosis, but like so many men he had probably ignored the telltale signs as though failing to see a doctor would make it go away. He had the face of a man who had suppressed pain for a long time and was still a little fearful of its return. "I'm sure you'd rather tell me about your family," he said. "You must miss them."

"Oh no, it's not really like that."

He glanced searchingly in Kristjana's direction, and she was aware again that she was being scrutinised. "So it's like that, is it?" he asked with unmistakable irony. "You are a runaway. Well, I suppose I had better distract *you* with a story then. It's not nice to live far away from home."

She blushed deeply, the humiliated do-gooder about to be ministered to in her loneliness by a terminally ill man who still had the energy to resent being patronised. "A story would be perfect, thanks," she said.

3

Liljana Camilleri walked down the street with the strident tread of a child hardened to life's many battles. She would not have looked very different—superficially at least—from any other schoolgirl of her time. Her appearance was formal, quite attractive and obviously very uncomfortable; from time to time her fingers strayed to the inside of her collar, where the lace trim was prickling her throat like a necklace of thistles. Her straw hat had slipped to an ungainly angle, possibly caused by the weight of her hair, but there was nothing jaunty about her demeanour at all. She marched along that steeply sloping Valletta street, glancing over the wide limestone steps like a cross-country runner contending with so many tiresome obstacles, head down, gloved fists clenched in front of her.

The popular imagination, with its fickle memory ever clouded by hindsight, would record these short years as a glorious time of innocence and peace for Malta, for Britain and for much of the Western world. The Old Queen had not been in her grave a decade, and it was still impossible to imagine the wars, riots and struggles for independence that would mark a century only just in its infancy. But not for Liljana, who in her nearly ten years of life had never once known the meaning of the word "peace". Or "family" or "welcome" or "friendship". If she walked quickly and determinedly enough, she could be sure that no one would challenge her or get in her way. By keeping her head down and staring fixedly at the shiny limestone she stamped on as though it had done her a personal injury, she could avoid the horror of being spoken to or even looked at.

Liljana knew from bitter experience that nobody would ever speak to her for a good reason. In a country whose culture was so famous for its hospitality and close-knit family networks, Liljana had only her mother for company, and most of the time she would rather have been completely alone. It was thanks to her mother—and it was hardly the poor woman's fault—that no member of Liljana's substantial extended family had spoken to either of them or invited them into their homes since Liljana's infancy. Their isolation from the happy realms of family and friendship was not just an unfortunate consequence of her mother's lack of a wedding ring or her mother's stubborn refusal to name the father of her bastard child. Liljana had other, more distressing troubles to contend with than even the absence of a father.

Her mother had been angry with her that morning when she had come downstairs in the desperate hope she might be given some breakfast before hurrying to school. It was not unusual for her mother to be angry, and there had been months when every day had begun with some explosion of rage necessitating a swift exit from the house, but today had felt a little worse than normal. Liljana had stepped into the kitchen to see her mother standing with her back to her, poring over Liljana's slate which was covered with the prep she had completed the previous evening. That she failed to turn round when she heard her daughter entering the room was an ill omen in itself, but from where Liljana stood she could just make out the sharp profile of her mother's jawline and the taut muscles stretched across her thin face from clenching her teeth. A second later, the woman wheeled round and gave her the full benefit of her thunderous expression.

"The answer to the third sum is fourteen not thirteen," she said quietly, "*fourteen*, do you understand?"

Liljana felt her heart sinking. "I'm sorry ... let me—"

"You really are a stupid little girl," her mother added as hushed as ever, but Liljana knew her mother's voice and braced for what was coming. "I told the priest years ago that school would be wasted on you. Stupid girl, making a mistake like that."

"I can change it."

But Liljana knew as she said the words that she was wasting her time and watched in dull horror as the slate was knocked repeatedly against the corner of the table until it smashed. "Shabby work! Shabby, lazy work! I expect you to be perfect! Is that so hard? I do not expect you to make mistakes!"

Liljana fled the house, her stomach rumbling with hunger and the encroaching horror awaiting her when she appeared at school without her slate. Of course, she could not possibly tell her schoolmistress that her mother had smashed the wretched thing; it would not have occurred to her to reveal an act like that even if she had trusted the teacher concerned. The only course of action was one she had taken many times before, to cover up the truth by saying she had left her slate at home, even though it meant Miss Josephine would accuse her of being a lazy little liar who obviously had not done the work at all and was pretending to have left the slate at home. She stood in front of sixty other children and took the tirade with an impassivity Miss Josephine unfortunately interpreted as insolence.

"You must think I was born yesterday!" It was an expression Liljana had heard once or twice before. "I know a liar when I see one. I've half a mind to send you home to fetch it directly." Liljana's stomach turned itself into knots. That really would be a disaster— going home, seeking out the broken pieces and taking them back, pretending that she had dropped the slate on the way. Another lie so soon after the first would be the last straw for Miss Josephine, who would probably dismiss her as a career criminal. "But that would be a waste of time," said the teacher. "I know perfectly well you have not done the work I set you, you lazy, lazy little liar."

Only as she returned to her place with Miss Josephine warning her that she had better remember the slate tomorrow was Liljana forced to suppress tears. She had not thought about what she would do when she could not produce the slate day after day, about the endless stream of punishments she would have to endure until she finally admitted that the slate was smashed and she got into worse trouble.

Liljana was still brooding over this problem when she came to a reluctant halt outside the door to her home and hesitated. Like most houses in that part of the world, the entrance was marked by two outer doors, one of them perpetually open, but today both doors were closed, and when she tried to push them open, she found them locked and bolted. "Is there anybody there?" she called through the letter box, but the house looked dark and empty from the little she could see when she peered through. "Mama, will you let me in?"

She tried hard not to think of the last occasion her mother had locked the doors against her, convinced that she had made a pact with the devil and was trying to steal her mother's soul. That time, she had hammered innocently on the door for ten minutes, imagining that her mother must have accidentally locked the doors and perhaps fallen asleep. When her mother had finally emerged, her face had been twisted with such terrible rage she had barely looked human, and Liljana had instinctively turned on her heel to make a run for it, only to be hit by a wave of domestic rubbish: eggshells, vegetable peelings, a small quantity of sour milk.

All Liljana remembered afterwards was standing stock still in the middle of the street, covered in filth, with her mother screaming, "You disgust me, you filthy little wretch! You did not make your bed this morning! Do not think I do not know what you were doing! You are trying to humiliate me; you are trying to turn me into a servant!"

Sometime later, as Liljana attempted to rinse the acrid fluid out of her hair, she heard two people talking under her window. "Somebody should do something about this. It has gone on far too long."

After that, Liljana became more cautious about exposing her mother's fragile condition and never again attempted to run away, afraid that her mother would follow her out into the street and be witnessed doing or saying something that would give away how terribly ill she was. Like so many children in her position, she became a master of secrecy and deceit. If she kept the windows closed, nobody would hear her mother's raised voice during her many prolonged outbursts of rage. It was fortunate for both of them that her mother was not given to committing acts of physical violence, that cruel words left no visible marks, or it would have been harder to hide her behaviour. There was not even the temptation to confide in anybody as there was not a single person alive who was remotely interested in Liljana. On Sunday, when she and her mother would enter their parish church—Liljana practically walking on tiptoe, her mother stomping defiantly across the marble floor—they would sit alone at the back; and even though the church would be heaving with people, there would always be plenty of space around them.

Liljana kept pushing the heavy doors in the childish hope that one of them would finally budge, even though she knew perfectly well that she was locked out. She did not dare knock any louder on the doors in case she inadvertently sparked an ugly scene. When she no longer had the energy to knock, she sat on the doorstep, tired and hot. Oh, she was very, very hot, now that she had the breathing space to notice, a state of affairs which only made her clothing more prickly and chafing. She struggled not to fidget.

For the present, Liljana could only hope that before too long her mother would tire of keeping her out and unlock the door, but she did not feel very hopeful. Typically, when her mother was angry with her, she would not speak to her for at least three days. She would exude so much contempt that she would glare and turn her back every time Liljana stepped into a room. Her mother usually got bored with giving her this treatment after a few days and would suddenly start talking to her again as though nothing had happened, but Liljana considered, as she sat on the hot stone step, that her mother must have taken the mistake on the slate very badly indeed not to let her into the house at all.

Whatever am I to do? she thought, after what seemed like hours, but then even a short space of time seems desperately long to a child in disgrace. *What if night comes and I am still here?* Liljana was just beginning to imagine curling up to sleep on the doorstep if she were still locked out as darkness fell, when she became aware of a shadow sliding across her and the sound of a man's voice.

"What are you doing here?" asked the man in English.

"This is my home, sir," she answered in English, without raising her head. "My mother has accidentally locked me out."

"Ah." The sound of the Englishman's awkward sigh made her look up at him immediately. He was just the sort of man she had imagined would own a voice like that: tawny brown hair, impeccably dressed, a little portly, with the leathery, prematurely aged skin of a man who has spent much of his life in a climate for which he was not made. "They did not realise she had a daughter," said the man as if to himself. "She told them she had no children."

Liljana jumped to her feet. "What has happened? What has happened to her?"

"You will have to speak in English please," he said, "I do not have the pleasure of understanding you."

Liljana swallowed hard and repeated the question in English, more calmly this time: "What has happened to my mother?"

"You had better come with me," said the man, extending a hand to her. Liljana ignored the gesture and folded her arms. "Don't be like that," he added, taking a step back to avoid alarming her further. "I mean you no harm. I know where she is and she is quite safe, I promise."

Liljana felt too dazed to resist and had nowhere else to go, so she got up and fell into step beside the stranger, walking with him the short distance to his house. As they approached the door, she noticed a brass plaque nailed into the wall with the words: "Dr A. Hampton, Physician".

"Is my mother sick?" she asked as she stepped inside. "Is she here?"

Dr Hampton wished afterwards that he had thought to take her somewhere other than his consulting room to break the news, but his first thought when he saw her on the doorstep was to get her as far from public view as possible. He was aware of the Spartan feel of the room, which he would normally have thought clean and efficient. "Why don't you sit down, my dear?"

They were both distracted by the sound of another door opening, and the carefully groomed head of Dr Hampton's housekeeper poked through from an adjoining room. "Oh, there you are, Dr Hampton," she said in the clear, precise tones of a woman whose plans for the day had been interrupted. "I wondered what had kept you." Noticing Liljana and giving her a disdainful look, she asked, "I say, am I interrupting you?"

"No, Mary, she is not my patient. How about a nice cup of tea?"

When the woman slipped away, as disgruntled as she had arrived, Liljana felt a knot of anxiety tightening beneath her ribs, accompanied by the sense that a very temporary distraction had disappeared. As she sat down, Liljana took in the faint smell of carbolic acid, the harsh, unforgiving benches and the right angles of the few pieces of furniture. Her mouth felt so dry that she could not bring herself to ask the question again.

"I am afraid your mother has been taken ill," said Dr Hampton when he thought she had settled herself. "She has had to be taken into hospital."

Liljana stood up only to be helped back into her chair by Dr Hampton. "I knew something awful had happened," she said breathlessly, "even my mother would not lock me out of the house for no reason."

"Your mother has been behaving a little strangely recently, has she not?" Dr Hampton ventured.

"No, not really," Liljana responded, not even aware that she was lying. Amazing the conspiracies children enter into to protect their families, even when they themselves are the victims. The next response was entirely reflexive: "Why do you say that?"

"Come now, my dear, you must have noticed she has not been herself?" The conversation was futile, he thought to himself, walking to the door to take the tea tray from his housekeeper so that she would not be tempted to intrude upon the situation. Of course the child had not noticed that her mother was behaving "strangely". The chances were that her mother had been mentally unstable for much of her adult life, since long before her daughter's birth, and the girl would never have known differently. Because her experience of life, particularly family life, was so limited it would not occur to her that other people had mothers who did not fly into blazing rages whenever they were crossed or blame their children for everything that went wrong or force them to submit to every bizarre whim.

Dr Hampton knew from the gossip he invariably overheard in his waiting room that Liljana had been forced to go to school one day dressed as a boy, all because her mother had got it into her head that she should have been a boy and would have got on better in life if she not had the misfortune to be born female. Liljana had run the gauntlet of derisive laughter and taunts all the way to school only to be publicly humiliated and sent home by a schoolmistress who had evidently thought the girl was making some kind of statement, showing her allegiance to the women's suffrage movement or something. The ladies who had tutted over the story in Dr Hampton's hearing whilst evidently finding it all quite entertaining, had been sure the girl had thrown herself out of the balcony window deliberately—not fallen out as she had claimed—so that she would do herself an injury (she managed a broken arm) and be confined to the house for a few weeks.

"Your mother has been taken to Mount Carmel."

"She is not mad!" cried Liljana immediately. "I tell you, she is not acting strangely. Do you think I would not have noticed?"

"My dear, she tried to burn the house down. She set fire to—" He swallowed the words a moment too late. Liljana's mother had set fire to the bedclothes in one of the rooms, convinced the linens were diseased, but not until he started to describe the unfortunate incident did it occur to him that the child's bedclothes may have been the ones she had burned. Nevertheless, the smoke billowing out of an open window at the back of the house had eventually caused a neighbour to raise the alarm.

Liljana moved towards the door to the outside world. "Take me to her," she said purposefully, "I want to see her."

"I'm afraid that is quite out of the question." Dr Hampton regarded the girl with unease. Like most properly brought up children she had been trained to be deferential to her elders and betters, and when

26

they had first met she had refused to make eye contact with him. The shock of what he had told her seemed to have had the effect of ageing her immediately, and this child, who could not have been more than ten or eleven years old, was behaving like a woman. To a large extent, he thought, not without a little regret, she was a woman. She could not realise it yet, but she would not be allowed to be a child anymore. Without a parent to provide for her even in the most eccentric of ways, she would have to leave school either to earn her own living or to enter an institution where her basic needs would be taken in hand. But if he had thought to tell any of this to Liljana, she might have pointed out to him that her childhood could not end because it had never truly begun.

"Please, Doctor, you do not understand. I must see her."

Dr Hampton took her hand and eased her back into the chair. "She would not want you to see her as she is now. It is not a fit sight for a child." Liljana tried to rise again, but he placed a resolute hand on her shoulder to hold her where she was. "I promise they were very gentle with her and she is being properly cared for. Your poor mother has been very unwell for a long time. At the hospital they can help her, they can look after her."

He did not think it necessary to tell her that men had to break down the back door to gain entry to the house when her mother refused to let them in and that they had to wrestle the screaming, scratching and cursing woman to the ground, because she was so determined to prevent them from putting out the fire. There were many, many things Dr Hampton did not see fit to tell Liljana that day, but which in the close, claustrophobic environs of Malta she was bound to hear from somebody else sooner or later. A less kindly informer was to tell her how her mother had been dragged out of the house, sobbing and raging, her hair unpinned and wild, while some onlookers thought her possessed and the neighbours who had shunned them both had spat on her.

"Is there anywhere I can take you?" asked Dr Hampton. Time was passing and he knew he would have to find somewhere for the child to lay her head that night. "An aunt perhaps?"

"No," she said immediately, "only my mother."

"There must be someone," he persisted. *The natives were good at family*, he thought, *the way they bred*. It was the only thing they were any good at, making more of themselves, and he imagined an army of relatives waiting to greet her: aunts and uncles, cousins, grandparents, a vast chorus of dusky people of all ages.

"Everybody hates us," she said without a hint of self-pity. "I suppose I have a family somewhere, but they never speak to us."

"What about a friend?" he tried, knowing that all girls have chums to whom they are devoted. "One of the girls from school perhaps?"

She looked puzzled and shook her head. In the end, out of sheer exasperation, he left her at a convent, promising to fetch her as soon as he had found a more suitable home for her. In his determination to protect her from the horrible nature of her mother's removal, Dr Hampton would not allow Liljana to return to the house to pack a bag, afraid that she would be faced with charred belongings and possibly overturned and broken furniture from the battle to get an unwilling, frightened woman away to the asylum. Liljana would never enter that house again. On an otherwise unremarkable afternoon in the year of our Lord 1906, Liljana Camilleri, possessing the clothes she was wearing and two school books that subsequently had to be returned, found herself facing a future without protection and without certainties.

4

Kristjana took some time to realise that Leo had stopped talking and was looking intently at her. "There, you see," he announced as though he had just passed an exam, "you should not have been so quick to sit at my bedside! You are troubled now."

"I feel sorry for her, that's all," she said. "Did she ever see her mother again?"

"Oh no, they never let the mother anywhere near her child again. I suppose they thought it would be bad for both of them to meet in such a place. Well, you can see their point."

"Not sure I can really, it's so cruel. How was she ever to recover without her child?"

"I say, are you all right?"

Kristjana looked up at the clock, which wobbled like something out of a Salvador Dali painting. "It's getting late, I'd better get my dinner or the kitchen will close."

"Are you all right?" Leo asked again. "You look troubled. I'm sorry, I've upset you, haven't I?"

"Of course not, of course not. I'm ... a bit dehydrated, that's all. It's hot. Good night, sweet dreams."

"Good night."

Troubled? Sweet Jesus, that has to be the understatement of the century, thought Kristjana bitterly; she had been troubled from pretty much the second she was conceived. By the time she had reached adulthood, Kristjana reckoned, she had moved on from troubled to just-about-in-possession-of-her-mental-faculties. To her intense annoyance, she felt herself trembling as the image replayed itself round and round her head of a poor sick woman being dragged from a burning building with a gaggle of spiteful neighbours enjoying every moment. Kristjana was so preoccupied she could not face the hospital dining room and the prospect of having to make conversation with other people over the bread and hummus. Instead, she stormed down the Neblus Road in search of solitude and refreshment, knowing, as anyone who has ever been the resident Nobody of a bustling boarding school knew, that the best place to find solitude was amongst many people.

The streets of the old city beckoned, so invitingly narrow and crowded, even at sunset, and Kristjana felt herself beginning to relax. It had been nerves, she told herself, some deep-rooted fear that she might find herself in a similar humiliating predicament one day. Some say the root of all prejudice is fear, and there are few worse stigmas in modern society than that of mental illness because everyone secretly knows that his own mind might break with enough pressure.

All Kristjana had been asked to do was to help him, most especially to be good company to him, and if he wanted to tell her stories—whatever kind he had to tell—she would sit patiently and listen to him. The thought came to her that it might be a good idea to write his stories down, since he would never talk to anyone else again, and she made a mental note to buy herself a fat notepad and plenty of pens on the way back to the hospital. Kristjana imagined herself sitting in her room with its distant view of the Mount of Olives, recording every word he told her, escaping into the realms of another person's life. Escape. She was running ever further away from her own life, to a hospital room in Jerusalem; to another city in another country; to a time before her birth, before her parents and her grandparents, before world wars and revolutions, before empires crumbled. She could extinguish herself by travelling back to a time that held no place for her. She was running away but no one else needed to know, not even that poor frail man on his deathbed with the ghost of his mother willing him to bring her back to life.

***

"She's very young," declared Susan Burnett, glancing contemptuously at the silent, rather cowed figure standing before her. Dr Hampton had escorted Liljana to the house of his old friend in the hope that Mr and Mrs Burnett might be prevailed upon to grant the girl a position. Dr Hampton's housekeeper had gone to some considerable trouble that morning to ensure that little Liljana was well turned out and the end result was quite pleasing. Her hair had been combed and tortured into tight plaits that hung like tarred ropes across the crisp white pinafore she had been lent to hide her regrettably faded frock. Unfortunately, Liljana had never been inside such a grand villa before, and she was so overwhelmed that she had not yet made eye contact with any of the people she had met, let alone uttered a word. "How old are you, child?" Susan looked impatiently at Dr Hampton. "I say, can this gal speak English?"

"Yes, Mrs Burnett," he put in, anxiously, "she speaks excellent English. She's very timid, that is all."

"Seems rather insolent to me." Susan glared in Liljana's direction. "Come along my gal, answer my questions please. What is your name?"

"Liljana Camilleri," she answered in a whisper.

"Speak up, I can hardly hear you."

"Liljana."

"What preposterously complicated names these people do have!" said Susan, addressing the comment to Dr Hampton as though she expected him to return the sneer. There was a harsh, scathing tone to every word the woman said, and Dr Hampton wished for the third or fourth time that his dear, gentle friend George had been at home when they had called. "That's far too much of a mouthful for me to remember," she continued, as though the priest who had baptised Liljana had christened her with that name specifically to annoy foreigners. "If you come to work for me, I shall have to give you another name. Lily will do perfectly well."

"Madam, my name is Liljana," she began, clutching her hands behind her back with sheer nervous effort.

As Susan Burnett eyed Liljana she reminded Dr Hampton of a bird of prey. The resemblance was in her combination of carefully preened haughtiness—grey hair perfectly coiffured, clothing elegant and neat to the point of looking artificial—and the faint sense of menace she exuded without ever raising her voice. "That is not a servant's name," she said coldly, "Lily will do perfectly well. Now," and the tone was suddenly business-like, "can you do anything?"

"She can read and write," said Dr Hampton, sensing that Liljana was struggling to find her voice, having so abruptly lost her identity.

"That is of no consequence to me."

"I have looked after my mother and her house since I was very young," said Liljana.

"Ah yes, she's the lunatic, isn't she?" smirked Susan.

She might as well have slapped the girl in the face, and Dr Hampton was not sure how he would have rescued the situation if George Burnett had not stepped into the room at that precise second, giving both females a healthy distraction. Susan forgot to taunt the child and Liljana dived behind Dr Hampton for cover. By the time she had been persuaded to tiptoe out again, Liljana found that she had been taken on as a domestic servant at the Villa Burnett and there was no further need for her to open her mouth.

She felt her head spinning with the suddenness of everything as Dr Hampton escorted her towards the kitchen. "Am I going to live here?" asked Liljana, taking his proffered hand out of sheer lack of an alternative. "Forever?"

"Nothing is forever," promised Dr Hampton, noting that she was trembling. "Come now, there's nothing to be afraid of here, nobody's going to hurt you. The Burnetts are good, upright people."

"What about school? What about my mother?"

Dr Hampton stopped outside the kitchen door. "Your mother is being taken care of now; the important thing is that you can stand on your own feet. There are many children in this world who go to bed hungry every night. Work hard and you needn't be one of them." He hesitated before knocking, thinking how harsh he had sounded without meaning to. "I'm ... I am very sorry that you will not be able to go to school any more, but you're a clever girl. Why don't you write me a letter every week telling me how you are getting along? You don't want to forget how to write, now do you?"

Liljana made a brave attempt at a smile as the door swung open and she was struck by the instantly reassuring sights and smells of a well-kept kitchen. An elderly woman sat at the kitchen table shelling peas; she looked up at them and quietly dropped her work. "Good day, Mrs Debono," said Dr Hampton, nudging Liljana in front of him, "I've brought you some assistance."

"Whoever's this?" she asked, indicating for Liljana to move towards her.

"Her name's—"

"If you'll excuse me, Dr Hampton, I was talking to the girl."

Liljana glanced back at Dr Hampton in surprise but he nodded politely. "Of course, Mrs Debono, Liljana can speak for herself. She has come to work here for a while. I'm sure you'll find her plenty to do."

"I certainly shall, but *Marija*, shouldn't she be at home with her mother at her age? How old are you, *sabihha*?"

Liljana opened her mouth to answer but felt a juddering sensation in her throat and knew she would burst into tears if she said a word. She lowered her head and shook it nervously. "Don't worry, Liljana," said Dr Hampton, touching her arm, "answer Mrs Debono."

That poor baby looks like a stray dog, thought Mrs Debono, getting up and finding somewhere for her to sit down. "Don't worry about anything," she said; then she looked up at Dr Hampton as though to check that he had not run away. "She will have to share my room," she said purposefully, "there is not much space but we can make some room for a little one. I shall ask Reno to put up a bed for her. Then I suppose I should ask Madam what her duties are to be. Dr Hampton, would you care for some tea?"

Dr Hampton stepped back towards the door. "Thank you, but I have much to attend to this morning." He hovered awkwardly, fighting the sense that he was dispensing with a problem. "Liljana, I shall leave you in this good lady's care."

Liljana watched as he pulled the door shut behind him and heard his footsteps on the stairs she already suspected he would never descend again. A sense of resentment nagged her, that he had not at least stayed to have the cup of tea he had been offered, but Mrs Debono was busying herself with bringing a tin out of a cupboard and Liljana allowed herself to be distracted. She would always remember how Mrs Debono looked at that first meeting, clad in the black she had never abandoned years after her husband's death; a set of keys hanging from her waistband, muffled in the heavy folds of her skirt; her plump face dominated by a pair of steel-rimmed spectacles perpetually drifting down the length of her long nose. Standing stooped over the dresser in a swathe of musty sunlight, she looked so much like any other elderly lady of the time that Liljana wondered—when the first grey hairs were making an appearance at her own temples—whether Mrs Debono had ever really looked like that or whether her mind had substituted the real woman with a comforting monochrome image of matronhood that suited her childhood memories.

"Dear me, you do look sad," said Mrs Debono, laying *pasti* on a large plate. "You'll see, everything is going to be perfectly well. It's just me and Reno down here, and Agnes in the mornings; nothing to be afraid of. You stay close to me."

Liljana needed no further encouragement. From that day, she barely left Mrs Debono's side and discovered very early on that the old lady was a good person to have on hers. For a start, the family treated her almost as one of them. She had served at the Villa Burnett for many years, and the now grown-up children regarded her as a fat, jolly aunt who could always be prevailed upon to hand over sweets and biscuits if she were pestered enough. Secondly, and this was rather more important for Liljana in her early months there, she had control of all the food. All of it. Lots and lots of food, lovingly prepared and served as though Liljana's skeletal figure were Mrs Debono's personal responsibility.

As it turned out, there was not quite enough space in Mrs Debono's room for an extra bed, so Reno unrolled a mattress on the floor between the brass bed and the wall which Liljana made into a nest of blankets. Liljana never knew it at the time, but Mrs Debono would often tiptoe into the room after Liljana was fast asleep and tuck up her bedclothes before turning in herself and would reach down and place a hand on the child's head if she murmured in her sleep, soothing her without ever causing her to wake up.

And if Mrs Debono needed a child to treat as her own, Liljana, who missed her mother terribly in spite of the troubles she had faced, needed a parent she could love unconditionally without having her love thrown back at her. Out of loyalty to her newfound patron, she was prepared to do virtually anything, even get up an hour earlier than was required (and she was expected to be up before six as it was) to accompany her to five o'clock Mass. They joined all the other domestics and fishermen and bakers, the many men and women whose hard work and poor wages made comfortable the lives of the privileged few who never acknowledged their existence.

Many years later, Liljana would recall those early mornings, sitting blearily in the folds of Mrs Debono's *ghonella* with the dolorous murmurings of the Rosary sweeping across the silence of the morning and the worn, tired faces of those good people all around her. Later she would wonder how she ever came to be parted from it all; how she came to be cast adrift; how a place and a people who seemed so permanent became the stuff of dreams within the space of barely a year. Was it really less than a year?

"Read it for me," whispered Mrs Debono, thrusting a holy picture into her hand. On one side there was a pastel sketch of a tiny figure in silhouette huddled up on a boat being tossed about on a vast, unwelcoming sea. She turned it over. " 'If I take my wings early in the morning, . . .' It's a psalm, Mrs Debono."

"Oh *ejja*, read it for me!"

" 'If I take my wings early in the morning, and dwell in the uttermost parts of the sea: / Even there also shall thy hand lead me: and thy right hand shall hold me.' "

"Now isn't that nice?"

Liljana rested her head on Mrs Debono's shoulder and closed her eyes, but she could still see a small, fragile boat swirling about before her eyes, ready to be swallowed by either the velvety blue waves or the fiery sunrise in the distance.

5

It was fortunate that life was so busy. A day filled from start to finish by an infinite list of exhausting tasks was a day Liljana could not spend brooding over or yearning for her mother, and in spite of everything she did yearn for her. The house was large, to her it was extraordinarily vast, and there were endless floors to scrub and surfaces to dust, including the slats between the wooden shutters, which turned out to be the most fiddly and time-consuming job of all. "Madam does not like dust," Mrs Debono had informed her on her first day. In fact, Madam loathed dust as a perpetual reminder that she lived in a hot, dusty country when she would far rather be at home in chilly Ipswich. Of all the many trials and tribulations of expatriate life that soured Susan Burnett's temper, the dust was the most constant cause of irritation and complaint.

"If she does not like dust, she should not have come here," said Liljana one day as she entered the kitchen, earning herself the mildest possible slap in the face from Mrs Debono for being impertinent. It did not occur to Liljana that the statement sounded political; she knew nothing of such matters and had only been thinking what a bore Madam was. It certainly did not dawn on her that Susan Burnett's perpetual ill temper could possibly be caused by unhappiness. What cause could she have to be unhappy? A woman living in a beautiful villa by the sea, waited on hand and foot with nothing to concern her other than the strain of sitting about all day, waiting for other ladies like herself to arrive at the house for tea. Liljana had never left her country before and had never felt the terrible yearning for the little details of home that had been left behind. In Susan's case, these were the sight of frost tracing elaborate patterns across the windowpane early in the morning; the first spring flowers, delicate and determined, breaking through the winter snow in carpets of crocuses and snowdrops; the spicy smells of Christmas pudding and mulled wine—those unimportant, superficial brushstrokes that make life, or a memory of a life, so vivid and so rich. Liljana had yet to learn what homesickness felt like.

One thing Liljana did miss, so much that it almost hurt, was school. She was not the sort of child who could ever have been happy at school. Her isolated existence had made it hard for her to make friends with other children, and her mother's quirky whims and fancies often caused her to stand out in the most unflattering way possible. The few school friends who had come home with her only had to be exposed to one dose of her mother's contempt in order never to enter the house or even to speak with her again, and her mother had a habit of disapproving of any friends she made. What Liljana had loved was the knowledge that she was learning about life; and once she had mastered the art of reading, she could disappear into the wonderful world of books for hours and even days at a time. During the school holidays, when she had had no reason to go out, she had stayed in the grim safety of indoors and read all day, sometimes only stepping out of her room when hunger forced her to go in search of food.

Fortunately for Liljana, one of her more enjoyable duties was to clean the master's library, airing the room and dusting off the seemingly thousands of books there. Great heavy bookcases covered every inch of wall from the floor to the ceiling. In the middle of the long, narrow room were a number of smaller book cases containing yet more weighty tomes. Books, books, books were everywhere—books on every possible subject in various languages, mostly English, but some Latin and French too; beautiful leather-bound books with gold leaf–trimmed pages; faded, creaky old books with broken bindings; new, unloved books with uncut pages. Master very rarely entered the library, which made her wonder why he bothered with it at all.

Perhaps it is the mere joy of possession, she mused to herself one day as she dusted down a shelf groaning under the weight of Ovid's *Metamorphoses*. She had overheard one of Madam's friends using the expression, and she had pondered it ever since. "Some men are satisfied with the mere joy of possession," Miss Norton had said, dropping sugar lumps into her tea with restrained violence. "They see a woman as a possession with which to decorate their homes, not a creature worthy of their confidence."

Liljana had been rather disappointed when Susan Burnett had cleared her throat awkwardly and muttered something in French, which had stopped Miss Norton in her tracks. Glowering at Liljana, Madam had then instructed her to get about her business. Mrs Burnett always muttered in French when she did not wish the servants to understand her; which meant she had not wanted Liljana to hear what Miss Norton had to say; which meant that it was something exciting and important; which was why of course she could not forget it now. Liljana was bright enough to have noticed that Miss Norton was not like the other ladies, either in her dress or her manner. She seemed rather dowdy compared with the others as though she were much poorer than her friends (though Liljana thought that highly unlikely—she was far too nicely spoken for that) or else regarded her appearance as unimportant. Best of all, unlike the other women who barely acknowledged Liljana's presence when she served them, Miss Norton appeared to be at pains to thank her as she took her empty tea cup or brought her a second slice of cake.

"You had absolutely no business listening in on Madam's conversation" was the only answer she could reasonably have expected from Mrs Debono, "Miss Norton ... well, she is different from the others. She is a ... a, well, I think the English call them whitestockings."

"But she wasn't wearing white stockings!" Liljana protested, "I'm sure she wasn't."

"That's enough! I should have boxed your ears for asking."

Possessions. Women. Books. And the most important of them all were books, which faithfully provided the answers without asking angry questions or suggesting she was being too inquisitive. And since the master did not seem to have much time for his books except perhaps as possessions, Liljana lavished them with the love and the attention they deserved. She worked out early on that if she cleaned the library as quickly as possible, avoiding tasks nobody noticed in the first place and doing some chores every other day instead of every day, she had a little time left over for dipping into one of the many books and practicing her reading.

"Books let us into their souls and lay open to us the secrets of our own," or so said William Hazlitt, but Liljana had yet to have her mind addled by such wayward English philosophers. When George Burnett caught Liljana curled up under the heavy mahogany library table with her nose buried in a book, however, he was more than a little surprised at her choice of author. He went in one morning to find a volume he had promised to lend Bertie Hampton; but unfortunately for Liljana, he hurried in a little too quickly for her to put down her book and pick up her duster. Instead, when she heard the sound of the door being thrown open she ducked under a table. The sight of his polished shoes coming to a standstill next to her hiding place she took as a sign that he had realised she was reading on the job and come to get her. As it happened, he was unaware that she was in the room, and if she had held her nerve, he might have walked out again without even noticing her; but she was so frightened she jumped up and slammed her head.

"Sorry! I am sorry!" she blustered, before George Burnett had managed to drag her out from under the table to see if her head was still on. "I was only here a minute. I stopped for a rest, just a little rest—"

"Be quiet," he insisted, casually. "Have you hurt yourself?"

Liljana had hurt herself quite badly as it happened; the blow to her head had left her feeling as though she were about to be sick and, worse, had caused her to bite the inside of her mouth, which began bleeding copiously. George took out an immaculate white handkerchief and pressed it to her mouth, which had the pleasing effect of staunching the bleeding and taking away the necessity to apologise further. "Now," he said, when normality had been recovered, "would you be so kind as to tell me what you were doing?"

Liljana was not sure afterwards what she had expected him to do to her but she was too terrified to speak, all the more so when he told her to go back under the table and pick up the book she had dropped in her haste. He took it from her wordlessly and looked at the title page. "Good heavens, can you actually read this?" he asked. "Aristotle is a little too much for me."

Liljana felt her fears dissipating with his shift in interest from her to the book she was reading—or trying to read at any rate. "It is harder than I expected," she lisped, guiltily. "Someone told me about Aristotle once, and I saw a book with his name on the spine. I thought I would take a look."

"Oh really? Who told you?"

"The priest who taught us catechism at school said something once about virtue," she said, with some difficulty as the sore place in her mouth was making it difficult to say the letter p and the letter s. She persisted, "My mother said afterwards that he was being silly, he should just have said what was in the book; but he said something about how Aristotle called virtue the Golden Mean between two extremes. Courage was the Golden Mean between cowardice and recklessness."

"That's a little much for a child," mused George out loud, but he found the sound of the girl lisping ideas she barely understood utterly adorable. "Dear me, I wonder why he troubled himself?"

"He talked about courage because I do not have any," she said sadly. "He looked at me as he said it and everybody laughed." She suddenly seemed to remember what the point of the conversation had been. "I'm so sorry I touched your books. Please forgive me."

"No need to ask forgiveness," he promised, giving her a benevolent smile. "It's nice to see somebody reading in here for once. But how about reading something a little more suitable? Hmm?" Liljana watched as he strode across the library and picked up a parcel she had noticed on her way in. "These came today from London," he said, cutting the string, "and I happen to think that there is a book in here you might enjoy."

Liljana had never received a parcel before and could barely contain her excitement as he peeled back the brown paper and pulled out three books, one of which he extended to her. "This one is quite new," he said, "and will teach you a bit about England."

She took the book in both hands. Encouragingly heavy it had a glorious odour of newness. It was the first completely new book she had ever held, a new copy of a new title that had only just appeared on the shelves of London's bookstalls: *The Railway Children*. She could tell already that this book was going to take her on a momentous adventure somewhere very special. Some green, fragrant place in far away, misty Albion. Somewhere where there were vast steam trains chugging for hundreds of miles through green pastures and leafy forests. "Thank you, sir. Thank you very much indeed."

"Read it and tell me what you think of it."

During the evenings that followed, in those few precious minutes before she fell fast asleep, she was the contented guest of the Three Chimneys cottage with Bobbie, Phyllis and Peter. She ran with them through the meadows to the railway line and waved to the old gentleman in the first class carriage; she quailed with fear in the gloom of the railway tunnel, praying like Bobbie for the safety of the poor boy trapped there during the ill-fated paper chase. In the idyllic English heaven she would soon discover existed only in books, she could dream of a family of her own, siblings who included her in their games and adventures, a mother who was effortlessly perfect and a father who would surely one day return.

It was a blessing that Liljana could not know quite how much trouble that particular copy of *The Railway Children* was going to get her into, but even Susan Burnett's long-suffering husband could not have predicted that the woman was capable of being quite as spiteful as she showed herself to be on the fateful morning when she went searching through Mrs Debono's room, convinced that Liljana was up to something. She could never have explained afterwards precisely what it was she had expected to find, but she had disliked Liljana from the first moment she had entered her house and was of a sufficiently arrogant disposition to believe that her first impressions of a person's character were always correct.

It was partly the girl's unnerving silence that irritated her as it could so easily be interpreted as dumb insolence. Susan had been able to convince herself the first time Liljana had been too frightened to answer a question that it was a clever form of defiance. She was not really timid and withdrawn as Bertie Hampton had so charitably suggested, she was simply insolent, determined to be dissatisfied with everything and everyone she met, haughtily, disdainfully silent. Susan made the wilful mistake Liljana's own mother had so often made about her motives and allowed herself to be annoyed and unsettled by behaviour that should have elicited sympathy. But Susan Burnett was not a woman easily tempted to sympathy, particularly when dealing with a person considerably more vulnerable and unfortunate than herself. So when she began searching the room whilst Liljana was busy in the kitchen and found a valuable book that was clearly not hers, snugly hidden away behind her pillow, she could barely contain her excitement.

"Run along, *qalbi*," chided Mrs Debono, when the parlour bell began to ring incessantly. Mrs Debono knew immediately that something was wrong, since it was really not necessary to keep ringing the bell like that, but she assumed that Madam was in a more than usually bad mood that day. "Hurry along before she wrenches that bell pull right off. *Marija*, what a noise she is making today!"

Liljana could hear the explosions of temper in the clatter, clatter, clatter of the tuneless bell as it jerked violently from side to side, and she could barely force herself to mount the stairs. She had some vague notion that no member of the household would hurt her without good reason, but nevertheless she was terrified of anger and knew how unpredictable people could be when they were enraged. Her tardiness would soon be used against her as proof of her guilt, but at that time all she could think of was the need to delay walking through that door. Liljana inched along the corridor, the sound of the bell resonating through the entire house, ringing relentlessly, and she knew that it would continue until she arrived; but her increasing sense of fear only dragged her back all the more. She felt her footsteps becoming fainter and slower, felt the horribly familiar sensation of sweat gathering at her temples—yet another symptom of her guilt, she would later be told—and knocked at the door as though she believed the devil was waiting behind it to drag her to hell.

At least the bell stopped ringing as soon as she knocked, though how her mistress could possibly have heard her was another question. "How dare you take so long to attend me!" came the shrill voice, before Liljana had even closed the door behind her, but she suspected Susan Burnett wanted the whole household to hear her. "Why has it taken you so long to answer my bell?"

Liljana found it impossible to answer. The years of female aggression she had lived with choked her like a poisonous vine wrapping itself around her throat every time an adult raised his voice, particularly a woman. She knew that her failure to answer immediately would be taken as a damning sign by Susan Burnett, but she also knew that every word she said would be twisted against her, no matter how carefully she phrased her answers.

> They'll have me whipped for speaking true; thou'lt have me whipped for lying; and sometimes I am whipped for holding my peace.

"Answer my question! Why were you so slow? Surely you could hear me ringing?"

Liljana glanced at the woman before quickly looking away. Another point against her, the bitter woman would assume she could not look her in the eye because she was hiding something, not because she could not bear the sight of her hate-ridden scowl. The eyes conveyed so much emotion, and in the case of Liljana's mistress, barely controlled rage and contempt were virtually the only feelings she exuded. She knew she would have to give some answer. "I was afraid," she said, quietly.

"Speak up! I can't hear you."

"I said I was afraid," she forced out.

"Don't take that tone with me, my girl!" she barked immediately, seizing upon the opportunity to shout like a rat tearing every last scrap of flesh from an emaciated carcass. "And, pray, why should you be afraid? Why should a good, innocent little thing like you be afraid of me?"

Because you are evil and I hate you, Liljana thought but did not have the spirit to say, *because you are a despicable bully and you want everyone to be afraid of you. Everybody must hate you; your husband must hate you.*

Liljana stood in silence, not saying a single word that exploded through her head. She was so well trained in concealing her resentment that she seemed as placid and calm as any happy child. Only when Susan Burnett picked up a rather heavy looking book did Liljana spring into action, convinced the woman was about to throw it at her. She was so quick to raise one hand to her face in self-defence and jump back several feet to a safer position that she did not realise Susan Burnett was holding a copy of *The Railway Children*. She saw only a weapon about to be launched against her and braced for the coming assault, giving a panicked squeak just to make sure her actions could be interpreted as badly as possible.

"You may well flinch," said Susan Burnett, waving the book at her, and Liljana was convinced she was only refraining from throwing it at her head because she did not wish to damage a blameless book. "You must surely have realised I would find out about your little theft sooner or later?"

"I am not sure I understand you, Madam," she managed to say, but a stinging slap in the face shocked her into silence once again. Looking at her mistress' expression, Liljana was not sure which of them was the more surprised, and she suspected the woman had acted entirely on instinct. She felt her face flushing with shame and the horrible sensation of tears springing up beneath her eyelashes, and she concentrated her attention on one resolve: she would not cry. Liljana had learned many harsh lessons in her short life and besides the need to remain silent as much as possible, the avoidance of any sign of emotion was near the top of the list. Not just because society demanded that emotion be concealed as though it were a faculty that disgraced human nature, but because it always seemed to excite adult rage, even if adult rage had provoked the scene in the first place.

Liljana could still feel tears perilously close to falling. She breathed slowly in and out as though breathing through pain; she swallowed once, twice, three times before she became aware that her eyes were dry again. She had almost been able to hear the sound of an authoritative voice in her ear snarling, "Enough!" Instead however, she heard Susan Burnett snarl, "Don't play the innocent with me, my girl! I suppose I can commend you on doing it very cleverly. You stole it as soon as it was delivered, didn't you? That way no one could know it had arrived. If it were missed, we would have assumed that it had been lost somewhere between London and Malta. Very clever."

Liljana felt herself flushing with what would have been anger in anyone else. "There were three books in that parcel," she said, "the other two are in the library. Sir said I could read it." Somehow she imagined that would settle the matter.

Susan gave an astonished laugh. "*Read* it? Do you honestly expect me to believe that a thing like you can *read?*"

"Dr Hampton told you, I went to school—"

"What else have you stolen whilst you have been in my service? I do not believe for a moment that this was the first instance."

"I stole nothing! I would never steal anything! I am a respectable girl . . . a Christian."

"You're a filthy little liar!" shouted Susan. The word "Christian" riled her English Protestant sensibilities, and she found it impossible to control her sense of loathing. "And you're not a Christian either; you are an ignorant, superstitious little papist! Do you really think any intelligent person believes all that mumbo jumbo you people prattle?"

Liljana had been warned that the English belonged to a bizarre sect set up by an evil king who wanted to divorce his wife, but she had never heard anyone say such horrible things and flailed around for a response. She remembered a line her mother had come out with once. "Saint Paul converted us when you people were living in the trees!"

Susan Burnett was not a woman who was used to being challenged, and in the absence of a considered answer she descended into further abuse. "You filthy little savage, I should never have allowed you anywhere near my home! I knew you were a thief the moment I set eyes on you!"

Liljana felt something snap. She could not account afterwards for how she had come to do it, but the sudden, unexpected tirade of abuse shocked her so deeply that she acted, as Susan herself had acted, on some powerful, tribal impulse to defend what was her own. She had no pretentions to great piety, but faced with this shrill, vindictive woman, Liljana felt the last vestiges of her identity being attacked. She stepped towards that glowering face, ugly beyond recognition and spat at her.

The rest of the scene melted away in a terrible blur of raised voices and violence, much of it directed at her, but it all felt so much like a dream that she felt and heard very little of it at the time. She was aware of being dragged bodily out of the room by someone—was it Reno?—who seemed to be trying unsuccessfully to avoid hurting her and of being locked in her room while the police were called. However, it was only much later, when Liljana heard the sound of a metal door clanging shut behind her that she appreciated that Madam really had had her arrested and that she really had been pulled out of that house in a humiliating spectacle not unlike the horror her mother had suffered when she had been taken away.

Liljana wondered whether her mother would have understood how it felt to be pushed and shoved and struck until the urge to resist became too much to bear and she began biting and scratching anyone who touched her. Just like her mother, so very like her mother except that the confinement of a straitjacket must have been quite comfortable compared with having her hands chained so awkwardly that the nerve damage took months to repair. And was Mount Carmel as dark as this? Had her mother flown at the locked door like a thing possessed, kicking and battering it with her fists, screaming at the top of her voice to be let out? It was so dark, so close and dark and hot, there was no air to breathe. In her panic, Liljana imagined that the damp walls were actually moving, slowly closing in on her like something from a Victorian horror story. She had been buried alive; she would be crushed, suffocated; she had to get out and this door would open if she could only apply enough force, enough strength.

The door flew open, throwing her backwards with such violence that she fell down and struck her head against the opposite wall. Slightly stunned, Liljana felt herself being hauled roughly to her feet and pulled out of the room. She knew she should not have panicked; she should have stayed quiet in the cell, the friendly cell where the walls had never been moving and she had never been likely to suffocate. As she tripped and fell in the middle of a narrow corridor, she opened her mouth to call for help but realised that she could not think of anyone who would help her, who would run to her side, ready to risk everything to protect her from harm. A wordless scream came from Liljana's mouth, but the force of the fall had winded her and she was choked into silence.

6

"Good God!" was all George Burnett could find to say when he arrived home the following day after a pleasing jaunt with friends and discovered that mayhem had broken out in his absence. "Are you honestly telling me you had that poor girl arrested because you thought she'd pinched a book? Have you taken leave of your senses?"

"It was the principle of it, darling," Susan protested in her most hurt tones, "and she *spat* at me, the horrid creature!"

Liljana would have been flabbergasted if she could have seen how fragile and tragic her monstrous mistress was capable of being when she was out to get her husband's sympathy. Susan began to sniff and pulled out a scented lace handkerchief to add to the effect, but George turned his back on her and began rearranging a small trinket on top of one of the cabinets.

"It was a disgusting thing to do," he said, "whatever could have provoked such an act?"

"I am sure I do not know," Susan replied immediately, dabbing her eyes. Annoyingly, tears refused to flow, which was unusual since she could usually turn them on whenever she wanted. "You know what these native girls are like; I suppose I should pity her really."

George Burnett knew perfectly well what native girls were like on this little island: polite, demure, pious, hard-working. He thought it singularly unlikely that a girl of Liljana's social class would have done anything as disgraceful as to spit in a grown woman's face unless she had been provoked to the point of madness. "You should certainly pity her where she's been taken. Honestly, Sue!"

The unspeakable man was on the wrong side. "George, how can you take that tone with me? I give the ungrateful little wretch a home and a position, then she robs me and insults me in the most despicable way!"

"She did not rob you; I let her borrow that book!" he exploded. "You might at least have asked me about it before you called the police in—"

"She *spat at me!* Does that mean nothing to you?"

George turned to the window and drew a long breath before responding. At moments like this, he knew why he spent so much time enjoying the hospitality of friends. "Of course it does. I would have punished her, but she's a child. How could you hand her over to the police like that?"

Susan glanced up at him and all George could see was a spoilt, pampered woman who was so used to getting her own way that she would never be convinced she was in the wrong. He doubted she had ever seriously questioned a single action of her life, and she could hardly be expected to do so now.

"It was a last resort," she said, finally, with the tone she might have used to point out that it looked like rain outside. "When the dust has settled, I am sure she will consider her actions and see that she owes me an apology."

George stormed out of the room without another word, called for Reno and prepared himself to make amends on behalf of his wife. It was by no means the first time he had been forced to smooth things over, but Susan's outbursts of nastiness usually never went beyond turning her nose up at another lady's hat or cold-shouldering the wife of a moderately important person over some imagined slight. He was too intelligent a man to believe that the hurt she had caused this time could ever really be put right; in the twenty-four hours that had passed since the girl's arrest, all manner of terrible things might have happened to her. Liljana might have been shackled, humiliated, locked up in squalid conditions, starved, possibly beaten, but he could at least rescue her and try somehow to put matters right.

The appalling thought entered George's mind, as he walked through the foreboding doors of the police headquarters, that Liljana might already have been forced to make a confession. If that were the case she was in terrible trouble and might have to go through the ordeal of a trial if he could not intervene in time. He noticed a corpulent, swarthy man sitting behind a counter and approached him. "My name is George Burnett," he said, calmly. "There has been a terrible mistake. I have come to ask for the release of Liljana Camilleri."

The man stood up nonchalantly and went over to a book that he opened and began to flick through. "What did you say her name was?"

"Liljana Camilleri. For heaven's sake, man, how many little girls come this way accused of crimes they have not committed?"

"Liljana Camilleri? Oh yes, I know who you mean," he said, closing the book gently, but George noticed that the man looked visibly shaken. "You cannot see her now, sir. Come another time."

"I want her released," said George, bracing himself for an argument. "My wife had her arrested for stealing a book I had given her. It was an entirely innocent mistake, and I would like her released. Immediately."

"I'm afraid this is quite out of the question, sir," he answered with a forced tone of surprise. "You cannot simply take her away; she has already signed a confession."

It confirmed his worst fears. He silently counted to five. "May I see it please?"

"If you wish." The man disappeared from sight and came back minutes later, extending a piece of paper. "You see, it is quite clear."

George's eyes went straight to the space at the bottom of the short document where a large, untidy cross had been made. "I want her released immediately. Liljana clearly did not sign this herself, certainly not freely."

He was aware of a nasty change of atmosphere encroaching upon the room. "I hope you are not suggesting she was forced?"

"That is precisely what I am suggesting. Firstly, this cross is a little ungainly, don't you think? Even for a child? It looks rather as though someone grabbed her hand and forced her to write it whilst she resisted. In any case, she would never have signed this piece of paper with a cross, she can write her own name, but you good people were not to know that." As a former military man, George knew how to stand his ground, but the fear of what might have happened to Liljana had unnerved him, and he could feel himself sweating with the effort of remaining calm. "You will take me to her."

Shades of the prison-house begin to close.

In later years, George Burnett remembered himself striding down endless corridors like an avenging angel, not the arguments and threats to which he was forced to resort until he was finally able to obtain the girl's release nor the sight, which kept him awake for weeks afterwards, when her cell door was unlocked. The stench hit him first, closely followed by the sound of her shouting two incomprehensible sentences over and over again. The sound of the key in the lock had evidently frightened her so badly that she had curled up in the corner as tightly as possible as though trying to disappear. He could not see her face, buried as it was beneath her arms and unkempt hair.

"This is disgraceful!" shouted George, but the sound of his raised voice only made the situation a hundred times worse, as Liljana thought he was shouting at her and began shouting her declarations ever more loudly. "What on earth is she saying? Speak up, man, I do not understand the language."

"She is saying she didn't do it." he translated. "That is all she has said since she arrived."

"What else? There's something else."

The officer shrugged awkwardly. "I cannot really hear her properly, she's hysterical."

"You're a liar, what else is she saying? There are two distinct phrases."

"She is saying ..." He fumbled for a lie, could not think of one in time and said miserably, "She says do not touch me."

"Leave us please," said George. He waited until the officer had discreetly slipped away before taking a deep breath and kneeling down on the filthy floor so that he was as close to Liljana's eye level as he could manage. "Lily? Lily, it's all right. Please calm down. No one is going to hurt you, it's all right. Calm down."

He was astonished with himself for feeling so protective. If one of his own children had so completely lost control, he would have given them a sharp slap to snap them out of it, but then he had never had a conversation with any of his children on the floor of a police cell and doubted they would have coped any better with the strain. Liljana barely seemed aware of his presence, and when he reached forward and lightly touched her shoulder, she jumped as though he had struck her; but at least she looked at him. "Lily, I am very sorry," he said as calmly as he could, but his voice juddered with shock. Her face was pinched and white with exhaustion; he suspected that they had not allowed her a wink of sleep. The grey, sleepy smudges under her eyes were so pronounced she almost looked as though she had been punched in the face. There was a thin film of dirt across her right temple and cheek which made him think she had been lying on the floor, possibly to take advantage of the cool draught coming from under the door. He braced himself. "I am very sorry, Lily; it was all a mistake. I am taking you home."

Liljana felt neither anger nor relief as George Burnett helped her to her feet and partly carried her through the dim labyrinth of corridors that led to the outside world. She was told afterwards that she had trembled and gasped with the pain of moving, but all she remembered was the searing, blinding light that struck her from all sides as she stepped out of the door: the sunlight in the unblemished blue arc of sky above her head and the white, unfriendly light bouncing off the limestone walls of the surrounding buildings. George placed a hand over her eyes and guided her very carefully into the back of a *karrozzin*, instructing the driver not to go too fast as one of his passengers was unwell. By the time he dared uncover her eyes, he discovered that Liljana had fallen asleep and decided not to wake her. He was beginning to think that sleep was the only real escape she had left.

7

"I'm sorry to see you like this," said Dr Hampton, standing awkwardly in the doorway of Liljana's tiny shared room. He had heard the sound of her scrambling to get up as he opened the door, as though she thought it improper for him to see her in bed, and she stood in her nightdress, as chillingly silent as ever, staring blankly through him. "You should not have got up. Why do you not get back into—" He looked at the pile of blankets that was obviously the child's bed and thought with some distaste that it looked like a very cosy nest for a small animal. "Why not get back into your bed?"

Liljana refused to move, and Dr Hampton noted that she was trembling and had clenched her fists in an effort to steady herself. "I prefer to stand," she answered tonelessly.

"Mr Burnett sent for me to look after you. I assure you, you have nothing to fear."

"I am not afraid of you." *No*, he thought, taken aback by her icy demeanour. *You are not afraid at all. You are angry and suspicious and have no reason to trust anyone ever again—myself included.* "Am I in trouble?" she asked. No, icy was the wrong word for her; fire and ice.

"Not at all. Why should you be?"

"I should never have spat at Mrs Burnett, it was a dirty thing to do."

Dr Hampton hesitated. He thought it singularly unlikely that Liljana would be called to account for her actions after the penance she had already suffered, but she did not know that and her uncertainty left him some room for negotiation. "Well," he said, "why do you not let me take a look at you and then perhaps I could put in a good word for you with Mr Burnett?"

If there was any emotion in her face at all, it was miserable resignation, he thought, but it was something. "Sir has been so kind to me," she said more gently, "if he has to punish me I shall die of shame."

"It's all right, I shall speak for you. Don't be afraid."

"I told you, I am not afraid. I said I would be ashamed."

A child without fear is a child without hope, he thought, stepping gingerly into the room and closing the door. "Are you in pain?"

"Yes," she said matter-of-factly, "the back of my neck hurts."

He moved towards her. "Will you let me look?"

"If you want."

"Thank you." Dr Hampton stood behind her and pulled back the curtain of her hair, drawing back her lace collar as carefully as he could. He had to bite his lip to stop himself from gasping out loud. "Lily, those men who hurt you … were they smoking?"

"Yes, I know what they have done; they said they would if I didn't say I was a thief."

Dr Hampton was hardly a squeamish man but the sight of those two red circles like bullet wounds across the nape of her neck, just starting to turn septic, left him feeling sickened to his very core. "Please sit down," he said, indicating a chair so that she would have her back to him whilst he brought a large bottle of iodine and a dressing out of his bag. "Listen to me, Lily," he said, turning his own back on her as he soaked the dressing in case she turned around to look at what he was doing, "this is going to hurt. Be a brave girl." He put down the bottle and extended his free hand to her. "You can hold my hand if it helps."

He felt Liljana's fingers grasping his hand gratefully, then her silent panic the moment the dressing touched her and she struggled to move away in spite of herself. He knew she was in agony and had to brace himself to hold on to her as she writhed and trembled with the burning sensation of the iodine attacking her. He was horribly conscious of how tiny she was, even for a child her age, stunted by years of undernourishment. She looked as though she would snap at the slightest rough handling. "Easy," he said, "steady now. Deep breaths." He heard the sound of her breathing becoming more regular and a low, almost inaudible groan of pain, which reminded him that she had not made a sound when by rights she ought to have been screaming. "I am sorry, Lily. I am so sorry. I promise things will be better from now on."

"Well, she's a robust little thing, I have to say," declared Dr Hampton, when George had ushered him into the privacy of his study and motioned for him to sit down. George's study was a gloriously male

53

domain, and Dr Hampton began to relax as soon as he had settled himself into the creaky wicker chair. The décor was a curious combination of English and Mediterranean, the walls fortified by rows of tired-looking watercolours, the delicate pictures faded from exposure to years of relentless sunlight. The heavy mahogany desk looked quite incongruous amongst the friendlier wicker furnishings and the marble floor adorned with soft rugs. Dr Hampton noted the slatted blinds like those in his own study and felt grateful for the protection they offered from the fierce sun outside.

"Is it as bad as it looks?" asked George, passing his cigarette case. "I was horrified by the state she was in."

"You were quite right to call for me," Dr Hampton reassured him. He understood the likes of George Burnett very well indeed and knew he was the sort of person who would not call upon a member of the medical profession unless he or somebody near him were minutes away from expiring. "One can never be too sure with injuries like that, and it might be an idea to have a record of what happened."

"What did happen?"

Dr Hampton shrugged. He had come to Malta shortly after the Boer War, having gone out there as a young army doctor, and he was capable of expressing considerable moral outrage without a hint of anger clouding his face. "She said they were trying to force her to confess to the theft. She refused to sign her name and things became a little unpleasant."

"That sounds like the euphemism of the decade."

"She has a few cuts and bruises from being thrown about. She said they threw her down a flight of stairs at one point—but she has got off fairly lightly under the circumstances."

"Lightly?" George exploded. "If Sue had known this would happen she would never have handed her over to the police, even if she had stolen that book. I feel simply terrible about this."

Dr Hampton peered impassively through the acrid cloud of smoke he was producing. They both knew Sue would care more about a dropped hem than the fate of another human being, particularly one who was too young and too foreign to be worthy of her attention. Dr Hampton could almost imagine her cheering the men on or offering helpful advice, but this was hardly the moment to go into all that. "Indeed."

"Well dash it all, *I* would never have handed her over! I would have dealt with her myself."

"What disturbed me the most, Burnett, was that she has a couple of cigarette burns on her neck. I have dressed them but they were turning septic and may well scar——"

"They did *what?*" George Burnett's attention was suddenly drawn to the cigarette sitting guiltily between his own fingers, and he stubbed it out before putting his head in his hands. "I regret ever going away. I shall never be able to light up again without thinking about this."

"She said that after it happened, a nice man came to her rescue and said she just needed to be a sensible girl and sign the confession, even if she didn't do it, and he would sort everything out for her. She still refused, so he forced a pen into her hand and drew a cross."

"Yes I saw that, that was how I knew she had not really signed. She would have signed her name."

"Naturally. Of course, it's none of my business," said Dr Hampton a little awkwardly, "but if she were anything to do with my house-hold I would take matters further. There is a certain type of man who thinks that a uniform gives him the right to do as he pleases. I saw plenty of those among our own men in South Africa. They are cowards posing as warriors who deliberately target those they know will not retaliate."

"Will you write a report for me?"

"Oh yes, I've taken very careful notes. I'll write it all down for you, and you can take whatever action you wish. Shameful. She could have been crippled for life." George flinched visibly. "No need to look so surprised, old boy. A little slip of a thing like that? They could quite easily have broken her neck. She only needed to have fallen badly."

"I suppose we should thank God for small mercies, then."

Dr Hampton was silent a long time, opening his mouth every few seconds then closing it again as though unsure how to phrase the next point. George, who spent much of his time stifling a natural impatience, had gotten up and taken two glasses out of the cabinet by the time his friend's calm, detached tone broke the silence. "Of course, this is none of my business either, but I cannot help thinking that that girl is wasted as a domestic. She should be at school."

"She has to work to support herself, her mother is——"

"Yes, I know about her mother. Look here, please don't think I'm interfering. It's simply a suggestion. Pour yourself a nice long drink."

"Not sure I like the sound of this."

"Relax."

Dr Hampton got out of his comfortable chair with some reluctance and stepped towards the covered window. He had developed the technique of turning to look out of the window during consultations when he thought his patient needed a little privacy. "It seems to me, as I have said, that Lily is rather wasted in her current position, and frankly, there is little to keep her in this country. Her mother is unlikely ever to leave Mount Carmel. Unusually for these people, she has no other family to turn to and faces a ... well, a rather lonely life as an unskilled servant. It is certainly not the life you would have chosen for your own children."

"Certainly not."

"Quite. My brother, as you know, is the headmaster of a small school in the West Country."

George guffawed with laughter. "For heaven's sake, Hampton, you're not seriously suggesting we send that child to an English boarding school? She wouldn't last five minutes!"

"Don't be so quick to write her off—or the school for that matter. It is a small establishment and somewhat *experimental*."

"How very unfortunate."

"I don't mean my brother's a crank; the school is similar to most but has some differences that might make it suitable for a ... well, a more unusual child, shall we say?"

"Well, she's certainly unusual. Oh do sit down, Hampton, I cannot bear a man pacing the floor like that."

"My brother lamented the fact that we were educated and our sisters were not. I have never seen what the fuss was about, they married well and have done very nicely for themselves, but he has always believed that a girl should have the same opportunities for study as a boy. I would never recommend such an institution for a young lady, but Lily is ... well, she is a splendid girl but she is no lady. Since she is likely to have to find her own way in the world, a good education, or at least a better education than she would get anywhere else, might do her good."

George shook his head. "She is ten—nearly eleven—years old. Plenty of children of her kind have already left school forever by the time they reach that age, if they ever went at all. I am not sure she could cope with it all, she's not really a child."

"Oh yes she is," said Dr Hampton, with a sudden, abrupt severity that made his old friend look up in surprise. "She may have been forced to grow up when she was a babe-in-arms, but she is still a child. For a few short years she should be in a place where she has permission to be one."

Happily unaware that her fate was being argued about, Liljana lay in her bed, floating on soft, warm, drug-embroidered clouds. In her confusion, she thought she could see her mother, radiant and smiling as she had been on those occasions when the gloom of her illness had lifted and she had experienced some peace. She truly was a beautiful woman, as lovely as a Pre-Raphaelite portrait, smiling as though it were the most natural thing in the world for her to sit at her daughter's bedside and talk to her. "You will be well again soon," she said, "and I will take you home. I've made up your room specially. Everything is going to be so happy. I want so very much for you to be happy."

As she lay cocooned in the happy isolation of her room, two men she barely knew were locked in negotiations about her future. It did not occur to them, as they plotted out the finer details of who was to pay for Liljana's eviction from Malta and how easily Dr Hampton's brother might be prevailed upon to grant her a scholarship, to ask Liljana how she felt about their plans. In the seen-and-not-heard world of Edwardian Malta, Liljana was silenced by the triple lock of being the wrong age, the wrong class and the wrong sex. It was not so much that they disregarded her opinions, it was more that she was not expected to have any opinions to disregard. On that otherwise quite unremarkable afternoon, as Liljana dreamed of her mother, George Burnett and Dr Hampton wrote a narrative that would part mother and child forever, and Liljana had simply to be dropped inside its chapters and guided from one episode to the next.

Liljana was kept entirely in the dark about the plan until it had been completed down to the tiniest detail: George Burnett agreed to pay her passage to England and to cover the costs of her modest needs for the time she was at school; Dr Hampton's brother was prevailed upon to give her a scholarship; and everything she required was quietly purchased and packed for her.

"They wanted it to be a marvellous surprise for you!" Mrs Debono promised her, as Liljana sat in the corner of the kitchen, staring into space. "What a blessed girl you are! England, who would have thought it? Travelling all the way to England in a boat! And all those pretty things they have bought for you. Why, I looked into the trunk myself before they locked it—what lovely warm frocks for the cold weather."

But as Mrs Debono prattled on and on with forced gaiety that grated horribly on Liljana's nerves, the child knew perfectly well that the plan had been kept from her not to give her a splendid surprise but to ensure that she could not possibly object if she had had the will to do so. Who could possibly be so ungrateful as to turn up her nose at a trunk full of goodies and a ticket to adventure? "I don't want to go," she said impassively, not moving her eyes from the cobweb draped across the opposite ceiling that Mrs Debono had somehow managed to miss.

"Nonsense, child, how silly you are! It is all so exciting! A proper lady you will be, you'll see."

Liljana continued to stare ahead, blocking out the steady stream of insincerities. She felt an irrational sense of injury that Mrs Debono had not broken down in tears when she had told her the news, not knowing that tears—and there would be many of them—would come after Liljana had left the house and could not be unsettled by them. There would be tears the moment the door closed behind her; there would be tears for months after she had gone every time Mrs Debono entered her bedroom at night and glanced at Liljana's empty nest of blankets; tears when Reno removed it because it seemed to ensure that Liljana would never return to her if she had nowhere to lay her head; there would be tears at Mass as Mrs Debono imagined her young charge snuggled up next to her, half-asleep; and endless, carefully concealed tears as she pottered about the kitchen and became abruptly aware of the emptiness of the room.

But all that grief was yet to come and would have been of little comfort to Liljana during those hazy, colourless final days as she battled with the thought that all that was familiar was to pass from her a second time, but this time more devastatingly than the last because there would be nothing left that she recognised or understood. Part of her thought that Mrs Debono should have been promising to help her to stay, begging for a reprieve, but here she was celebrating the news that they were to be parted. There was no such thing as justice.

Liljana bore much the same impassive expression as she sat at the dockside on her trunk, the picture of Edwardian misery in her little white gloves and hat. There was no one to see her off. Her mother, drugged and bewildered, was not told that her only daughter was leaving the country forever because at that time she still could not remember ever having had a child of her own; by the time she would call for her she would be long gone. Liljana's whispered request to see her had been met with incredulity and then a clumsy attempt to distract her attention, as though her desire to spend an hour in her mother's presence could be removed from her mind with a promise of *pasti*.

She glanced wearily at the other passengers waiting to embark—English men and women cheerfully awaiting the journey home; her own people tearfully parting company with family and friends for the promise of a better life. Liljana had no inclination to cry and observed those who did with something like envy. She thought about her last hour in the house and the enormous breakfast Mrs Debono had made especially for her, how she had smiled as Liljana had tucked in. She had not even been hungry, but she had known Mrs Debono would be crestfallen if she pushed her plate away and so ate with apparent delight. Then there had been embraces when Liljana had felt herself disappearing into the safety of the swathes and swathes of black material that covered Mrs Debono's vast person and she had so very nearly cried. She was still a little worried that Mrs Debono would think her heartless for not weeping, but all she had felt was a dull ache where her heart should have been, as the old lady had slipped a thin chain around her neck with a small silver crucifix.

"Thank you," she had said.

"It was my mother's," Mrs Debono had told her, "but I have no one to pass it on to. Do not forget who you are, will you?"

"Never," she had said without understanding what Mrs Debono had meant or that she would almost certainly never see her again. As it happened, by the time Liljana did return to Malta, Mrs Debono had gone to her Maker and Liljana had long ago stopped wearing the crucifix.

"I hoped I would catch you in time," said a man's voice. Liljana looked round and saw Dr Hampton moving breathlessly in her direction. He handed her an envelope with a name written in black ink on it. "Be sure to give this to Mr Hampton when you arrive," he said.

"Yes, Doctor."

"Good. You know, don't you, that there will be someone waiting for you when you arrive?"

"Yes, I was told."

Dr Hampton was not a man given to throwing his emotions about, but he felt desperately sorry for Liljana sitting there, prim and quiet, looking every bit like the unfortunate subject of a maudlin parlour song. She was the loneliest person he had ever come across and yet seemed almost unaware of it. It had been for that reason, more than any other, that he had suggested sending her away to start a new life, but now he almost wondered whether he had made a disastrous mistake. "Have you everything you need?" he asked.

"Yes, thank you, Doctor."

"Good." He reached into his pocket and brought out a small paper bag bulging with mint humbugs. "I bought these for you. They might help if you feel queasy on the way."

She smiled. "Thank you. He is not angry, is he?"

"Who? Oh, no, of course not. Not at all." He looked at her and noticed no sign of reassurance on her face whatsoever. "I promise you, no one is angry. None of this horrid business was your fault." He knew he had to make her understand now, once and for all, or she would go away to England wondering what she could have done to escape the punishment of exile to an educational penal colony. "It's a reward, Lily. You have shown yourself to be honest and brave, and Mr Burnett wants to help you on your way in life. Think of it as a chance to make a fresh start."

Dr Hampton knew, as any sane person who had ever been the unfortunate inmate of a British boarding school knew, that no child could ever imagine it a reward to be sent to a world of cold showers, poor diet and excessive discipline, but he could not bear the coldness she exuded. If she had burst into tears or protested volubly, he would have remonstrated with her, but as it was he felt utterly locked out of her life. "I wonder if you could help me get my trunk aboard?" she asked, rising to her feet.

"Of course, let me find a porter."

Dr Hampton watched her diminutive figure stepping hesitantly across the gangplank and comforted himself that English children scattered across the empire made lonely journeys like this at younger ages than hers. Except that such children invariably came from affluent families and had mothers to wave them off and to send them sweets and hand-knitted vests to keep out the chill of the winter. He raised a hand to wave to her, but she never turned her head to look at him, and he fled the scene before the ship began to move. It was incredible, he thought, as he stepped casually back into his otherwise undisturbed life, how much heartbreak there was to be found in the absence of a return ticket.

As for Liljana, she watched in silence as the waters of the Mediterranean swallowed up her island home and, with it, the world she had known. In spite of the hot weather and the layers of petticoats and flannel she wore, she felt chilled to the bone. Thoughts scattered themselves around her, grazing her memory like fragments of broken glass: Mrs Debono busily at work in her kitchen; Mrs Burnett sitting in the drawing room oozing self-pity to her lady acquaintances; her home and its every familiar detail—the furnishings, the rugs on the floors, the frayed mosquito nets, the possessions she had left behind and her mother with no one to love her. Her mother, still angry with her for some slight for which Liljana had never been able to apologise, locked up in an asylum away from the malicious eyes of a society that held no place for either of them anymore.

II

8

The question pestered Kristjana every time Leo took her on one of his little trips down memory lane: If she were mad would she know it? She was beginning to think that it was this irksome question that had brought her to Jerusalem, because in a place where there were so many damaged people walking the streets, her little eccentricities could slip easily under the radar.

Damaged people: men and women from both sides of the divide who had lost brothers, fathers, children in the recent conflict and were trying to build a lasting peace; families who had lost their homes years ago and still held on to the front door key because they could not let go of the hope that they would one day return and everything would be as it was when they left; people who had walked away from massacres, leaving behind everything including the unburied bodies of their murdered loved ones; the very old who remembered Auschwitz and the liquidation of the Kraków Ghetto. Set against such devastation, such inhumanity, Kristjana's small losses and struggles counted for so little that she was ashamed by how gracelessly she had borne them, ashamed that she had gone to such desperate lengths to run for cover.

The question barely needed asking: If she were mad, would she know it? Kristjana feared so many things, but nothing more so than the thought that she might lose her mind without knowing it or, much worse, might have already lost her reason and was living the lie that the rest of the world had gone mad while she was the only one who had kept her head. Would a person in possession of her mental faculties have fallen apart because her boyfriend went abroad for a few months, when others had hung on to their self-possession on the Burma railway or in the Gulag? It was too ludicrous to contemplate. Would anyone who even knew the meaning of the word "rational" have absconded from life and travelled abroad so as to avoid living like an adult?

As soon as Leo's sleeping drugs took effect, Kristjana packed a bottle of juice and a box of baklava into her rucksack and left the hospital, heading for the old city walls. There was no sight more stunning than the most loved and fought over city in the world. At the very brink of sunset, the sky above her head was pink and orange and yellow—every warm, inviting colour—so perfect it could almost have been painted. Further down, as the light began to fade, she saw lights going on in the many houses as those happy enough to have homes settled down for the evening, and she felt the luxuriant ache of the perpetual outsider. Perhaps it was this pain that made her feel so close to Liljana; Kristjana knew she must have felt it, for she was an outsider in her own country and in everyone else's.

On her way back to Damascus Gate, Kristjana found herself hovering at the door of the Al-Arab youth hostel before the temptation to connect with someone took over and she stepped inside. She knew there was an Internet café past the lobby, where two American backpackers talked politics aggressively over the sound of *The Bold and the Beautiful* prattling inanely on the television set elevated in a corner. "Camp David will fail" was all she heard, spoken as though the man wanted the region to descend into another bloodbath to prove how insightful he was. A bespectacled man she seemed to remember from her previous visit, sat behind a counter reading a book. "*Marhaba*," he said, looking up at her with a smile, "can I help you?"

"Ten minutes on the Internet please." She handed over the correct number of shekels and sat at the battered-looking computer he indicated. She did not attempt to look at her work e-mail because she had resigned and her absence from meetings and seminars seemed pretty academic from a stuffy, smoke-filled Internet café in East Jerusalem, but the in-box of her personal account was full of e-mails from one person.

Sweetheart, I'm really sorry I haven't heard from you since we parted at the airport. I realise this is a very bad time for me to be away but I had no idea you would be feeling like this and I don't want you to hold it against me. You have to understand, this is such an important opportunity for me. If it were you, I would want you to do it, even if it meant you going away for a long time. The project is quite exciting and I like the team here at the lab, though I'm glad you can't see the accommodation I'm living in. I'm renting a room right opposite the accident and emergency unit of the local hospital and there are sirens blaring all night. I even dream about them!

Please drop me a line when you get this message. There's no need for this to come between us.

I love you XXX

Darling, it's been three days and still haven't heard from you. I know you must have read my e-mail by now, you always check your e-mails. I'd really appreciate a response, even if you're still hopping mad. Please write soon. If it helps at all, I'm pretty lonely here too. It makes me realise how miserable it must be to be a post-doc when you're single and have no one to share your life with. I don't ever want it to be like that for me. Lots of love from far away. XXXXX

Kris, I think you've made your point. Please remember how miserable you felt when one of your friends stopped talking to you. Silence is a horrible thing when it comes between friends and I don't want it to come between us. I know you're very upset about us being parted but it's only temporary and academics have to do this all the time. It won't always be like this. When I get a permanent position we can make a life for ourselves. I'm only doing this because I want to make sure we have a future together. Please do me the courtesy of answering. I check my e-mails every hour when I'm working at the computer, hoping to find a message from you. I know we can work things out but we need to communicate. Love you. XXXXX

My darling, what on earth is going on? I tried calling your mobile but just got a message saying that your Sim card was unassigned. When I rang your office, the receptionist said that you had not turned up for work and just sent some weird text message to your manager. They called the police because they thought something terrible had happened to you on the way to work since you are never late and would never take time off without asking. The police started investigating what had happened to you, even interviewed your landlady and she discovered that your passport was missing from your things. When they checked with your bank, they found out that you had bought a ticket to Tel Aviv on your debit card and left the country but the trail went cold as soon as you arrived at Ben Gurion Airport.

The police aren't taking things any further because it appears that you went of your own accord. I'm guessing, since no one has heard anything else of you, that you must be working somewhere in Israel and earning enough money not to have to use your card anymore or it would have shown up. FOR PITY'S SAKE WHAT ARE YOU PLAYING AT? You can't just disappear like this, everyone has been worried sick! PLEASE PLEASE tell me what's going on, nothing is worth running away like this. If you're having a nervous breakdown or something, you must come home where people know you and can look after you. Please e-mail me immediately to tell me you're all right. I'm worried about you, my darling. Please don't do anything else on impulse, there is always an alternative.

I love you, whatever you are feeling. Please don't leave me in the dark anymore.

By the time Kristjana had finished reading through the e-mails, she was not sure she deserved to belong anywhere. She had walked out of his life without a second thought; heaven only knew what he had been through in the days that had passed since his first e-mail. She had *known* he would try to contact her before very long, and it had not even occurred to her to tell him she had left the country. In her infantile rage she had barely given him a second thought.

"Time is up, I'm afraid," said the man with the glasses, appearing awkwardly at her side.

"Give me five minutes," she begged him, "I'll pay the difference before I go."

It was absurd. Kristjana sat in a stiflingly hot room, made all the more uncomfortable by the row of computers being used by a row of silent individuals all churning out heat, trying to write an e-mail to a man in another country, another continent, another time zone, to reassure him that her disappearing act from yet another country, continent and time zone, was nothing to be concerned about.

My darling Benedict, I am so sorry for causing so much bother, I'm really not sure what got into me to run off like that. It was very selfish and I should have thought about what I was doing. It didn't even occur to me the police would get involved.

I wasn't ignoring you when I didn't answer your e-mails, it was just that I don't have internet where I am living and I have been too busy to get out to an internet café. I promise I am not having a breakdown. I am very well and have a job looking after a man dying of cancer. Please don't waste your time worrying about me. You do your job in Harvard and I will do mine in Jerusalem.

Lots of love, Kris xx

She was still not sure she was as sorry as she should have been for the trouble she had caused, particularly to Benedict, and finding out that she had left such a trail of mayhem in her path—including wasting police time—gave her even less incentive to go back to England than Benedict's pleading. Panic was quietly taking over. She could stay where she was. She could make a life for herself in this city. She had a bed to sleep and dream in; she had food awaiting her at every meal time; she had a job to occupy her time and a story-teller to draw her away from her petty unhappiness. If she could just make amends to Benedict, properly make it up to him, there was nothing else to consider.

At the entrance to the hospital, doctors and patients were sitting on the steps and benches enjoying the cool evening breezes. As soon as Kristjana stepped into view, she noticed a sudden fluttering of interest amid the otherwise peaceful company, a whispering that travelled from person to person up the steps and through the entrance to the reception desk, causing Issa, the hospital director, to emerge. He was in his early forties, she guessed, dressed in the jacket-and-tie uniform of a man with a desk job, cutting an impressive figure among the sea of hospital gowns and scrubs. Kristjana was immediately on her guard. She liked Issa, but he was the director of the hospital and therefore an authority figure, one of those people a bit like the head-master who might be a very nice chap but only ever wants to talk to you if you've done something wrong.

"Kristjana?" he called, waving a set of papers. "There you are! The gentleman in room 37 asked for you hours ago."

He did not need to say anything else. She raced past him, past the gaggle of patients and doctors and the haze of fruity smoke, through the reception area, through the empty outpatient clinic, up the stairs and onto Leo's ward. She did not even bother to knock at his door—she no longer needed to—and rushed straight in to find him rocking from side to side in his bed, his eyes screwed shut, his lip bleeding with the effort of trying to keep quiet. When she reached his bedside, she could hear the gravelly sounds of his voice, strained and barely audible, whispering, "Oh, my Jesus, so much pain, so much pain."

"Why on earth didn't you call the nurse?" she asked, grasping his hand. "She could have arranged pain control for you."

He looked up at her like a child frightened by some abstract nightmare and pressed his free hand to her face. "I was offering it up."

69

Kristjana had no idea afterwards why she felt so angry, but she pressed his alarm button as though she would rather wrench it out of the wall altogether. Bernadette appeared after a couple of minutes that ticked by like the seven ages of man. "Oh my word!" she exclaimed when she saw the state he was in. "Why you didn't call me before?"

"He was offering it up!" Kristjana all but shouted, then immediately became aware that she had broken some trust he had placed in her. "Or something like that anyway. Is Dr Khoury on duty?"

"No, Dr Nasser. I'll call him."

Dr Nasser duly appeared, and Kristjana backed away into a corner while he and Bernadette made Leo comfortable. She knew her place, but even more so, she was beginning to feel quite squeamish about watching Leo going through the ordeal of tubes and needles, as she would if she were forced to witness a member of her own family being treated. She was on the point of closing her eyes when the whole exercise came to an abrupt halt and both doctor and nurse moved towards the door.

"*Wardi*, don't stay too long," said Dr Nasser, turning to look at her. "You are supposed to be off duty."

"I won't be long."

He nodded with a patient smile, knowing that she certainly would be, and left. She could sense Leo glancing in her direction and moved back to her station in the easy chair next to his bed. The muscles of his face relaxed slowly as the powerful pain-relieving drugs coursed through his bloodstream. "You know why he calls you *Wardi*?"

"No idea. I quite like it."

"It's a beautiful word. It means ..."

"Flower. Yes, I know, it's the same in Maltese."

Leo managed a smile. "He had a daughter called Warda. She died when she was about your age."

"I'm sorry. Was it an accident?"

"No. Dr Nasser came here from Lebanon. He lost most of his family in the 1981 massacre. That's why he pretends not to understand Hebrew."

She had never noticed that and was ashamed to admit that she had no idea what the 1981 massacre was, but this region had seen so much bloodshed she could almost see it unfolding in front of her eyes in an array of BBC news reports: burning cars, blood on the streets, women screaming, and in the midst of it, dear, gentle, grey Dr Nasser staggering through the smoke and carnage, carrying the body of a young woman he could not cure with his tubes and needles and life-prolonging drugs. "What were you offering up the pain for?" she asked, as nonchalantly as she could manage.

"My mother, since you ask."

"It sounds as if she had enough of her own to offer up."

"I'm not sure she offered it up very much. She ... drifted." He peered at Kristjana through the haze of morphine. "It's all right, *qalbi*, I know you think it's crazy. But I think it's crazy to waste suffering. It's not good to drift away, but I can't say I blame her."

***

Drifting was the only word anyone could have used to describe Liljana's plight. Once the ship had cleared the Mediterranean, Liljana was overcome by seasickness and stood out on the deck, gulping the fresh sea air in the hope that she would not disgrace herself completely. She felt bile in her throat, felt the terrible wrenching of her guts churning inside her and sucked in air as though there would soon be no oxygen left in the whole world. The spasm subsided; she crumpled slightly, clinging to the railing to prevent herself from sliding onto the deck, then jerked upright again, convulsed by another spasm of nausea. Liljana remembered a teacher at school talking about remembering happy things to sweeten bitter experiences such as having a tooth pulled. She tried to remember a rare visit to Caffe Cordina with her mother, the glimmering interior of marble and polished metal, the imperious curved ceiling. There were waiters, immaculately dressed, walking ramrod straight, carrying gleaming trays laden with every delightful treat: pots of tea and coffee; plates of *pastizzi*, pastries stuffed with ricotta cheese; *pasti*, sweetmeats made of almonds; *helwa*, sticky and crumbly at the same time, a heaven of sweetness. She smelled again the intoxicating odour of coffee swirling around her, heard that cheerful, busy purr of conversation and people coming and going—lawyers rushing in for a break whilst the jury adjourned, businessmen talking animatedly, retired colonials lost behind English newspapers.

Liljana crunched one of Dr Hampton's humbugs between her teeth, but its only effect was to make her vomit taste minty when she gave in to the urge and threw up noisily into the sea, to the considerable consternation of the dainty people around her. She had to go back. She wanted somehow to turn the clock back and to be back at the port, sitting on her trunk with Dr Hampton asking her if there was anything she needed so that she could tell him she had changed her mind.

If Liljana were in Malta, she would be there when her mother recovered and came home. She would be there to welcome her. She saw herself spring-cleaning the house in preparation—she had learned so much about that art at the Villa Burnett, she could do wonders for her mother's tiny house. She planned every detail of it: she would scrub the floors, remove the cobwebs from the corners, dust every single surface, polish the metal bannisters, air the rooms, turn the mattresses, and make the beds with fresh linen. The cupboards would be bare after so long; she would find the money to buy food and drink and replenish the empty jars of olives and capers. She would haggle with the paraffin man when he came by on his donkey, or she would not have any fuel for cooking. She would have to watch Giuseppe when he measured out her paraffin, since they all said he was crooked and used false measures. He used a trick involving a piece of rubber at the bottom of the metal jug.

Stop it! An invisible voice of reason shouted in her ear. *You are not going back. Do you not understand? You are not going back.* She knew she was not going back to any of it. The house would have to stay dusty, become more and more smothered in the dust of neglect with every passing day; the jars would remain empty; the rooms would be unaired, the beds unmade; her mother would stay in the locked and bolted sanctuary to which she had been so unwillingly dragged; and Liljana would drift away from her. She was drifting, drifting, drifting away.

9

And did those feet in ancient time
Walk upon England's mountains green?

Liljana had drifted into a dream and was not sure whether it was a good or a bad dream; it simply felt strange and confusing. She wondered, as she disembarked at Southampton, if this might be the sort of dream impossible to remember a few minutes after waking up. After days of misery at sea, perpetually seasick and unable to sleep, she stumbled about in a haze of exhaustion, only fleetingly aware of the misty drizzle of rain spraying softly across her face and the whirlpool of activity all around her: so many men and women hustling and bustling about, men carrying cases and trunks around, passengers like her gratefully arriving on dry land, others preparing to leave, meetings and partings, people of all ages who had friends and family to greet them or bid them farewell.

"Lily?" called a voice, shortly before a gloved hand tapped her on the shoulder. She turned and saw a smiling middle-aged woman, the shape of a cottage loaf, who had obviously been calling her for some time but had not wanted to raise her voice in public. Liljana nodded. "Frightfully sorry, my dear," continued the woman, "but I simply cannot pronounce your surname. I'm Mrs Davies, Dr Hampton's cousin."

Liljana scrambled her best manners together and gave a small curtsy. "How do you do, Mrs Davies. Dr Hampton told me there would be someone to meet me."

"You're to stay the night with us, my dear. My brother thought you would be far too tired to make the journey to the school as soon as you arrived. You will travel there tomorrow."

Liljana nodded, too tired to argue even if it had been in her character to do so. She managed to say thank you before drifting back into a dreamlike state, aware that nobody wished or needed her to say anything else; she was simply required to follow. She listened to the clip-clop of the pony that drew them along, thinking in a rather muddled way that even horses sounded prim in the heart of the empire. Liljana took her first bleary glimpse of an English street when they arrived at the door of the Davies' house, and she noticed a man ascending a ladder to light the street lamps one by one as it was already getting dark. The trees that lined the way rustled eerily in the gloaming. She paused to take in the sight of the first place in the country where she laid her head, a neat red-brick townhouse with a front door inlaid with coloured glass and bay windows poking out at either side. When Mrs Davies walked imperiously past her in the direction of the door, Liljana hung back and watched as the door opened as if by magic, letting the lady in before she turned around and gestured for her guest to follow her.

Liljana was startled in the hall by the presence of children, a boy and a girl some years younger than herself who had evidently been instructed not to harass her as they acknowledged her appearance politely before scuttling away. "I say, isn't she dark?" she heard the girl state as they disappeared. "Just like an Indian princess." It was only later that Liljana realised the children had not known she understood English or they might not have talked about her within earshot. It hardly mattered. Susan Burnett and her friends had had a habit of talking about her as though she were invisible or did not understand them, and they were seldom so flattering in their comments.

She was immediately shown upstairs to a spacious guestroom with yellow-and-white-striped wallpaper and a pale yellow eiderdown. Out the window, she could see one of the gas lamps casting a soft, almost plaintive glow across the ever-darkening street, and she felt the ache of homesickness for the first time. It was all so very strange, so completely alien, every tiny detail from the colour of the brick that made up the house, to the damp grey street where rainwater was still trickling into drains. Even the smell of the room felt wrong. She slumped onto the bed and felt her face burning with emotion, but before she could give way to tears, there was a tap on the door and a friendly voice inviting her to come down to dinner when she had refreshed herself.

Whatever else she was, Liljana was extremely hungry, and she jumped to her feet in a panic, hurriedly digging out an appropriate frock for the evening. The clothing she was wearing was quite cold and damp from being caught in the rain, another detail that felt wrong for she was more accustomed to clothing that was warm and damp from being worn in hot, humid weather. As she struggled to remove her clothes and slipped into clean ones, she thought of the ferocious downpours of rain that swept Malta during the winter months. They would come on very quickly, the sudden appearance of ominous black clouds allowing just enough time to find shelter. The roaring rain would fall in sheets, on and on sometimes for hours, causing so much water to cover the land that the floods had been known to sweep horses and even men out to sea.

When the rain was accompanied by equally ferocious lightning and thunder, Liljana had spent many contented hours huddled under the stairs with her mother. They were both afraid of thunderstorms, but in a nervy, girlish way that rather enjoys hiding and views it almost as a game. They had been close during those times, wrapped in thick blankets like a pair of hibernating animals, shrieking every time their secret nest was lit up by the lightning stabbing the sea with gigantic, white-hot barbs.

Liljana stood before the looking glass, swallowing as though she were trying to force down the most disgusting medicine created by grown-ups to torment her. She was ready. She had fought the battle of removing the endless layers of cloth in which good Edwardian children were perpetually trapped, undone the rows and rows of fiddly buttons and repeated the entire exercise in reverse. She had found the time to untie her hair, comb it a little more harshly than she needed to and restrain it in two thick, dark fountains rippling down either side of her head. Dark hair. Dark face. Dark eyes. She had never even noticed before.

Liljana was interrupted by another soft tap on the door and hurried out, afraid to keep her hosts waiting.

Time and the hour runs through the roughest day.

She was in the country where the stories and plays and poems she had read in Mr Burnett's library had been written, works by Shakespeare and Lord Tennyson and Charles Kingsley and E. Nesbit and William Wordsworth—all those famous people who had captured the spirit of a generation that had lived and dreamed before passing into history.

The family were exceedingly kind and attentive during dinner, going out of their way to converse with her, asking if she liked the food that was placed before her or if she found it too strange to eat. She was so ravenous after the days of sickness that nothing was too strange to satisfy her appetite; her biggest challenge was to check herself from eating too much or too quickly. Before long the younger children were packed off to bed, and Mrs Davies took her by the hand and escorted her away from the dining room to the glorious comfort of a chair in front of the fire. She felt full of good things, with a curious feeling of safety all around her. In the corner of the room, a grandfather clock ticked lazily as though the whole world were winding down for the night, too warm and too satisfied, too *still* to move. Her eyelids became heavy and insisted upon closing. She felt the soft heat enveloping her, the ticktock of the old clock rocking her to sleep like the strangest of lullabies, and she slept. When she awoke briefly, she found herself tucked into bed and realised that someone must have carried her to her room. She must have been too tired to wake up when they got her into her night things, since she did not remember ever getting ready for bed. She buried her head in the pillow and slept on.

When Liljana woke again at first light, she heard birdsong outside her window and was thrown into confusion because she had slept so deeply she could not even remember that she had slept. It was the first night she could recall when she had not had any dreams at all or at least none worth remembering. She lay absolutely still, aware of the creeping cold across her hands—it would not be long before she learned to sleep with her arms tucked under the bedclothes—and she slowly began to remember where she was. She was in England, in a house in Southampton belonging to one of Dr Hampton's many relatives. She was on her way to school. Everything was new. She sat up, braced herself for another battle with tears but found instead that her heart was fluttering with nervous excitement. Everything was *new*, an adventure like the stories in Mr Burnett's library, except that this story was happening now and was her adventure; it was her story and she was the heroine.

By the time Mrs Davies knocked gently on the door to see if her young guest was awake, Liljana was dressed and ready, answering the door with the closest thing to a smile she could manage. "Good morning, *Sinjura* Davies," she said, in her delightful, singsong accent, "I trust you slept well?"

Then there was another flurry of activity, a hurried breakfast while her repacked trunk was carried to the brougham that would take Liljana to her destination. She was to be accompanied by the family nanny, an elderly lady dressed in black because she was still in mourning for the Old Queen. Before she left the sanctuary of the Davies' house, Liljana was handed another bag of sweets, which had the unintended effect of dampening her spirits as it reminded her of her final moments before leaving Malta. She was beginning to wonder whether giving sweets to children was the English equivalent of giving cigarettes to a man before he was hanged or of giving sugar to an animal before its throat is cut, "to sweeten death" Mrs Debono had said about the Turkish custom. Managing to suppress the morbid thought sufficiently well that nobody noticed her turning a little pale, Liljana said to Mrs Davies, "Thank you very much for your hospitality" and bobbed a curtsy. All the family could say about her afterwards was how beautifully well-mannered she was, so much so that they had barely noticed her presence among them.

Maybe it was not a storybook she had fallen into, thought Liljana, as the streets of the city gave way to a paradise of lush green fields and an unpolluted sky, clear and flawlessly blue after the previous day's rain. Maybe she was the heroine of an epic poem in which the Garden of England, green but dusted with gold from the creeping hand of autumn, would form the landscape through which she would have to journey to find—to find what? The meaning to some mystery? Some elusive treasure? She might even have to write it herself because she already sensed that she could have the most overwhelming, the most scintillating adventure in the whole of human history and still go unnoticed.

Season of mists and mellow fruitfulness. That was how she would begin it, even if there was no mist yet. She was sure Keats would not mind if she borrowed the first line of his poem as long as she acknowledged him properly at the end.

***

"'Season of mists and mellow fruitfulness,'" recited Kristjana, "'Close bosom friend of the maturing sun.'"

"I thought you would know it," said Leo, "'Ode to Autumn'. I had to write it out as a punishment once."

"That's a pity, you must hate it," replied Kristjana. She wished she could remember the rest of it now. She could almost hear her own teacher reading it aloud at the start of the autumn term of her first year at secondary school. She saw Mr Quest's balding head and his look of genuine surprise when he discovered she already knew it, because Kristjana's father had been in the habit of reciting poems to her on the long journey to school to distract her from the torment waiting at the end. It was the first time she had ever succeeded in impressing a teacher, and it was not long before he was recommending long lists of books he thought she would enjoy. Like Liljana, she had spent many happy evenings slipping away from the tawdry dormitory and its resident camp commandant into the many different worlds to which her teacher guided her: lands past and future, blitzed London, Captain Bligh's mutinous ship, time machines, Shakespeare's Verona. Worlds where demons could be fought and conquered.

"Of course, she did write some poetry when she was older," Leo explained, breaking abruptly into Kristjana's thoughts. "During the First World War everyone was at it, fancying themselves the next Rupert Brooke. But she said they were no good, and I think she destroyed most of them."

"A pity."

"Not really, I think her life was a poem in itself. It should have been me who wrote it down."

"Is that why you are telling me the story?"

"Seems a shame to waste it. You'd never burn a book, would you?" He yawned luxuriantly. "I need to sleep."

Kristjana took the cue and pulled his bedclothes over him, lowering the bed until it was not quite flat. Prone to heartburn, he liked to be a little propped up because it helped to keep the acid in his stomach where it belonged. "I haven't written poems in ages," she told him, placing a hand on his head. "It felt a bit adolescent. But if I was going to start again, this would be the city to do it. Good night."

"Good night."

"Sweet dreams."

It crossed Kristjana's mind, as she walked down the pink corridor, that Leo's mother had the sort of name every literary heroine should have: Liljana. Florid, romantic, enigmatic, and if the real Liljana was any of those things, she was certainly enigmatic. But if the poem of Liljana's life was to be written down, she had a feeling it should really be written in Maltese, a language that would somehow suit her: exotic but earthy, rooted in the past but still in its earliest flowering, a Semitic language written down in Roman script, the language spoken by a tiny, scattered people doomed to wander through the world in search of new homes and new identities. As one of Malta's abandoned children, Kristjana felt a gnawing sense of shame that she could never write anything in the language of her parents or her many ancestors. Liljana's memory would have to settle for second best, with the hope that her spirit might make a poem rise from English prose.

10

Liljana never forgot the moment Harewell School jumped into view. There was a long, winding path lined with beech trees that partially concealed the acres of farmland on either side, then a small stone bridge that crossed a river marking the end of the avenue and farmland, and the beginning of vast, landscaped gardens interspersed with tennis courts and areas for sports Liljana had never heard of. Quite suddenly they turned a corner, and a building Liljana fondly imagined to be a castle appeared as if by magic. It was a majestic miracle of grey stone and leaded windows, with little turrets, chimneys and wisteria creeping across the walls on either side of the front door in a blur of green and lilac.

"Is this a school?" asked Liljana incredulously, turning to the nanny for help. "Is this it?"

"Yes, my dear," came the croaky voice of the chaperone, who had been silent for virtually the entire journey, "this is your school. You are a very fortunate girl. Young ladies of your kind are not normally graced with such an education."

The unintended insult was lost on Liljana, who was busy climbing down whilst the driver stepped round to help Nanny. The old woman stepped briskly ahead, leading the way to a not entirely welcoming oak door, which looked to all intents and purposes like a gigantic chocolate bar that had been left to grow stale and unpalatable. Liljana could already feel herself losing her nerve and stepped back whilst Nanny rang the bell and spoke to the uniformed servant who answered. She was even more overcome when they stepped indoors and she found that it was as impressive inside as out. The entrance, like much of the school, had a polished wooden floor and oak-panelled walls. A wide wooden staircase swept majestically up to a gallery, which she was soon to discover acted as a crossroads between corridors and a narrower flight of wooden stairs that led to the dormitory Liljana was to call her home for her first year.

During her early weeks at the school, Liljana spent almost as much time dreaming about the possible history of the building as she did getting lost amid its dizzying, daunting corridors. For the moment, however, a guide had appeared in the form of a smiling girl Liljana's age. "I am Emily Sheppard," she said, in an accent Liljana could not place. She reminded Liljana of a small woodland creature, with her thin, expressive face and thatch of flaxen curls unwillingly restrained. "I am from Gibraltar. Mr Hampton thought you might like that."

Gibraltar was separated from Malta by a thousand miles of sea and, as far as Liljana was aware, the only thing the two places had in common was that they were both under the rule of His Britannic Majesty, but she appreciated the gesture. "How do you do?" she said.

Little did the girls know, as Liljana followed Emily up the two flights of stairs to the dormitory and Emily talked as though the fate of the empire depended upon it, that their friendship would endure through the years of growing up, their emergence from this place as polished young women and the suffering they would both face when August 1914 brought the world's youth to its knees. On that sunny afternoon shortly after the start of term, all Liljana knew was that she was very tired, exceedingly cold and utterly lost for words, but thanks to the flow of advice and information streaming from Emily's mouth, she had no need to say anything.

"The dormitory's quite comfortable really, as they go.... You'll be in the bed next to mine in Far End ... right next to a window, you lucky thing ... splendid view of the lawns ... even see the apple orchard in the distance on a clear day.... Extra blankets in the cupboard if you need them.... Matron thought you might find it cold ... get used to it ... always cold.... I'm to help you unpack.... Any books to go past the prefect first? ... Hope you've brought plenty of food."

There are certain places in a person's young life that he never forgets—a building, a garden, a room—and the dormitory where Liljana laid her head every night for her first year at the school was one such place. To be exact, it was more like three rooms connected by a meandering corridor than one. Far End, as it was called by virtue of being the furthest section of dormitory from the door, contained eight beds, with a set of curtains separating them into two groups of four. There was another cluster of eight beds in a middle section, also cut off by a curtain, followed by Near End, which was an exact mirror image of Far End. Each section of dormitory had its own coloured curtains and bed linen: pink for Near, green for Middle and blue for Far, and Liljana quickly associated the colour blue with bedtime and its routines, her favourite being reading time before lights out.

As a Roman Catholic, Liljana had the added luxury of not having to attend chapel after dinner. "Almost worth being a Papist to get out of that," Liljana once overheard another girl muttering resentfully, as she walked back to the dormitory to say her own prayers whilst the rest of the school groaned and shivered in the dour, chilly chapel with its hard wooden benches, musty prayer books and whitewashed walls covered in ominous Bible verses. For Liljana it was a sacred time, when she was alone with her own thoughts, and she would often find the rosary beads sliding out of her hands as her mind wandered to the worship of home. She saw it all in a series of picture postcard images that would have moved her to anguished tears if she could have allowed herself that luxury. Instead, she felt the dull throbbing of a grief that could not be described or shaken off as the lost, half-imaginary world of her past fluttered before her eyes: the honey-coloured houses and the tumbledown limestone walls, the whispering breezes through the palm fronds and the sun, blood red, melting into the sea at nightfall as though it were being sacrificed to a wrathful deity.

"Don't you know what's so special about this windowsill?" asked Emily. They were perched on the dormitory windowsill, and Emily's eyes were wide with wonder; she was clearly having the time of her life drawing her friend into the story. "Take another look."

Liljana looked more closely at the oak panel she had been leaning against. Not only was the windowsill made of wood but the entire window frame was lined with oak panels. Her fingers wandered to what appeared to be a small metal clasp, which she pressed carefully until there was a click and the whole panel began to swing open. She gave an uncharacteristic squeal of excitement. Liljana was fascinated with the past; it was difficult not to be, growing up in a land of knights and noblemen as she had done, but this was particularly exciting. "It's a secret chamber!"

"It's more than that, old girl," said Emily importantly, "it's a priest hole."

"Whatever is that?"

"In Elizabethan times, they used to hang Catholic priests and tear their guts out," Emily explained with relish, not considering that Liljana might be unsettled by this information, "so wealthy Catholics used to hide them in their houses. They built priest holes behind oak panels and pictures and things like that so that the priest hunters wouldn't find them."

"What nonsense you do talk, Emmy!" came a withering comment, and the two girls looked up in alarm to see an older girl standing before them. She had sharp, pale features and a perpetual smirk on her face, which was not softened by the odd angle at which she held her head. It might have been simply her haughty manner, but it seemed to Liljana that the girl was giving her a perfect view up her nose. "This house is not Elizabethan, it is less than a century old. It was built to look older. And even if it were, that chamber is tiny; a grown man could never fit into it. Even teeny tiny Lily here would struggle."

"People were shorter in those days, Millicent," Emily suggested, determined not to be humiliated. "And perhaps the house is older than you think."

"Priest holes were built not to be discovered," said the girl, wrinkling her nose and giving the other two some relief from having to look up its cavities. "If someone with her tiny mind opened it that quickly, it would hardly be a very good hiding place, would it?"

"Millicent," spluttered Emily, kicking her heels against the wall, "that's uncalled for! She has *not* got a tiny mind!"

Millicent shrugged. "Of course it is tiny. My father was horrified when I wrote him that some other creature from the colonies had arrived. He said education is wasted on people like that; it makes them forget their place. But then I suppose the same could be said of you."

Liljana had to give Emily credit for making the most of the element of surprise. Millicent may well have been expecting a sharp retort or even an irate swipe of the hand, but evidently had not expected Emily to fly at her from the height of the windowsill, knock her down and start screaming accusations in her face. But then, when a grown-up came running and dispatched Emily and Liljana to the headmaster in the belief that they had both been involved, it was Lily's turn to be surprised. She was only at the school because she had been falsely accused once before and was fully prepared to face the consequences of yet another injustice, but Emily would not hear of it.

83

"This had nothing to do with Lily!" Emily protested, as they handed Mr Hampton the tickets they had been given by the mistress who had rushed to the scene. "She was insulted and refused to rise to it. She does not deserve this."

"She was trying to help me!" pleaded Lily in turn, too astonished at being defended to take it entirely graciously. "Millicent would never have said all those beastly things if I had not been there."

The bizarre *Alice in Wonderland* logic of her argument would have caused Mr Hampton to burst out laughing anywhere else, but it was that comment—unbeknown to either girl—that caused him to leave her alone. There was something so pathetic about a child sincerely believing that a situation was her fault simply because of her existence. She had not said, "She would never have said those things if I had not provoked her" or "if I had not said such and such a thing" but rather "if I had not been there". He would have blamed her Catholicism for inducing instinctive feelings of guilt in the child if he had not been painfully aware that she had been a scapegoat before and might simply think like that. Whatever the cause, it occurred to him much later that sparing her had probably made the situation even worse, as she would no doubt reproach herself for the rest of the day for leaving her friend to take the rap, even though he had had to throw her bodily out of the room when she refused to leave.

"Thanks," said Liljana, when they were once again sitting on the dormitory windowsill and Emily was sitting on her hands, her face still blotched red with the effort of controlling herself. "It was awfully decent of you."

"Think nothing of it," Emily giggled, a little too long. "You look so fragile, you've no idea! Funny little thing!" The laughter petered out and Emily descended into uncharacteristic silence. "Why did you not answer back? She insulted you, the horrid little brat."

Liljana hesitated. "I suppose I thought it would be more dignified to remain silent—isn't that what the English do? Anyway, people can be so nasty, it is hard to know when to fight back."

Emily giggled again, and Liljana found it so infectious that she was soon giggling herself. "Very well then, I'll do the fighting, you provide the dignity. We shall make a formidable team."

"I'm so sorry you were punished."

"It's all right. I suppose dirty little colonials like us should stick together."

Liljana looked askance at Emily, then realised she was joking. It had been a day of firsts: the first time a child her own age had shown herself willing to be a true friend to her, the first time anybody had suffered for her and the first time she had experienced the wonders of English humour. And if being at the receiving end of Emily's affection felt a little peculiar, she thought that she could grow to like it.

Oh, the vanished world of the Edwardian school, described with such love by a dying man born when that world was already engulfed in a miasma of artillery smoke and poison gas. It was every bit as harsh, as petty, as spiteful as any insular little institution, particularly an educational establishment, but Liljana was quietly determined to live with every miserable detail. She excused its many privations and cruelties on the grounds that the alternative was domestic service and a lifetime of drudgery.

The minutiae of daily life in the classroom lingered in Liljana's memory until her final hour: the long benches, the high windows, the faint cloud of chalk dust hovering in the air. In winter, a small fire burned sulkily in the grate, fighting the encroaching chill.

And there Liljana would sit, a dark, diligent head bent over a puzzling piece of work: "Describe a journey from Moscow to Vladivostok, noting the products of each region." Anyone observing her could have been forgiven for thinking that Liljana's greatest ambition in life was to keep her head down and be as little noticed as possible. She was a discreetly industrious child making the most of a difficult situation, for whom work—any work—offered a diversion from painful subjects and the promise of a happier future. There was even a certain novelty to their housekeeping classes, in which they were taught how to remove stubborn stains from clothing and how to manage a household laundry. She was rather better at the tasks they were set than the other girls and ignored the steady stream of catty remarks that only a common servant could be so well-versed in the intricacies of cleaning and mending. As Liljana sat stitching a sampler or darning a sock, she dreamed her way into life as a grown woman with her own household to run, her own home to tidy, her own children to mind, and her own husband to cheer after a long day's work as they sat together by the fire. The life that future generations of women would dismiss as dull and degrading offered Liljana the liberating prospect of being mistress in her own home rather than living to serve others.

Liljana remembered much of her first year as a series of snapshots: a moment during a lesson she had actually enjoyed, the interior of a room, an exchange with another child. With hindsight and memory of the watershed awaiting her near the end of that academic year, Liljana chose to forget the aching homesickness she had experienced during the early weeks, the perpetual hunger and cold that hit her during the winter, the persistent sense when she first arrived that she was being got out of the way because there was no longer anybody in the entire world who really cared what happened to her. By the end of her first fortnight at the school, her knuckles were cracked and bled constantly, partly from the bitter cold and partly because she had had her knuckles rapped every single day since her arrival—always for being late for class because the school buildings were so very large and confusing that she was perpetually lost—but she stubbornly remembered it in later years as a time of innocence and safety when she had not had a care in the world.

The one break in the weekly routine was her Sunday visit to Mass. Matron would tiptoe into the dormitory two hours before reveille and quietly nudge her awake, then she would dress in the semidarkness and walk alone through the dewy fields the three miles to the nearest Catholic church. The first time, a mistress had been prevailed upon to accompany her to Mass to show her the route; but ever after she was left to make her own way, and she preferred solitude to the company of a sullen female who spent the journey expressing her resentment at being expected to assist with such superstitious claptrap.

A walk alone as the sun was rising felt exciting and mysterious. The countryside seemed virgin, as though Liljana were an explorer stepping through some unconquered land untouched by man. She would hear the birds singing and watch the weak early morning light fluttering through the tiny gaps in the clouds, revelling in the freshness of a world waking up all around her to start a new day.

It was on these early morning walks that Liljana discovered that most mysterious quality of the English climate—the four seasons. Back in Malta there was no such thing, not really. There was the summer when it was blisteringly hot and all the vegetation died except for hardy, unfriendly plants like the cacti that grew wild along dry stone walls; then there was what she might have called the wet season, when the rain suddenly fell upon them, drenched and flooded everything and then stopped as abruptly as it had started, with dense grey clouds dispersing, and sunlight and wind drying everything out. But the English countryside was a land where subtle change was written into the very earth: the spring with tiny green shoots piercing the frost and delicate pink blossoms everywhere; the long, lazy summers where the sun if it shone at all beamed gently down upon the teeming fields and hedgerows, and the days were so long that Liljana would go to bed with faint sunlight still trickling beneath the edge of the curtains and wake to find that dawn had already broken; then autumn, the first season she ever witnessed unfurling, when the countryside she crossed seemed to have been sprinkled with gold—or rust, if she felt sad—and the branches of the trees groaned with fruits and nuts she had never seen before and the warm, fertile earth waited in silent dread for winter to strike down all that was life-giving and nurturing.

Being of a wistful disposition, Liljana came to love the passing seasons but could not help feeling saddened by the constant reminder that time was passing when she should have been too young to care. For all its beauty and promise of perpetual rebirth, the rhythms of the seasons she discovered in England, the predictable slide from spring to summer to autumn to winter, was also a reminder to a mind grown old before its time that all things must pass and all life must end.

"I say, you are frightfully morbid," Emily would remark when Liljana tried to speak of such things. "What you need is a jolly game of French cricket. Blow the cobwebs away."

If Emily had been less determined to bundle Liljana outdoors for a game she thought entirely pointless, Liljana might have confided an even sadder activity she was wont to indulge during her weekly visits to church. When she arrived, she would sit at the very back of the church, as far from every other member of the congregation as possible out of sheer force of habit. After Mass, she would visit the side chapel dedicated to Saint Anthony and light a votive candle. Her silent prayer was always the same: *Let my mother get better and send for me*. It took her years to admit it, but as she lit a candle to the saint popularly believed to be the finder of lost things, she nursed a secret desire for her mother to be well again, to be her old self so that they could make a home together back in Valletta. She was not sure which of them needed to be found but eventually was forced to consider that they were both lost.

***

"Her mother never called for her, did she?" asked Kristjana desolately. She was not sure why it mattered so much, but she wanted that child's prayer to be answered. "She never recovered."

"Of course not, it was impossible. A woman so ill and so little the doctors could do about it in those days." Leo spoke with his eyes closed, in the weary tone of a man about to nod off. Kristjana almost felt guilty for keeping him up. "There's plenty the doctors can't do anything about." He made the remark without bitterness, without energy, but he clearly meant it to apply to his own situation. "It's all right, part of her must have been resigned to the fact, but children have a remarkable capacity for hope."

Hope, like diligence, like innocence, like the need to be found is the stuff of which dreams are made. "I don't want to be lost," Kristjana found herself saying out loud, then cursed herself for saying something so ridiculous.

Leo chuckled though he evidently did not find the remark as silly as she did. "Then why did you run away?" he asked, peering at her from beneath half-closed lids. "Why did you lose yourself? Perhaps you too are hoping to be found." He closed his eyes again and turned his head to one side. "Not that it is any of my business, my dear. I'm sorry. I say stupid things when I'm tired."

I say stupid things when I'm wide awake! Kristjana thought. *I always, always have something stupid to say!* "Don't worry. Why don't you sleep now?"

"Good night then."

"Sweet dreams."

"I hope he does find you. Whoever he is."

"Good night!"

11

Liljana was so good at keeping her head down during her first year at school that once she had settled in she seldom found herself in trouble. Consequently, when a prefect discreetly tapped her on the shoulder during breakfast and told her to go to the headmaster's study immediately, she felt none of the stomach-churning fear she ought to have felt. Nevertheless, as she walked down the corridor and mounted the stairs, she found herself searching her conscience for a possible reason she might be in trouble—a poor piece of work perhaps, an unguarded comment, a forgotten chore—but by the time she arrived outside Mr Hampton's study, she was still none the wiser and felt a grim curiosity as she knocked quietly on the door.

"Come in."

And all our terrors freeze in memory.

Years later Liljana remembered the headmaster's turned back as he stood by the fire, apparently warming himself. It promised to be a bitter April, and as a fire roared in the grate, huge flames leaped up the chimney with such violence she remembered being amazed that the fireplace could contain them. Outside, the sky was so over-cast with impending rain that the room felt quite dark in spite of the ferocious fire and Mr Hampton's having lit the lamp. In amongst so many swirling shadows, Liljana stood still and silent. "You called for me, sir," she said quietly, when she had begun to wonder if he had failed to notice her entrance, "am I in trouble?"

"No trouble at all," he answered tonelessly without turning around, "not with me anyway. I'm afraid I have some bad news for you. Please prepare yourself."

Liljana felt her chest tightening and struggled to draw her next breath. "News from home?"

"Yes. My brother sent me a telegram early this morning. It's about your mother."

"She's dead, isn't she?"

He flinched at her taciturn response and turned to face her. "Yes."

"I knew it," she continued, with chilling matter-of-factness, "I think I knew it as soon as I stepped through this door. I was almost hoping I was in trouble. What did she die of?"

He stumbled over the word, still reeling from her cold tone. "Pneu ... pneumonia."

"I see. Did anyone go to the Requiem?"

"My ... my brother will have paid his respects, I am sure."

Liljana stared across at the ragged hearthrug and noticed a few charred holes where the cinders of past fires had scattered themselves. "I always hoped she would get better and we could go back to our little house, but I knew she would never come out of that place." The sound of the clock chiming the hour made her jump. She looked up at him. "May I be excused, sir? I have to go to class."

Mr Hampton reached out a hand to her. "Don't be silly, you don't have to go to lessons this morning. Here." He motioned for her to sit in the armchair near the fire, but she refused to move. "You've had a shock, Lily, you're trembling. Why do you not sit down for a while?"

"I shall be late," she insisted, "Miss Carson hates us to be late. I shall be back here with a little lavender slip if I am late."

"You will not get into trouble with Miss Carson, Lily. She's not expecting you in her class this morning. Please sit down."

"I promised I would never be late for lessons again," said Liljana, in the relentless voice of a child on the run. She turned around and walked to the door, then paused with her fingers on the brass handle. "It's all right, sir, you did not have to lie to me," she said, almost in a whisper. "I know my mother did not die of pneumonia. I know there was no Requiem."

The chill of the outer corridor hit her as she left the warmth of Mr Hampton's study, but she would not have noticed if a grown man had slapped her in the face. She marched towards her classroom as though she were marching mindlessly towards a battle she was certain to lose. She halted when she reached the main hall, disturbed by a sudden lurching sensation in the pit of her stomach that quickly overcame her. She had the dimmest recollection of grasping hold of the windowsill and seeing raindrops bursting against the leaded window, trickling in every direction. It looked as though the whole world was weeping, the world and all its peoples, all the angels safe in the heavens, every living creature was weeping except her.

They all tried so hard to be kind to her. Whatever else Liljana could say, she had to admit that they tried. She woke up in the sanatorium with a bruised head from having hit the edge of the windowsill as she fainted. Unusually, she felt warm, tucked up so tightly under several thick blankets that she found it impossible to sit up when she tried. Matron appeared by her side surrounded by an aroma of carbolic soap, but she was making a supreme effort to smile for once. "There we are, my dear," she said, putting a cup of tea on the table beside Liljana's bed. "You stay exactly where you are. Girls who bump their heads and have nasty shocks need plenty of rest."

"I am supposed to be taking part in the class debate this afternoon," she protested, but was surprised by how lethargic her voice sounded. "Emmy will be awfully put out if she has to do it on her own."

"Lily—"

"She hasn't read the book yet, I was going to talk about it."

"Lily, it *is* the afternoon," said Matron, stooping forward to help her sit up. "Emily understands. Bless her heart, she's already been down here asking after you."

"May I see her?" Liljana blushed, noting for the first time that she was in a nightgown and that Matron must have personally changed her clothes.

"No visitors for now. You just drink your tea. Nice hot sweet tea."

Tea, with its mystical powers to cure absolutely any ailment, from a broken head to a broken heart. Liljana watched as Matron walked away with a firm clip-clop tread. She could not understand it, but a storm cloud seemed to have descended upon her as she lay unconscious, and she felt no inclination to drink the tea. She felt no inclination to do anything, even lie down again, and when Matron returned she found Liljana exactly where she had left her, staring into space, the cup of tea cold and untouched by her side.

Two days later, she still could not be interested in food or conversation, and Matron summoned Emily to Liljana's side in the hope of lifting her spirits. The visit lasted ten minutes. "I hope you don't mind me saying so," Emily pronounced, when she imagined she was out of Liljana's hearing, "but I cannot help thinking she would be

91

happier if she were out of here. She's nothing to distract her lying in bed, and you know what a girl she is for brooding."

"I'll be the judge of that, Madam," answered Matron curtly, indicating the door. "She's in no fit state to get up."

"We'll look after her, Matron," promised Emily, taking her arm, "you'll see. We'll soon get her back to her old self."

Matron could not help thinking that Liljana's old self—quiet, reserved, unnervingly guarded—had not been a particularly healthy disposition for a young girl in the first place, but compared with her current state of near-trance it seemed positively gregarious. And whatever she could say about the other youngsters in Liljana's class, they were quite sweet-natured; it might do her good to be back in the thick of things again. "You know something, Emily? You may be right. Perhaps getting back to normal would help."

Emily jumped with excitement. "You'll see, Matron, she'll be smiling and laughing again in no time at all!"

Matron raised an eyebrow. "If you ever make that girl laugh I'll give you a medal."

Emily was never destined to be decorated for any achievement—Mr Hampton had written on one of her school reports: "This young lady's confidence outstrips her ability." Within a week of her friend returning to the schoolroom, Emily was beginning to wonder whether Liljana's bump on the head had altered her character forever. For her own part, Liljana could not explain the terrible transformation that had occurred. Cold resignation was part of her identity, it was the only way she felt able to cope with the uncertainties of life, but never had she felt this aloof from everyone and everything. It was as though she were floating in the middle of a vast ocean, far beyond the reach of any other human soul, beyond their kindness and their patience. All around her, there were people trying to make her feel better. She would find boiled sweets under her pillow or waiting for her on her desk. She was aware of teachers being uncharacteristically forbearing with her, not asking for work, not asking her questions in class, failing to notice when she sat staring out the window without once opening the book in front of her. But none of this kindness touched her; none of it brought her back to life.

"I've had enough of this," said Miss Carson, one dreary afternoon a fortnight or so after Liljana had received the news of her mother's death. Miss Carson had dismissed her class a few minutes early and instructed Liljana to stay behind, an instruction she had obeyed with an air of silent insolence. It was the first time since her brief conversation with Matron that Liljana had been forced to communicate with anybody, and she felt thrown by the air of confrontation in the room. Miss Carson stood in a square of weak sunlight, looking as she always did—red hair pinned neatly away from her pinched, frowning face, gown hanging neatly about her in crisp, heavy swathes—but Liljana found it impossible to look at her for more than a minute before glancing down at the floor. "Do you hear me, Lily? You're to pull yourself together."

Liljana felt silence descending all around her. "I cannot help it, Madam," she said finally, so quietly the slightest noise would have drowned her out.

"Yes you can!" snapped Miss Carson, and Liljana was shocked enough to look up for a moment. "This will not do. I am sorry about your mother, Lily, but I am not prepared to countenance this self-indulgent behaviour any longer. I have not received a single word from you since it happened."

There was something in Miss Carson's tone that reminded Liljana of a cracked bell clanging. It irritated her just enough to force her to answer. "I cannot help it," she said again, a little more strongly.

"You can help it," said the cracked bell. "Now you listen to me. You're a good girl, Lily, and I know things are very hard for you, but I will not allow this to go on."

"I cannot help—"

"I will *make* you help it!"

It seemed a long time since anyone had raised a voice to her, and Liljana flinched visibly before taking several steps back as a precaution. Miss Carson did not strike her as the sort of person who ever acted rashly; but one could not be too careful, and in any case the cold, calculating types were surely the most dangerous if they wanted to hurt a person—they were capable of holding back and thinking up the cleverest way to do harm. Millicent was like that; she would smirk in her victim's direction, giving her a second's warning to brace herself, then out would come some wounding dose of sarcasm immediately followed by a raised eyebrow and an "Oh I say, did I really say that? Oh gosh, I'm so tactless, I'm not sure where that came from."

Liljana knew she should make a polite response to Miss Carson, an assurance that she at least intended to mend her ways, but she could not open her mouth to speak and glanced blankly ahead, giving Miss Carson the uneasy feeling that she was not really there at all. "You are here to learn, Lily," she said, falling into a preaching tone out of sheer exasperation. "From now on, I expect to receive work from you when I ask for it. If you fail to do so, I will treat you the same as everybody else. Do you understand?"

The slightest, most reluctant of nods did little to reassure Miss Carson that Liljana had taken in a single word she had said, and she knew she had no business feeling any surprise when the essay on the life of Florence Nightingale failed to emerge by the end of the week. Nevertheless, as she went around the classroom collecting pages from eager hands, she felt a nagging sense of irritation descending as she approached the dark, tousled head lowered as had become customary so that it was impossible to engage the girl's attention without rapping sharply on the desk in front of her. "Lily, where is your work?"

Lily looked slowly in her direction, like a sleepwalker peering out at the world through a bewildering dream. She made no effort to speak and shrugged her shoulders by way of answer, which riled Miss Carson even more. "Lily, I did tell you I wanted your work. Have you done anything?" Lily shook her head, and her teacher was reminded again, most unhelpfully, of a small animal. "You haven't even started it, have you?"

Miss Carson heard a quiet, drawn-out sigh as she turned on her heel and walked the short distance to her desk, only realising as she brought out her lavender-coloured pad that it was her not Lily who was sighing. Of course, it would never occur to her pupils that she loathed the rare occasions when she was forced to send them to the headmaster with a lavender ticket containing the brief details of their offence and her signature. It was not that she cared particularly about their mortification and panic—she was far too hardened by spinsterhood for such sentimental feelings—but it was the thought that she had failed. She should not *have* to send them to a higher authority to face horrible retribution.

I am a monstrous coward, she thought to herself, as Lily wearily reached out and took the ticket, then left the room soundlessly without even bothering to look at the thing to discover what penalty she had incurred. The teachers were forbidden—theoretically at least—to lay a finger on any of the children and were instructed on arrival at the school to pack offenders off to the headmaster or the prefect to be dealt with. The system had been cleverly designed to protect children from short-tempered, aggressive teachers, but for the first time Miss Carson wondered whether it was really there for the benefit of teachers like her, who either did not trust themselves to act justly or were too squeamish to do so. She knew she would have ignored the absent piece of work if she had had to punish the girl herself in the face of howls of protest from the rest of the class.

"I am very sorry to see you here," said Mr Hampton, when Liljana stepped through his door. He had witnessed some impressive scenes in his study before, from eloquent protestations of innocence to uncontrolled histrionics, but never had he seen such a display of cold misery. She was not even afraid, he thought, as he gestured for her to come closer. She was not hiding fear as some of the cockier miscreants did, the shock of her mother's death had left her incapable of feeling any normal emotion whatsoever. He glanced at the ticket she had handed him and tore it in half before dropping the pieces into his wastepaper basket. Laziness was a vice he took very seriously, but he knew she was not lazy, and he knew, as Miss Carson had evidently not known, that no shock tactic would have any effect on her whatsoever. "It's all right, Lily, put your hands down. I want to talk to you."

She almost looked old, he thought, like a person reaching the end who is so burdened by aches and pains and illness that the effort is too much to be borne any longer. There were dark patches under her eyes from lack of sleep, and he was sure she had lost weight in the short time since they had last spoken. "You cannot go on like this," he said finally. "I know that something very terrible has happened to you, but you must stop this."

"I wish I were dead," she said so blandly that it took him a moment to comprehend her words.

"That's a wicked thing to say at your age!"

"I should never have been born. My mother said she only had me because a man took her by force. Then they hanged him. That was why she went mad."

Mr Hampton clenched his fists under the table to prevent himself from shuddering. "Are you ... are you sure?"

"She showed me the court papers once, when she was explaining why I was a mistake. She said God didn't want me to be born because he didn't want anything bad to happen to anyone, so I must have been the devil's idea." She let her head rest on one cupped hand, the only sign that the story troubled her. "It didn't seem to matter so much when she was alive because I thought I could make it up to her one day. Now I think that if I stop trying I shall just drift away before long."

Mr Hampton stood up abruptly, like a man suddenly aware that he is being hypnotised against his will. "Lily, *no*. Listen to me" Her hand slipped across her eyes but she showed no sign of breaking down. "You did not owe her anything; it's a wicked thing to say to a child. I should not have told you about it if I had been her."

"But you are not her! You know *nothing* about her!" He was not sure which of them was the more surprised, but Liljana had leaped to her feet and shouted the words, one hand clenched in front of her as though she seriously meant to attack him.

"Lily . . ."

But she never heard the stern, warning tone, and in any case they were both about to discover which of them was the angrier. "She could be so . . . so wonderful when she was herself! She could love better than anyone else in the whole world. Better than *you*." She could hardly breathe. "I thought . . . I thought if she could only get better and come out of that place. I thought if she could be well again . . . it would all be all right. We could be . . . happy. I could look after her."

"Lily, she was too ill for that," he tried, childishly grateful for the desk that stood between them, "she would never have recovered—"

"Perhaps she would—"

"She would *never* have got better, you must understand that!"

"Perhaps she would. She never . . . never gave herself the chance!"

"Lily, for pity's sake, will you be quiet!"

Liljana looked up at her adversary like a gladiator seeking out the weakness in a toweringly powerful opponent. She drew back, gasping for breath. "Please don't shout at me, sir."

"You were the first to raise your voice," he said quietly. "Sit down. There. Please sit down this time."

She sat stiffly in the chair he indicated, looking every bit as though she were waking up from a powerful anaesthetic. If she was at all afraid, she was afraid of herself not him. "I am sorry."

"It's all right, we won't say any more about it," he answered, matter-of-factly, "but you will now be quiet and listen to me. Nobody dies simply because he cannot make the effort to live any more. If you had truly wanted to end your life, you are clever enough to have found the means to do so by now, but you will not do it. The Roman Catholic in you will not allow you to do it." He noticed her twisting a clenched fist against her open hand, which he took as a sign that she was at least listening to him. "The only result you will achieve through your behaviour is failure. Now, if that is what you want, I can spare this school the nuisance of your presence and send you back to Malta tomorrow, but you know you can never go back. You are alone. Do you understand? You are entirely alone in the world."

Liljana felt an unfamiliar sensation of tears clouding her head. The room lurched around her for a moment as though she were going to faint again, but instead, she felt strange watery patterns tracing their way down her face and was thrown into confusion. "Why do you say these horrible things to me?" she whispered, but she could not speak properly either; she was out of control. "I ... I want to go back to class!"

"And indulge yet more of this absurd behaviour?" he asked coldly. "You will not leave this room until I am sure you mean to put an end to this."

Liljana struggled to make a response—any response at all, even a plea for him not to be so unkind—but her whole body seemed to be in rebellion, determined to silence her and every word choked in her throat.

"Try to hear what I am saying," he said. "Calm yourself." He waited what seemed like an age as she gasped and hiccupped, not realising that Liljana was releasing more grief in those excruciating seconds than she had expressed in all the years of her life put together. He waited until she was crying more softly, calculating that she was quiet enough to hear him but still too overwhelmed to answer back. "You have much to learn about the people with whom you share this school. With one or two notable exceptions, this establishment is populated by pampered little girls with wealthy papas to rescue them should they ever need help. When they are grown, however little they have retained of the excellent education they have been offered, they will marry well and live very comfortably indeed. You, on the other hand, will have to fend for yourself. You do not have a wealthy papa."

"I know that!" she wailed, finally. "Why are you telling me this? That's the terrible thing. Even when my mother's madness made her hate me, she was still my mother. Now I have *no one* ..."

"For your own sake make the most of the chance you have been given to better yourself, because there will be no one to catch you if you fall."

He told himself that it was best to let her cry. Watching her shuddering head buried in her arms, he wished he had dealt with the situation a little better when he had first told her about her mother's death. Now that he thought about it, he should not have allowed her to leave the room until he had been confident that she had taken in the news, then she might not have sunk into such an unhappy state in the first place, but it was easy enough to think that now.

Liljana wept relentlessly. Mr Hampton watched with the awkward bemusement of a man for whom life had been a quiet but satisfying experience with little to trouble him or any member of his family. He thought of his own children, his young son and two daughters, hedged in by certainties Liljana had never known, whose only recurring complaint was that life held no adventures in store for them. "Lily, if it helps, it needn't be like this," he said. He had no idea what would comfort a girl in such a miserable situation, but he knew he had to offer her some vision of a happy future. "I know it may seem a long way off now, but it needn't be like this forever. You could marry one day and have a family of your own. A family of your own making."

She did not look at him, but he noticed she seemed to be trying to control herself in order to hear him properly. "I think I am meant to be alone," she answered. "Some people are made like that. I cannot imagine myself any other way."

Mr Hampton felt himself blushing. He should never have permitted himself to get into such a ludicrous situation but he could not escape now. "You will not live your life alone," he said. "I promise you, you will not be alone."

And she chose to believe him—chose because the alternative was too dreadful to bear. He made her stay where she was until she had calmed down; but when she went back to class her eyes were so swollen that the other children thought she had been beaten to within an inch of her life, and Miss Carson went running to Mr Hampton at the end of the day to ask what on earth he had done to her. It would be many years before Liljana lost control again in such spectacular fashion, and when she did the consequences would touch the lives of countless unnamed people, including a troubled young woman born long after her death.

"I am not troubled," declared Kristjana to the world in general. Leo had taken to telling his story almost entirely with his eyes shut or staring fixedly into space as though she were not there, which made her want very much to remind him of her presence.

"I didn't say it was you."

"I know perfectly well you meant—oh skip it. What happened? It must have been fairly devastating to affect that many people."

"We are not there yet; I like linear narratives." He was teasing her, which came as a relief. If Leo had the energy to tease her, Kristjana mused, she was in no danger of losing him yet. "So he promised her," he continued. "It's silly to make promises to children, they never forget anything. They hold you to things." His eyes had closed again, but he had been very lucid in his storytelling throughout the afternoon and had the wistful smile on his face Kristjana remembered from their first encounter. "Could you pass me some water please?"

"It was the least he could do," she retorted, getting up to fill a beaker from the water jug. "Saying all those nasty things to her—talk about rubbing salt in the wound!"

"He was being honest."

"Heartless. I went to a school where they talked to you like that. The lower school boarding mistress' motto was, 'It's cruel to be kind.' She ought to have known." Kristjana succeeded in splashing water across the starched front of her white uniform and cursed mildly. "Sorry, but I hate the way the English make a virtue of being so cold."

"Not cold, careful." He reached forward to take the glass and chuckled at the sight of the wet patch on her clothes. "He was right. If she had clung to the past and wasted her time at school, she would have been completely helpless when she left. As it was, she left school an educated and accomplished young lady." He sipped from the glass, and she noted that he seemed to be finding it harder and harder to swallow. "Of course, what the poor man was not to know was that his children and all his pupils would grow up in time for the First World War. There were many lonely women by 1918. Millions of them."

"Was Mr Hampton's son killed?"

"Yes, at the second battle of Ypres. His wife died shortly after the war. There was a flu epidemic."

Kristjana remembered that from history lessons. She could still see the black-and-white photos of coffins piled high and harassed-looking nurses in overcrowded wards. "Was Liljana always alone?"

Leo tittered rather naughtily as though he was laughing in his sleep after an unrepeatable dream. "She had me, didn't she? And rather enjoyed the experience, I suspect."

Kristjana took the half-empty beaker from his hand and put it aside, ashamed to discover that she was blushing. Kristjana belonged to the generation brought up to believe that nobody had sex before 1965, or at least not meaningful or enjoyable sex. If their parents were to be believed, love as a concept was invented in the same decade as the Beatles and the Mini. Before that, couples partook of a reluctant act of intimacy for the purpose of conceiving children and protecting the empire; nice women closed their eyes and thought of England. The notion that those prim little girls in their starched white pinafores and lacy collars and long hair tied up with white ribbons could possibly have grown up to surrender to such heady passions and desires was almost offensive. Leo could read her mind. "You young people do make me laugh! Look at your face!"

The case was hopeless; Kristjana could feel the crimson spreading right across her neck. Time for a change of subject. "Your fluid intake is too low with this heat" was the best she could manage, and she began the ritual of making him comfortable by tucking in his sheets and stepping across the room to close the shutters. "I might ask Dr Khoury about getting you put on a drip tomorrow. Would you be happy about that?"

"Delighted, *qalbi*." His look of amusement remained unchanged as she folded his arms in front of him and plumped up his pillows. She had a sinking feeling he might burst into gales of laughter the moment she left the room. "Good night."

"Sweet dreams."

12

She knew Leo could not let it go. If Liljana belonged to the generation destined to die in the squalor of Flanders, Leo belonged to the generation born amid the carnage, the many lives conceived during brief moments of hope by men and women thrown together by a conflict that would eventually claim them all. But he did not want to come into being yet. He lingered in the happy tranquillity of a country school where his mother slowly learned the art of contentment. Like a dying man travelling the world to bid farewell to his favourite cities one by one, Leo was making a pilgrimage through his heritage, taking his leave of it chapter by chapter. But for a moment he was too tired and too dehydrated, too entranced by this innocent Edwardian world to go any further. Leo and Kristjana rested in the garden of July 1910, clinging to a world of tea parties and harmless pranks and deportment and straw hats and manners and frivolity and music halls and gas lamps and punting on the Thames. Like time travellers aboard the Titanic, watching the merriment of men and women who do not know they will never see another dawn, they watched Liljana's youth unfolding.

If there were ever a time in her life when Liljana discovered happiness, it was then, amid the books and chalk dust and green spaces of Harewell School. Her friendship with Emily Sheppard gave her companionship with a girl her own age and entrance into the mysterious realm of family life. Whatever she had imagined before setting foot on English soil, Liljana was pleasantly surprised by how hospitable people were. Hospitality, she had once imagined, belonged to Latins, with their culture of welcoming any person who appeared at the door, even a stranger, the social obligation of putting food and drink before him and offering him shelter should he require it. Only whilst in the service of English colonials had she discovered the bizarre world of appointments and letters of introduction and calling cards, the tendency to treat visitors as if they were mild nuisances to be tolerated and treated with courtesy but hardly *welcomed*, hardly made to feel at home.

In their natural habitat, Liljana discovered, the English were capable of being as welcoming as anyone, and she was never once left to while away the holidays all alone at school. As the end of term beckoned and she began to dread the prospect of being left to her own devices amid the empty school grounds, a friend would tap her on the shoulder and ask her very formally if she would like to join them should she have nothing else planned for Christmas or Easter. And she trained herself to thank them and to accept the offer very politely, stifling her excitement long enough to lock herself in the lavatory and jump up and down with glee at the prospect of a warm bed, good food and treats so novel and so wonderful she would live off the memories of theatre trips and picnics for weeks afterwards.

Her summers were reserved for Emily Sheppard and her delightful family safely ensconced in a thoroughly splendid London house containing every modern convenience. She would dream about the coming adventure for weeks beforehand: the long journey on the train that chuffed into Paddington Station with its vast arched roofs, the welcome—oh, the welcome so like the greeting she might have received from her own family at the end of term!—and the glorious feeling of waking up on the first morning of the holidays idyllically comfortable, in a room of her own lined with floral wallpaper and a thick woollen rug near her bed for her feet to sink into when she took her first steps of the day. Before she had been awake very long, Emily would tap on her door and two of them would sit in bed planning the day. "Mama thought we might have a walk in the park today," Emily would say, or even better, "Mama thought we should do a spot of shopping this morning" or even greater bliss, almost too marvellous to contemplate, "Papa has tickets for *Peter Pan*. He very much wants you to visit the theatre; it really will be perfectly wonderful!"

In that house, among the sumptuous rooms and the walled garden, Liljana and Emily felt the first unsettling stirrings of growing up. Proper growing up this time: the slow, inevitable process of looking ahead at a mysterious future from the safety of childhood. Childhood had come late in Liljana's life, and more than most children on the cusp of maturity, she felt a sense of exquisite terror while leaving childhood behind and at the same time flirting with the promise of womanhood. She and Emily posed before mirrors, imagining longer skirts and pinned back hair; they held secret vigils on the landing when they should have been long in bed, peering down through the bannisters at the grown-up world of parties and overhearing strained conversations and jokes that never made sense. They spun elaborate future plans when their elders thought they were talking about school.

"I shall have a very tragic romance with an artist or a poet," declared Emily, sitting astride one of the stronger branches of the chestnut tree at the end of the garden. "Then when he has died of consumption I shall marry some gentleman with a country estate."

"I shall sail home to Malta," said Liljana, for the hundredth time. "I shall live in a cottage on Sliema Front with Mrs Debono."

"Who's she?"

"She was the—she was a friend of my mother's." Liljana sank her fingernails into the bark of the tree, loathing herself for feeling ashamed. She knew Emily viewed her time in domestic service as a tragic accident, which she sportingly avoided mentioning, but Liljana was already mature enough to know that she had betrayed the old lady's kindness to her by denying the association. "A good friend."

"Whom will you marry out there?" asked Emily, noticing the change of atmosphere. "An Englishman or one of your own?"

A valiant effort, but Liljana could feel her spirits sinking even further with the question. She stared up through the leaves at the mottled pattern of clouds as though for inspiration, but no answer came. Plenty of Maltese girls married Englishmen, but she thought it unlikely that she was of the right class to do the same, and she was already distant enough from her country that the thought of marrying a fellow Maltese frightened her although she was not sure why. "Whomever I fall in love with," she answered in a small voice, then scrambled down the tree and threw herself backwards onto the grass. "Gosh, it's cold!"

The perimeters of Liljana's dreamy future home with its own painted balcony overlooking the sea and vast airy kitchen, tended to shatter into a thousand pieces when inconvenient realities like marriage markets began to emerge. She closed her eyes, willing herself to cheer up, but the image that had haunted her since she had first seen it returned to her again: a figure in a tiny boat being tossed about on a stormy sea before a blazing sunrise. And Mrs Debono's matriarchal presence was not there, and the words she had read out for her did not come to mind with the picture. "You shall have to come and live on my estate," Emily volunteered from her vantage point, noting her friend's furrowed brow. "I shall find you a splendid little cottage with roses growing up the walls."

Liljana shrugged. "I don't mind as long as there is plenty of space for books."

Emily jumped down from her perch, sprinkling Liljana with leaves as she descended. "Don't worry, old thing, you'll have your house by the sea. And a husband, and twenty children, and . . . and . . ." She ran to the safety of the other side of the tree as Liljana pulled herself to her feet and ran after her. It was a clumsy distraction, but Liljana wanted to be reminded that she had not yet left the walled garden.

And in the dusk where fell the firelight gleam,
Softly it wove itself into our dream.

III

13

Leo's strength had grown a little since the doctor had made some alterations to his cocktail of medication and decided to have him artificially hydrated to increase his fluid intake. When Kristjana came back from her lunch break, she was pleasantly surprised to find him smiling and alert after several days of lethargy, clamouring for her to tilt his bed so that he could be as upright as possible. "Fetch my box from the drawer, would you please, *qalbi*?"

Kristjana rummaged in the drawer in the bedside unit, making a mental note to herself to tidy it up before Bernadette found the used tissues and food wrappers she had stowed in there and forgotten to throw away. "It does sound funny, you calling me *qalbi* when you've such a plummy English accent," she remarked, bringing out the box he had requested. "Don't get me wrong, I like it but ..."

"My mother used to call me that," he explained, reaching out to take the box from her, "and she had a pretty plummy accent by the end, though it always had a certain ... a certain *lilt* to it. They say it is the speech patterns that never really disappear when a person learns another language, even if they lose their accent. You know," he indicated the box, "I've carried this around with me all my life. I've always taken it in my hand luggage on flights in case my suitcase went missing. I could lose anything except for this."

The box in question was slightly larger in length and width than a hardback book and about the depth of a Bible or a dictionary. It had been carved out of some dark wood or other that Kristjana did not recognise, engraved on the lid and sides with Maltese crosses. The catch had evidently broken years ago, and the box was tied shut with a length of black ribbon Leo no longer had the dexterity to untie. "Allow me," said Kristjana, applying her fingernails to the stubborn knot. "There we go."

"My father gave this to my mother when they were engaged to be married. She used it to store letters and photographs, precious things like that." With the ribbon untied, he opened the box very slowly, with an obvious sense of reluctance. "It's strange the way memories work, isn't it?" he mused, stroking the side of the box as though it were a sacred relic. "It would destroy me to be parted from these things, but I hardly ever look at them, they make me so sad."

"Don't look if you'd rather—"

But he was already passing her a stack of monochrome photographs one at a time, and whatever sadness he felt was lightened by the excitement of having someone with whom he could share his mementoes. There were remarkably few moments of Liljana's existence immortalised on celluloid, but they marked out the salient points of her life as photographs so often do: a rather dour snap of her in a classroom, holding what looked like a certificate; a posed photograph in full nursing uniform; a less formal picture of a young woman aged around thirty, smiling in a garden in the company of an older man Kristjana guessed to be her father-in-law or perhaps her childhood guardian on a visit. Then there was a family group, which did not make sense since Liljana had had no family.

"I'm sorry, the pictures are in the wrong order," said Leo, taking them all back except for the family group Kristjana had just begun to puzzle over. "That was taken in the summer of 1914. It's the Sheppard family during one of her holidays there. Her last holiday, of course. She never went back to school."

The last summer of youth. They huddled together, squinting a little in the sunshine, three older people—Mr and Mrs Sheppard and the family nanny—seated regally in front of a row of smiling members of the younger generation, all in the first flowering of adult life. Emily and Liljana flanked by two boys looking very dapper in their summer attire. "Emily's brothers?"

"Yes," said Leo, "Richard and Harry, God rest their souls."

"Were they both killed in the war?"

"No. Richard was killed three weeks before the armistice. Harry lied about his age. He went so far as to memorise the letters on the doctor's chart to hide his terrible sight, but he came home from the front alive, minus an arm."

"Poor man."

"Oh, Harry was one of the lucky ones. He came back to Blighty a week before his regiment was decimated at the Somme; not that there were really any survivors. I remember him." Leo pondered the photograph. "All those dead faces. All those dead, unsuspecting faces."

"Emily and your mother stayed close then?"

"Like sisters. I must have spent as much time in that house as a child as in my own. Mad, sad Uncle Harry. He never married, never *smiled*. He was dead before he was forty. But then the whole house felt a little sad when I was a child. They left Richard's room exactly as he had left it on his last leave—I only saw it once—bed carefully made, a copy of *Bleak House* on his desk with a bookmark left at the last page he'd read."

Kristjana squeezed Leo's hand. "Don't, Leo, you're crying. Can I . . . can I do anything for you?"

He lay back, signalling for her to straighten the bed so that he could lie back. "Don't go, will you? It sounds so foolish and selfish, but I feel like the last survivor of a disaster and I wish I wasn't the last. Richard died with his men; Harry died surrounded by his family. The old ones died together without time to be afraid. . . . Oh I'm sorry, *qalbi*, I'm sorry. I keep forgetting how young you are."

Kristjana felt suddenly exhausted and allowed herself the unprofessional luxury of resting her head against the side of Leo's bed. "It's me who should be sorry." She hesitated. "'We that are young shall never see so much . . .' Lear or Hamlet?"

"Lear," he said, "the last words." He gently continued:

> The weight of this sad time we must obey.
> Speak what we feel, not what we ought to say.
> The oldest hath borne most. We that are young
> Shall never see so much, nor live so long.

She felt the weight of his hand coming to rest on her head, almost in blessing. "I hope you do live long."

"I'm not sure I want to. The world's such a mess."

"You're far too young to talk like that. If the world's a mess, do something about it. That's what my mother thought—she tried to help."

"She became a nurse?"

"Yes. Lied about her age—for the sake of the war effort."

Leo reached back into the box and took out the photograph of Liljana in her nursing uniform, followed by another photograph Kristjana had not seen before. "Is that your father?"

"Naturally. Can you see a resemblance?"

Kristjana was not sure she could, but the young man looked like so many pictures she had seen from the same period that his face certainly felt familiar. It was the face that had greeted her generation as schoolchildren when they had opened the pages of their history textbooks, the face that glanced in their direction as they wandered into some room of the Imperial War Museum. He was in his early twenties at most, looking directly into the camera with that serious, soulful look that so epitomised Britain's lost generation. He was a private soldier, and even the details of his uniform formed part of the national heritage, from the rifle he would never have had the time to fire when staggering through no-man's-land to the heavy regulation backpack. "It weighed over 50 kilos," she could almost hear her history teacher informing them. "Imagine trying to make a dash for it with that on your back." This was Joseph Radcliffe, taken the day before his regiment embarked at Liverpool bound for Lemnos and finally Suvla Bay—where most would remain, interred in unmarked graves hurriedly dug to avoid the horror of human corpses left exposed to the elements in a hot climate.

Joseph peered at Kristjana now, his living, watchful eyes meeting hers as though they could somehow communicate across the decades—more than decades, not much less than a century—that divided their youth. Joseph Radcliffe of the Sixty-Fourth East Anglian Regiment. Joseph Radcliffe, the Cambridgeshire shopkeeper's son who queued with his friends for five hours in his desperation to enlist, convinced he was witnessing some epic moment of history. Joseph who celebrated with a gloriously drunken evening that had involved dancing all the way down Mill Road singing at the top of his voice: "If you were the only girl in the world and I were the only boy!"

"Are you sure you can't see a resemblance?" pestered Leo, placing the photograph near his face. "Allowing for my very great age?"

But that was the problem. So few of those First World War combatants seemed to have made it to any great age, their photographs looked quite generic. "The eyes?" she ventured, but even the look in the young man's eyes could not be replicated. *My God,* she thought, *why do they always look so pure?* These young men were not so very different from any other generation: they went to school, they earned a living, they got drunk, they fell in love with pretty girls—but there were things they had yet to learn about humanity's inhumanity with which future generations would be burdened. Kristjana wondered, glancing fixedly at that photograph, whether the Great War killed off not just a generation of youth but the very notion of youth, by creating the epoch of trenches and machine guns and chlorine gas and flame throwers, and not so very long after that, concentration camps and gas chambers and Hiroshima and the Gulag. All that unremitting evil unleashed upon the world in the space of a single lifetime.

"You are very proud of him, aren't you?"

"I am proud to be his son," said Leo, and for once his smile was just a smile, warmly affectionate. "Wrong side of the blanket, but still his son. It is hard not to be proud of reluctant heroes."

"He doesn't seem to have been so reluctant." *And hardly a hero, he had no idea what he was letting himself in for,* but even Kristjana was not churlish enough to say as much to a dying man clutching the faded monochrome photograph of his soldier father.

"Oh, it was easy enough for these young men to enlist," Leo conceded, "because they expected a short, heroic war they could boast about to their wives forever after. The real heroism was sticking it out, when the months passed and they realised how squalid and long it was going to be. Think how hard it must have been to return to the front after a short leave when you'd spent a few precious days doing normal things—sleeping in a comfortable bed, shopping, enjoying dinner with your family. Now *that* was heroism."

"Is that how they met? When he was on leave?"

"No, he was badly wounded. He fell in love with his nurse, as so many men do."

Kristjana felt herself blushing; but he had obviously meant nothing by the comment, and she struggled to pull herself together. "In London?"

"No indeed, in Malta."

We that are young shall never see so much.

14

Joseph had no idea where he was going as he lay on his stretcher in the hospital ship. All he knew was that it was taking him away from Gallipoli and that was all that mattered to him. The multiple wounds that had brought him out of battle were causing him unremitting pain, but pain was a sign that he was alive and he knew he was one of the lucky ones. Unlike Geoff Kennedy and Michael Bennett and Daniel Margolin and all the others. He felt tears pricking his eyelids, but he was not thinking of his friends tumbling helplessly into the dust like rag dolls all around him. There were some sights so unspeakable that only his dreams—over which he had no control at all—brought those moments back to life. Joseph was not even imagining his friends before they were soldiers, and there were so many touching moments he could have conjured up since they had grown up on the same street and dragged their feet every step of the way to the same school every day until they were fourteen.

What brought him so dangerously close to weeping was the thought of how desperate they had been to march to their deaths in the first place. They had been so frustrated by how long it had taken to see active service, as though they had truly believed the war would pass them by and fail to offer them the promise of a place in a mass grave somewhere far from home.

Joseph could see them all now, their uniforms clean and new, the seams yet to be colonised by those invincible regiments of lice, bored and resentful that other soldiers were heading for the front and they were being moved from inglorious place of safety to inglorious place of safety, from the dullest most provincial little East Anglian town in the world—Bury Saint Edmunds—to Saint Albans, where they were at least thankful that the travel broke up the excruciating boredom of waiting. History would surely record the battles, the salient points of interminably long campaigns, the eleventh-hour rescues, the daring raids, but would anyone think to record the weeks and months of tedium in between? The unbearable stretches of time when men got on one another's nerves and the biggest battles to be fought were with anxiety and the wearying discomforts of army life.

Joseph wondered now whether they had really been bored and resentful of their safety back in Blighty or whether they had secretly known they would eventually be shipped out to some disastrous campaign to be offered up as sacrificial machine-gun fodder to the Germans or the Turks, but of course they had not thought that. It was so hard to remember any of it with any clarity. The early days of their training, when they had been instructed in the art of warfare— dear God, he knew how to stab the Hun to death with a *bayonet!* Never, during his painfully brief active service had he ever got within *firing* distance of the enemy, let alone close enough to stab a man in the heart even if he had been of a strong enough constitution to commit such an act. They had clambered up ladders over the protective lip of the trench with many of them dead before they had properly emerged, picked off by the enemy like pheasants on a shoot. But that was not for the hours of daylight; he would not see them, hear them, remember them dead.

"I am alive," Joseph said out loud, but he was overwhelmed by the agony of his guts knotting up and his eyes began to mist over.

"Steady on, old chap!" called a voice from the end of a long tunnel. "Steady!"

Joseph clenched his teeth, braced every muscle in his body, but the effort of tensing up set the pain off again and he retched repeatedly. It was not so much the motion of the ship that was making him sick, it was the miasma of foul smells that seemed to erupt every time any other patient moved. It was the stench of infected tissue, of pus dripping from suppurating wounds. Perhaps it was his own wounds he could smell, which was why it suddenly seemed so close. "Sweet Jesus!"

"You need to find your sea legs, old man."

The throbbing across his temples slowly subsided. He felt bile rising in his throat, swallowed hard several times and felt it slipping away again. When he was sure he would not vomit, he opened his eyes and saw the owner of the sardonic voice for the first time. An impossibly young doctor with a head of wild black curls, blinked at him through steel-rimmed spectacles. "I'll be fortunate if I end up with any legs at all, Doctor!" Joseph retorted.

"Not a doctor yet, I'm afraid, just a lowly medical student helping the war effort."

"That's very decent of you."

"Not at all. The white feathers handed out by worthy ladies became a little tiresome."

"I can imagine." In fact, Joseph had no idea how it felt to be accosted in the street by women dripping with spite and righteous indignation. He had enlisted too soon to have been subjected to the humiliation of being presented with a white feather—in full view of every bystander in the street—and a bitter enquiry as to why he was not fighting for king and country. All delivered by a woman living in the happy knowledge that she would never have to march to her own death. In his uniform, Joseph had been greeted by smiles and cheers. "Where are we going?"

"Malta," said the lowly medical student, "the perfect place to convalesce. Good weather, fine food, pretty girls, and it's as far from the line as one could possibly ask."

"It sounds like paradise."

"Oh yes." He took out a cigarette case and offered it to Joseph, who took one with shaking hands. "Matthew Horton, by the way."

"Joseph Radcliffe." He took several puffs of the cigarette and felt the nicotine calming him down almost immediately. "I shall be able to walk again, shan't I?" he asked finally. It was the question he had been desperate to ask since he had first been carried off screaming to the field hospital. "It either hurts like the blazes or I can't feel anything at all."

Matthew Horton gave a reassuring smile. "It's all right, old man; you've had a rough time of it. They'll probably need to operate when we reach Malta."

"But I shall recover, shan't I? I shouldn't be able to bear sitting in a wretched chair for the rest of my life. The only men who seem to escape the front go home without a leg or an eye."

"Try not to think about it yet," said Matthew. "Wait until the doctors have had a proper look at you. In the meantime, you've a good long rest from the war to look forward to, being waited on in some nice Maltese hospital."

"I've never been to Malta before," said Joseph, "I'd never been anywhere before we landed at Lemnos, and it was hardly the nicest way to see a new country."

Matthew chortled. "You'll love Malta, visitors always do. It is the most beautiful little island in the world—excepting our own, of course. A country of enchantments and mystery. I say, do you have a sweetheart you would like me to write to?"

Joseph shook his head with a little regret. "No sweetheart, I'm afraid, but I dare say it's for the best. So many of my friends left girls waiting for them and now ..." He blinked through the dreary cigarette smoke and spluttered to a halt. All along his street in faraway Cambridge, fragile young women had watched the telegram boy stop his bicycle outside their front gates before handing them a piece of paper that would smash their world to smithereens. "KILLED IN ACTION, DIED OF WOUNDS." Or what was almost worst of all: "MISSING." With that word came futile hope, since the missing were virtually never found alive; but futile hope was still hope, and it meant a lifetime of wondering whether a lover were secretly alive somewhere and might one day knock on the door.

Matthew saw the soldier's sorrowful face and realised that his palpable, overwhelming sadness was almost as familiar a sight to him as the many ghastly physical injuries a soldier could suffer—bullet wounds, shrapnel wounds, blindness caused by poison gas, lung damage from gas and smoke, burns, trench foot. He endeavoured to distract him. "You'll never guess what happened to me the first time I worked aboard a hospital ship?" he said, offering Joseph another cigarette, which he took gratefully. "I was helping out in theatre when they were amputating a leg. It was all going very nicely, thank you very much, when the surgeon handed me the leg as though it were a Sunday joint and said, 'It's all yours, sonny.'"

Joseph looked at him in thinly amused horror. "What did you do?"

"I passed out, old man. Next thing I knew, I was the patient and the nurse was slapping me in the face, shouting, 'Pull yourself together, boy!'"

Joseph laughed, and for a moment he almost felt young again. But when Matthew Horton left his side to attend to his duties and the cigarette was a dead stub between his trembling fingers, Joseph found himself whispering the question over and over again: "Will that be me? Will they do that to me?" And in the murky background were the faces of his dead friends and the bent weeping heads of the girls they had once embraced.

There was screaming all around him. It was a familiar sound, but it set his heart racing all the same. Screaming, the screaming of men as they were cut to pieces—those who had the chance to utter a final cry before they died. It was the most desperate, the most pathetic of noises, somewhere between an animal shriek and a plea to be spared when they were already beyond human mercy, but almost worse than that was the piercing, screeching noise of death raining down on them, churning up the dusty ground, ripping powerful men into fragments of flesh and bone. Joseph staggered down onto his knees. For a moment, he thought he had been hit—he had been told that some bullet wounds were painless because they severed every nerve they hit instantaneously—but he had simply fallen because the ground beneath him had juddered so violently. He shielded his eyes from the blinding light of a nearby flare and saw a man lying face down beside him, the head crushed and open, revealing a mess of blood and brains and splintered bone.

The fragments of a human life. What disgusted Joseph so much in the brief, dazzling glimpse he caught, was not so much the raw bloodiness of a man lying dead with his head blown open, but the thought of everything that had been contained within that head that he could not see trickling away—all the songs the man had known; the facts he had absorbed at school, historical dates, mathematical equations; the blur of consciousness and memory, likes and dislikes, fears, amusing anecdotes; the universe of emotions and thoughts never to be replicated by any other human mind. And Joseph ran. It was fortunate for him that he happened to run in the right direction or he might have been charged with desertion, because at that moment he could think only of running and would have run anywhere. Running towards the enemy lines made him a hero, running back to his own trench would have made him a coward, but what the military police did not know was that he truly was a coward; he was a coward and he was running; he was running because death was coming to take him.

Joseph woke up to find himself screaming, but he was not the only one making a noise. Instead of waking to the sounds and smells of a hospital room, Joseph found that he was still surrounded by death-making noise. The ship seemed to be lurching from side to side, so much so that he imagined he might be thrown out of bed altogether and clung to the sides for dear life. He was engulfed by a cacophony of shouting, of alarms being sounded and explosions churning up the water from all sides. They were under attack. The ship that should have been carrying them to safety was being bombarded by an enemy so relentless it had chased the survivors all the way from distant no-man's-land to the sleepy Mediterranean, determined to claim them all.

Joseph struggled to sit up, but all he succeeded in doing was opening up wounds that the likes of Matthew Horton had been patiently dressing and trying to heal. Not that his ingratitude could matter now, they were trapped. They would all go down, all of them with their dressings and their plaster casts and their fevers. These excombatants and nurses and doctors, these lowly medical students pining for their studies, every passenger who could be of no danger to anyone any more would go down with this besieged ship. And he was trapped in every sense of the word. Trapped in a body that could not run or even struggle against the murderous waters as they clawed at him; trapped below decks in a ship bombarded on all sides. He imagined himself floundering around with the sea water creeping up his crippled body, desperately seeking a way out, and he realised that he was screaming for his mother. She was the only person he could imagine who would risk the freezing darkness to save him, and he called for her in savage panic, willing her to pull him to safety.

Matthew Horton was at his side with another man. "Steady on, old chap," he called over the noise, with alarming calm. "We're taking you onto the upper deck. You just sit tight."

Joseph screwed his eyes tight shut as they carried him away, forcing his fist into his mouth when the pain of being jolted made it almost impossible not to start screaming again. He felt the torment of overwhelming relief that he was being rescued and the horror that he was putting two blameless men in danger of their own lives as they tried to save his. "Leave me!" he ordered them, but the words spluttered with insincerity. "Save yourselves, I'm as good as dead anyway."

The two men ignored him and continued the laborious process of moving him, slipping and staggering every step of the way. At the base of the ladder, they were joined by two others who began lifting him upwards. He felt the night air against his face and the howling rage of the raid, which seemed so very much louder with not a single shield of metal to soften the sounds. Another lurching movement caused Matthew Horton to fall over, but he sprang to his feet again with the determination of a man who knows how much depends upon his actions. "Leave you indeed!" he shouted back at Joseph, with an indignant smile. "No heroics please, this is war!" Joseph opened his mouth to respond but was interrupted. "No, no, no. You've done your job, old man, now you leave us to do ours. There are no heroes here."

There certainly are not, thought Joseph and he felt himself slipping in and out of consciousness again as pain and shock spun their wicked spells around him. He suspected Matthew Horton had heard such empty pretences at valour before and had learned to ignore them. In the end, everyone wanted to be rescued, and he had wanted to be rescued, whatever the cost. There were no heroes.

When Joseph was woken again, it was by the gentlest of sea breezes touching his face. He could feel the mild movements of the ship sailing unaccosted along peaceful waters towards the haven of Malta and could almost have believed that the events of the night had been a terrible dream. But when he opened his eyes, the sky was blue and vast and radiant above his head, and he realised he was still on the upper deck, where he and the other wounded men had been moved during the raid.

An exhausted-looking orderly moved towards him, his haggard face unshaven, bleary, the only reminder of the savage night they had survived. "We'll be carrying you back down now," he said blankly, "the danger's past."

"Thank you," said Joseph. "Will you thank Matthew Horton? I suppose he must be resting now."

"None of us are resting, mate," the orderly retorted with thinly disguised resentment. "There's far too much to do and we're a few hands short now. Horton was thrown overboard last night."

***

Kristjana found herself blinking repeatedly with the effort of keeping calm, but Leo was no fool and knew her too well to avoid noticing. He reached forward and touched her face, a gesture so unexpectedly affectionate that she jumped back in alarm. "I'm sorry, my dear, have I offended you?"

"No, not at all," she promised, "I just wasn't expecting it. Why on earth didn't they try to rescue him?"

"How could they? In all that darkness and panic, they would never have been able to spot him in time."

"They might at least have tried! 'A few hands short'? That's a nice way to talk about a person!" Kristjana could hear herself talking too loudly and allowed herself a moment to calm down. "I suppose I thought a medic had a get-out-of-the-war-free card."

"You know nobody did. Medics get killed all the time in wars," said Leo, "and few would ever abandon their patients. I don't think you would abandon me if it came to it, would you?"

The awkward question at least had the effect of drying Kristjana's eyes. "It's easy enough to say I wouldn't. I hope I wouldn't." This was ridiculous! The man was fishing for compliments and she was indulging him. "Why don't I put that photograph away for the moment?"

He handed the snap back to her, and she slipped it carefully back into the box. "You have a photograph of your young man?" he asked, nonchalantly.

"No. It was ... it was on my mobile phone and I lost it."

"The picture?"

"The phone. Shall I turn the air conditioning up a little? It's very humid this evening."

"We're in for a storm. Horrid, noisy things."

"At least it will clear the air. Sweet dreams."

"Good night."

Kristjana suspected that neither of them was in for a particularly good night by the looks of things. By the time she had returned to the nurses' quarters, the sky on the other side of the window was menacingly black for the time of day and the air inside the normally cool and draughty hospital building felt as thick and sticky as treacle. She could feel sweat gathering in pools across the back of her neck, under her arms, around her waist where the elasticated band of her nursing uniform pressed awkwardly. It was one of those stifling evenings when even taking a shower made very little difference. After bracing herself under a freezing cold torrent of water, Kristjana found herself sweating again by the time she had changed into clean clothes, the droplets of water from the shower mingling for a moment with the droplets of sweat before evaporating.

Down in the hospital canteen, Bernadette was sitting with two male nurses, Sameer and Sharif, eating the regulation hospital supper of hummus, a tomato and a round of unleavened bread. "Come and join us!" she called cheerfully. "How are you getting on with your patient?"

By the time Kristjana had sat down with her own plate of supper and a plastic cup filled with hot, sweet black tea, the conversation had moved on and the two men were recounting a blazing row that had erupted in the operating theatre earlier that day over the unconscious body of a patient having his hip replaced. "You should come and work with us in theatre some time," suggested Sharif, as though he were inviting Kristjana to a family dinner. "Some really bloody operation perhaps, bowel surgery!"

"No thank you." She peered at the fat, over-ripe tomato posing uninvitingly at the edge of her plate and suddenly didn't fancy it any more.

"You'll love it!" He gave a mischievous little boy grin, "I stick your hand right in somebody's abdomen!"

Fortunately for Kristjana's self-esteem, she was saved from throwing up or passing out by a flash of lightning powerful enough to illuminate the whole sky outside. Sharif and Sameer raced to the window. "Wow! You gotta take a look at this!"

As Kristjana reached the window a mighty roar overhead like the descent of an Apache helicopter shook the building. She had seen violent storms in Malta, but never had they felt quite so threatening. Rain hurled itself at the hospital garden, churning Sister Pauline's horticultural efforts into a hideous quagmire within minutes, whilst above them forks of lightning slashed the sky into burning shards, leaving her and the others standing in awed silence as though they were watching Armageddon descending. In the distance the Mount of Olives, that loneliest garden in the history of the world, lit up then plunged into darkness again, a second before the lights tripped and they were thrown into pitch black gloom.

"No panic, it is power cut!" announced Sharif, bumping into her as he turned around.

"What about the patients? What about all the machinery?"

"Don't worry, there are generators to power the wards."

Kristjana's mind drifted to Leo lying in bed all alone with pandemonium erupting outside his window, and she started feeling her way through the darkness of the canteen. "I've got to go."

"Are you crazy? You will break your leg!"

But she was skidding out of the canteen and along the dark corridor already, helped along by the sudden flashes of light that blazed through the windows at discreet intervals. It was fortunate that she knew the hospital well as there were no windows to illuminate the stairwells and she found herself in virtual darkness when she ran through the door to the first staircase. *Fortunate I'm not afraid of the dark either*, thought Kristjana, feeling her way along the wall until her fingers brushed a cold metal handle and she threw open the door, only to be dazzled by the blinding light of the ward. The generators were indeed working; the refrigerators hummed earnestly, and the ventilators and monitors did their work without interruption from the storm outside.

Sister Pauline was on night duty and glanced at Kristjana in surprise from the nursing station. "What are you doing here, Kris?"

"I wanted to check on Leo."

"He's fast asleep, darling. They're all asleep."

"Would you mind if I popped my head round the door?"

Sister Pauline shrugged in mild exasperation. "There's really no need, you'll only wake him up."

Not for the first time, Kristjana felt like a complete idiot. "I thought he might be worried about the storm."

Sister Pauline giggled, and Kristjana would have found her laughter quite infectious if she had not been on the receiving end of it. "He's a big boy, Kris—are you going to sing to him about his favourite things?"

Kristjana had already noted that the only film available in the convent appeared to be *The Sound of Music*, but she still felt irrationally annoyed, as she walked towards Leo's room, by the sound of Sister Pauline singing sweetly, "Girls in white dresses with blue satin sashes. Snowflakes that stay on my nose and eyelashes...." Kristjana had never even *liked* that film. Nuns never sang in tune; naughty children *never* reformed.

Kristjana opened Leo's door and stepped noiselessly inside. It was almost completely dark in the room, except for a few blinking lights here and there, but Kristjana could just make out the outline of Leo's body, hunched up under the bedclothes in what looked like the foetal position. A bizarre, unsettling noise emanated from the bed—a grating, rasping sound—and for a few tortured seconds she could not tell whether he was asleep or awake.

"Leo? Leo, it's me. Are you all right?"

The rasping noise became a wail. Leo was wide awake and weeping, so violently that when Kristjana reached his bedside and placed a hand on his head, his hair felt wet and hot from sweating profusely. A flash of light illuminated the room, and she saw Leo's face for a single dazzling moment, wet, contorted; then they were both plunged into darkness again. A thunderclap erupted a few seconds later. "My God!" he sobbed.

"It's all right, the storm's moving away. Not long now and it won't sound so loud."

"My God, my God! So much violence, so much noise!"

"It's all right, it's just a thunderstorm."

She felt her way to the bedside table and switched on the Anglepoise light. He was holding his head, his fingers twisting his hair, whilst his body shook so badly that Kristjana felt herself beginning to shake as soon as she sat beside him and placed an arm around his shoulder. She knew he was not hearing a thunderstorm but had no idea where he thought he was and could not reach him. "My God, so much violence, so much death every day! Day after day after day they came!"

"Leo, where are you?"

"I knew they would come for her! The only woman I have ever loved!" He grasped her arm so tightly she nearly cried out with pain. There was a savagery about him Kristjana had never seen before, and part of her wanted to scream with him, not just because he was hurting her but because she was afraid of him. In his delirium, he was out of control, frightened, angry, grieving; she was not sure what or for whom he was grieving. All she wished was that she had never entered the room. For the first time since she had started on this journey with him, Kristjana wanted Leo to leave her alone; she wanted his memories to leave her alone. She was a hostage to this man's past and knew she could not escape.

"Leo, who was she?"

"They killed her! With their planes and their bombs, the dirty, filthy cowards! They killed her from on high." Before she could grab his hands they had slipped to her face and held her head so close to his that she could feel the heat of his tortured, agitated body. "If they could only have seen her, seen her face. They would never have done it. I could have pleaded her case; I could have stopped them, but they never gave me the chance! I would have taken her place. I was not there; I was *not there!*"

He slumped back onto the bed, and Kristjana gave in to cowardice and pressed the alarm button, knowing that in his distress Leo would never hear its distant ring at the nursing station or notice the small, round red light flashing near his head. By the time Sister Pauline had walked the length of the corridor and opened the door, Leo was lying silently in his bed, still trembling beneath the bedclothes and still weeping, the steady stream of tears sliding inoffensively down the side of his face.

"Could you call the doctor?" asked Kristjana, turning to meet Sister Pauline's enquiring glance. "The sedatives aren't working."

Sister Pauline darted back out of the room, leaving Kristjana to stand guard over her patient as he walked invisibly through the dream worlds of his past, unable to extricate himself. He began to whisper. "I can still see her lying in the rubble as though she were falling asleep in her own bed. So peaceful, absurdly peaceful in such a place. I could have believed she would wake up and everything would be as it was before—or I would wake up and find that it had never happened. So peaceful she was, so very beautiful."

"Leo, who was she?"

"I still find myself turning the clock back in my mind and taking her somewhere far away from that place, or warning her to walk away just before. If we could only know a few minutes into the future ..."

If we could only know, thought Kristjana. *What tragedies we would avoid and what horrors we would inadvertently cause, simply by having a few minutes' warning.* She heard Leo's breathing pattern slowly changing and realised he was falling asleep without the aid of the doctor's hypodermic needle. His eyes closed, and she noticed the slightest reddening of his cheeks brought on by his feverish behaviour. Or perhaps by the memory of a nameless woman he had loved once. The only woman he had ever loved.

15

"There is something holding my legs down," said the soldier. "Are you holding my legs? It feels as though they're in clamps or something ..." He strained to shift position, simply to convince himself that he could shift position, but Liljana placed a hand carefully on his shoulder and pushed him gently back into his bed. She had never been possessed of great physical strength, but the young man was painfully thin and weak from an infection that had set in shortly after his arrival at the hospital and, as he was just beginning to suspect, he was paralysed. He had taken a shrapnel wound to his lower spine and lost all feeling from the waist down, but he had been delirious with fever for so long that he had been blissfully unaware of the disaster that had befallen him. "Nurse?"

Liljana could hardly bear the searching way he looked at her. Like her, Liljana suspected, the lad had lied about his age to play his part in the war; he looked no more than sixteen. "You just be a good boy and rest. The war's over for you now."

She could not bring herself to tell him that he was most definitely paralysed, but there was a nasty possibility that he would die before it fully dawned on him that he would never walk again. She had never learned the art of powerful emotion, but she did feel pity for him; she felt pity for all of them. When the war was long over, that was the word that would always spring to mind: the *pity* of it all, the pity of war, as Wilfred Owen put it.

The paralysed boy was called Edwin Collins. He was a little short and had rusty-coloured hair. He spoke with a slight lisp, and in his feverish ravings he had called out repeatedly for his mother. But then they all called for their mothers. The seasoned soldiers who had seen active service long before Germany violated Belgium's neutrality, the navvies and labourers who had enlisted to escape the drudgery of a life they could not otherwise hope to escape, the fresh-faced boys who just a few short months before had been safely incarcerated in their public schools. When pain or disease or panic hit any of them, they became weeping infants again, calling for their mothers to comfort them and to make it all go away as though the entire war and all its carnage were a mere child's nightmare that had fleetingly found its way into the nursery.

And Liljana gave them her pity. During the early months of the war, Liljana and Emily had trained and worked in London, lodging at the home of Emily's parents, though the days were so long that they were scarcely seen there during daylight hours and arrived there late in the evening, too exhausted to answer the many questions with which they were bombarded. Liljana had felt a certain grim amusement at the pride Emily's parents felt for them both and the praise that was heaped on them by Emily's parents' friends. It was so very good of them, and particularly of a foreigner like Liljana, to be showing such support for the war effort. It was very pleasing to see that the empire could be relied upon to do its bit for the cause of freedom.

Liljana was beginning to wonder whether anything was quite as it seemed. Would they think her work so laudable, she wondered, if they knew that she saw it as an escape? Would they think her such an angel in her starched nursing uniform if they knew that the most she was capable of feeling for her patients was pity? Not pride, not admiration, not gratitude, not grief but childish, female *pity*?

"Hif you were an 'alfway decent nurse, my gal," Matron had stated on more than one occasion, as publicly as possible, "you wouldn't waste yar time pitying hanybody." It was a tiresome cliché, which Matron always delivered with her arms crossed in front of her for the first half of the pronouncement, then she would fling her bony hands out to the side in a swift, cutting motion to ram the punchline home. A cliché and rather unfair, since Liljana certainly did not waste her time and threw herself into every task, from scrubbing floors to dressing wounds. She had had a bet with Emily about which of them would faint first, and she had won the sugar mouse when Emily had stooped forward in a kindly manner to hear what the patient was trying to tell her and he had vomited directly into her face.

Liljana still wondered, four months later, whether she should have given back the sugar mouse the following day when she had been asked to change a young man's dressings and came within inches of passing out. The dressings that bound the soldier's arm had looked quite presentable from the outside, and she had unwound them without hesitation, pausing only when she felt the fibres of the bandage sticking to the man's flesh and he shouted loudly as it gave way. The most disgusting stench she had ever come across in her entire life hit her like a punch on the nose, a second before she saw the raw, grossly infected wound tear open before her eyes. Green and yellow matter trickled over her hands, closely followed by a spurt of blood that seemed positively clean by comparison. With the hellish odour sticking to the back of her throat and nostrils, she felt as though she were swallowing and inhaling the putrid tissue. Her sight blackened, she braced, held her breath, then fled the ward blindly, almost colliding with a doctor who roared at her back as she vanished. Even after Liljana had washed her hands more times than she could count, she could still smell infection all over them above the sharp, institutional scent of carbolic soap.

If Joseph's youth was cut down with the first volleys of machine gun fire on a desert battlefield, Liljana's melted away by degrees, scorched a little further and a little further with every new injury she stumbled upon, with every man who left the hospital maimed for life or who never left it at all. By the end of the war, she had closed so many dead eyes that it had become yet another unpleasant detail of her life as a nurse, but the first few times, the sight of those staring, sightless young eyes had haunted her nightmares. She had still been capable of musing during those early days and would find herself wondering as she summoned up the courage to touch the cold, moist eyelids, how many beautiful and terrible things even a young man must have seen during the short years of his life. Liljana would think of those eyes in the face of a tiny baby, looking longingly up at his mother, and then she would think of the man's mother and the news she was soon to face. All in all, it was a relief when such acts as closing eyes became a chore rather than a horror.

"I thought you'd be delighted, Lily!" exclaimed Emily, as they discussed the plan over breakfast. They were making the most of their day off by eating a leisurely breakfast at a rather later hour than would normally be regarded as proper—if there was such a thing as normal anymore. Mrs Whitehead, the Sheppard family's housekeeper, had lovingly presented them with boiled eggs and hot buttered toast, accompanied by a vast pot of steaming tea, and the two girls ate and drank with alacrity. They had both lost weight in the preceding months, and Mrs Whitehead seemed to believe it her patriotic duty to fatten them up again. "Oh don't be a stick in the mud, Lily! I could hardly wait to tell you and here you are looking as though you were on your way to your own funeral!"

"It's been an awfully long time, Emily," said Liljana in a low voice. "More than six years. I'm not sure I could bear to go back now."

"Oh come now, it's your home! Everyone wants to go home. I'd do anything to see Gibraltar again."

"You haven't been anywhere near Gibraltar since you were four years old," answered Liljana, breaking up her eggshell in a way that jarred Emily's nerves terribly. "If there had been anything to keep me in Malta, I should never have been sent away. What on earth should I do there?"

"Precisely what we have been doing here, of course. What a question! They're desperate for nurses out there with all the casualties coming in from Gallipoli. One must go where one is needed, as they say." *Who on earth had* ever *said that*, thought Liljana. "And since you speak the language and know your way about . . ."

Liljana let Emily's shrill, persistent voice wash over her in chilly, undulating waves until her mind had wandered away from the breakfast table altogether. She could not pretend that the first two months of the New Year had been especially happy. Christmas and New Year had been quiet, predictably melancholy occasions with the boys away at the front and precious little worth celebrating. With so many women already donning black, it had been celebration enough that the boys were alive, but Liljana could not help feeling that the world was in a pretty sorry state if not being killed were a cause worth celebrating. Now, with a reluctant spring struggling to emerge, she was left wondering whether a change of scene might help somehow. "I haven't been back since before my mother died."

Emily was at her side immediately, clasping her hand. "Oh Lily, my poor darling, I'd forgotten about all that! I'm sorry, but perhaps that is all the more reason to go back. You could visit her grave."

It occurred to Liljana that Emily did not know the exact circumstances of her mother's death. The shame of losing a loved one to suicide was so powerful that she had never told anyone, even her closest friend to whom she had confided so much. Mr Hampton had been the soul of discretion and never told anyone else to her knowledge. He was so discreet he would not have even told *her* if she had not guessed herself how it had happened. Visit her grave, indeed. Visit her unconsecrated grave in some shabby, unloved corner of the cemetery; visit her grave when she had never been permitted to visit her hospital bed. The haunting thought emerged again, as it did every time she thought of her mother, that perhaps she would have never met such a wretched, lonely end if they had not taken away from her the one person in the world she might have learned to love again. "I am being indulgent," said Liljana emphatically. "We must go where we are summoned. Little Malta needs nurses, so to Malta we shall jolly well go."

Malta. The very word threw Liljana into a state of confusion, all the more so because she had dreamed so many times that the island would call her back one day. She knew she should be in ecstasy as they made their preparations to travel when all she felt was a numb sense of panic. Her picture postcard recollections of Malta had become more and more fanciful as the years had passed and the grittier details had slowly given way to a series of abstract images: blankets of vivid, aromatic flowers covering the rocks in early spring when she had been a townie and virtually never saw such sights; the view down a Valletta street, the many glistening limestone steps, the painted balconies high above her head. Malta. Tawny, dream-scented Malta, a childhood playground where she had never been a child; a mystical land of refreshing breezes and blasting sirocco dust and chiming bells and balmy evenings and bustling markets and a language that called back across the centuries to the days before the British colonials and the Knights of Malta and the Normans, before words and histories were written down.

And somewhere, in the midst of all those shimmering fragments, she saw the shadow of a life cowering in a boat as it was flung across a deep, merciless sea.

Liljana closed her eyes and tried to remember. " 'If I take my wings ...' It's no good, I can never remember the words."

"Psalm 139, you heathen!" wailed Emily from her bed. "When was the last time you opened your Bible?"

"A long time ago," Liljana admitted, mopping her friend's clammy brow. "Let us hope we are not going to judgement tonight or I shall be in terrible trouble with the Almighty."

Liljana had discovered, soon after they embarked from Southampton, that she had grown out of her childhood seasickness and felt quite at ease on board the ship that was to carry them to Malta. Emily, on the other hand, had not been to sea since before she could remember and lay in the cabin they shared, protesting that she would die one moment and begging to die the next. Added to her misery, she had discovered virtually as soon as the dry land of Albion had vanished from sight that she was utterly terrified. "I keep thinking of all those poor souls on the *Titanic* fighting for their lives in the freezing darkness."

"Don't Emmy. They're all at peace now, and we're unlikely to hit an iceberg on this stretch of sea."

"We'll be torpedoed! We shan't even have time to run onto the deck, we're below the level of the water! I can almost see the headline—'VADs Go Down with Ship.' "

Liljana bent her head closer to her friend's to command her attention and placed a finger over her own lips. "Shush. You're hardly helping yourself. We'll be all right, you'll see. We'll laugh about it when we're on dry land again."

Emily looked up at her friend's Madonna-like face, which looked as it always did—calm with a whisper of melancholy—and she reached instinctively for her hand. "Dear Lily, I doubt you will laugh. Aren't you afraid of anything?"

"Oh yes, but so many men our age are dying who desperately want to live, it seems wrong somehow to make a fuss about the prospect." She shrugged. "Anyway, I've always thought that if God wants to claim me, he will take me wherever I am, however safe I feel."

Emily laughed lightly. "Dear me, you always were a tragic little thing."

"I'm sorry, I'm afraid I'm poor company. Do you need anything?"

"Your company." Emily stared vacantly above her head, but her eyes began to mist over in spite of her best efforts. "I know I'm being a dreadful coward, Lily. Please don't tell anyone, will you? But I do so wish we had stayed at home."

"It will all feel different when we arrive and settle down," promised Liljana. *It certainly will*, she thought, feeling that terrible knot of anxiety tangling itself inside her chest. *Then you shall be as fit as a fiddle and I shall be the one being the dreadful coward.* She tried to think of the young men who were sailing away from home to the front in the unhappy knowledge that they might never return. She talked to Emily about how very fortunate they were that, however dangerous the voyage might be—and in truth it had thus far proven uneventful—they would soon set foot on a peaceful island far from any fighting or killing, where they would sleep in comfortable beds at night and wake to hearty breakfasts. Indeed, it was almost shameful to think how few dangers and privations they would know compared with the menfolk trapped in their trenches and dugouts, contending with mud and rats and the maddening roar of German bombardments. Except that, for all her talk, Liljana could not imagine arriving safely anywhere or being one of Rupert Brooke's "hearts at peace". She simply saw the shadow of herself thrown into relief by the savage all-consuming sunrise, thrown about for eternity on a hostile sea.

16

"There now, don't cry, old thing," pestered Emily, handing her a clean handkerchief, though it seemed perfectly right and proper to her that even a stony-heart like Lily would shed a few token tears on her return to the motherland. And she was not to know that Liljana's tears, which she blinked away with what was almost rage, had been prompted not by her return home but by the shattering of a ridiculous, childish fantasy that had persisted throughout the long years of exile. It had somehow survived that harsh encounter with Mr Hampton during the months following her mother's death; it had survived her sitting at the back of church and no longer going up for Communion or lighting a votive candle to Saint Anthony; it had survived the morning, shortly after that, when she had picked up Mrs Debono's crucifix to slip it around her neck, changed her mind and tucked it safely away with her few keepsakes. It had survived the long road of disillusionment, silently walked, but then so much of Liljana's life was lived out in silence, and it had survived the voyage back to Malta with Emily. Somewhere in her mind, which was only just on the cusp of womanhood, there had been a ludicrous, impossible dream that the telegram Mr Hampton had received from his brother five years before had been an unfortunate mistake and that her mother might be alive to greet her when she stepped off the boat. Stranger things had happened after all. It was so absurd and so infantile that Liljana was grateful to Emily for being prosaic enough to assume that she was overcome with emotion by a mere homecoming.

Insofar as it was a homecoming. Liljana had her first unpleasant moment as they disembarked, when she gestured to a porter for assistance, only to see him turn to a companion and comment: "These English whores should be good for a few shillings. You fleece one, I'll fleece the other."

"I am not English, I am not a whore," Liljana retorted in Maltese, "and I find that I do not require your services after all."

The man's smirk evaporated and he fled as though taking cover from a volley of gunfire, leaving Liljana just seconds to compose herself before the matron's gloved hand touched her shoulder, prompting her to turn around. Matron, who cut as embittered and contemptuous a figure as her rank appeared to demand, was glaring at her with undisguised disgust. The other VADs who had overheard her seemed to be doing the same. "You will speak English, my girl, if you please. I'm not sure that gibberish belongs in the mouth of a lady."

Liljana mused, as they were transported to their hospital, that Matron would have been a good deal more appalled if she had understood her precise use of language, as she had inadvertently repeated the extremely crude word for prostitute the porter had used, but it hardly mattered how she had spoken the language, simply that it had occurred to her to speak it at all. The reprimand at least had the effect of keeping Liljana's eyes dry as she was engulfed by every flawlessly unchanged sight and smell of home. They had arrived at Grand Harbour, just minutes from the street where she had lived out the drama of her early childhood—for one tantalising moment she had thought they would pass by the very house, and she felt the ache of dread followed immediately by regret.

"I don't suppose much has changed, has it?" Emily mused. She was recovering rapidly from the horrors of the sea and breathed in the balmy air with enthusiasm Liljana evidently did not share.

"I have changed," answered Liljana, softly. "I used to know every inch of this city. I suppose I still do, but I doubt it knows me."

Emily gave her friend a quizzical glance. "You do talk in such riddles! Come now, a few days and you will feel perfectly at home again. Do buck up!"

Liljana had to admit that she cheered up somewhat when they were shown to their unexpectedly comfortable quarters, a shared but spacious and airy room with a balcony overlooking the sea. As they unpacked, Liljana thought of the cramped room she had shared with Mrs Debono years before—stiflingly hot in summer—and the nest of blankets where she had rested at night. "I suppose it might be worth pretending to be English to live like this," she said out loud, lying on her new bed with its springy mattress and crisp, laundered sheets.

"Oh come on, Lily, you are *entirely* English now," answered Emily, as though no girl could ever be paid a weightier compliment. "I declare we have fallen on our feet being sent here."

They certainly had. Over the next few days as they began their work, they discovered that their duties in Malta were a good deal lighter and the discipline less severe than anything they had known in the London hospital in which they had trained. With the brilliant clarity of hindsight, Liljana would wonder whether it would have been better for her to be worked to the bone than to have spare time to get herself into mischief, but at the moment it came as the greatest possible relief to be given time to collect her thoughts. And she had plenty to think about.

Early the following week, in the absence of her friend, Liljana made the journey to Mount Carmel Hospital. In her memory, the sun had always shone on little Malta with a warm, benevolent glow that had never failed to give Liljana a spring in her step. She had forgotten how harsh it could be, how stifling, as though she were walking through treacle or an invisible hand, hot and clammy, were pressing itself over her face to arrest her breathing. The glare of the unrelenting, early summer light bouncing off the limestone buildings had given her a rumbling headache by the time she arrived at the hospital and staggered in the direction of a small, reluctant square of shade. Liljana glanced up, cursing herself for ruining a perfectly pleasant day off. She had left her comfortable, shady quarters that morning without the slightest idea of what she intended to do when she arrived at the hospital that had sheltered her mother during her final year of life. Had she meant to knock at the door and request admittance? A guided tour of the wards perhaps? A look through the records to convince herself that her mother most definitely had died while residing in this secluded little prison of soundproof walls and closed wooden shutters?

Liljana allowed her struggling attention to be grabbed by an intricate sculpture above the main gate, some kind of English heraldic shield denoting the different nations of Britain. It looked rather too regal an ornament for a lunatic asylum, though in many ways the whole edifice looked no different from any other hospital. It could have been any one of the hospitals she was to work in during her time as a nurse in Malta, but it also seemed to her like so many other places—and people—in this country to which she had returned with such reluctance: closed, unwelcoming, a little hostile. Nevertheless, here she stood, searching for something.

"You should come out of the sun, my dear," said a voice in English that startled her. "A good Maltese girl ought to know better."

Liljana looked around and saw a grey-haired Englishman, dressed exactly as she remembered him on the last occasion their paths had crossed. "Good heavens, Dr Hampton," she said, "whatever brings you here?"

"I might ask the same of you." He moved towards her and she nodded gravely in his direction. "I see England has made a lady of you. I knew it would. I do hope you have not returned to brood over the past."

"I was curious, that is all," she assured him. "There can be no harm in that."

"I hope not. Well, you have seen the place now, and it is hardly seemly to loiter alone like this. May I escort you home?"

Liljana was hardly a lady yet, thought Dr Hampton, as they sat facing one another in the *karrozin, it was only the long years apart that made it seem so.* She had struggled through those critical years of transformation and emerged a woman; poised, serious—but then she had always been serious—well-spoken without a trace of an accent; and yet she was so slightly built that she retained the doll-like look of a girl who had been dragged unsuspectingly into adult life before she was quite ready. "You are far too young to be caught up in all this," he said cautiously, "you should be safely ensconced in my brother's school. Did you lie about your age or did they forget to ask?"

"Plenty of young men are at the front, as we speak, who will never reach their majority," she answered with a piercingly cool tone he remembered all too well. "Nursing is harsh but unlikely to be the death of me, I suspect."

"It is hazardous enough to travel the seas these days," said Dr Hampton. "A ship was torpedoed only last month."

Liljana sat back in the carriage and watched the threads of light fluttering through the gap in the curtains. "I trained as a nurse to help with the war effort. I did not ask to be stationed here, nor did I desire to be. It seemed wrong to object when soldiers are expected to go where they are sent."

"You ring true every time," mused Dr Hampton. "Well, perhaps it was Providence that brought you here then. You know you have been assigned to my hospital? That was how I knew you were here. Your friend Miss Sheppard told me you had gone out on your own, and I thought I had better find you."

"I am not sure about Providence," said Liljana tonelessly. "In every possible way, it would have been better for me to stay in England. This is no country for an orphan. 'To lose one parent may be considered a misfortune ...'"

"I see you are familiar with Oscar Wilde," said Dr Hampton, then he lowered his voice. "If I were you, my dear, I should be grateful for being an orphan. It sounds frightfully callous to say it, but being an orphan may be pitied. Other misfortunes of birth, sadly, are not."

Liljana felt herself blushing slightly as she looked searchingly at his face. "You know, don't you?"

"My brother did tell me what you said to him after your mother's death. If it helps at all, if it gives you any peace at all, your father was not hanged."

"Doctor, she showed me the papers!"

"Lower your voice, please. I have no notion of what papers your mother showed you, but there is no record whatsoever of a man being hanged for—for violating a woman during the years following your birth."

"I remember her telling me, over and over again ..." but her voice trailed off. "No part of my life feels entirely real." The thought crossed her mind, so squalid and so macabre that she felt shamed by its very presence, that if her father had been a criminal she could at least have identified him if only to despise him. As it was, another void was opening up where there should have been a certainty.

"I thought you would be relieved. It was a terrible burden she forced you to bear by telling you such a thing."

Liljana looked at him again and felt a rare desire to trust another human being. "What did happen then? Who was he?"

"I'm sorry, Lily, but that is impossible to know. Your mother was never married, and there is no possibility of finding out who your father was. If he was what she said he was, it can never be proven. It may be that she convinced herself that she was forced because she was ashamed; it may be that she really was. Sadly, justice is rarely done in these cases."

Liljana looked at him with the cold composure he remembered in her face on the afternoon long ago when he had found her sitting on her own doorstep and he told her that her mother had been taken away. "I will find him," she said, finally.

"You will not." Risking immediate retribution from her, Dr Hampton placed a hand on her arm, but she was not affronted. "You cannot. Whoever your father was, he left no trace of his existence. Only your mother knew who he was and she has taken that secret with her. For all I know, even she may not have known his identity. Now," and suddenly his tone was brisk and pragmatic, "you people are very good at brooding over the past. I have seen it in so many of your kind. You can never let anything go—the slightest grudge, the most insignificant event—so I knew as soon as I saw your name on the staff list that you would start raking over the past the moment you arrived."

"I am not like that."

"Then why, when you have barely arrived back in the country, did I find you standing outside Mount Carmel Hospital? Why do you suppose I knew you would be there?"

"I went there today to lay the past to rest, not to rake over it."

"Good. That's my clever girl." He sat back in his seat. "I suppose I should be grateful it was a war that brought you here. I'm afraid you will have more than enough work to keep you out of mischief. And there will be more, I fear. There will be very much more before long."

With or without work, Liljana could not help herself. During her first month in Malta, she frittered away her precious hours of leisure making enquiries and having doors—literally and figuratively—slammed in her face at every turn. Her father, whoever he was, had indeed disappeared without a trace. She was a woman destined to have the most important facts of her life hidden from her, to be cheated by a world that exposed every woman's least fault and hid men's shame for all time without leaving behind so much as a footprint in the collective memory. Whoever Liljana's father was, whether he was a shy lover struck down by some misfortune, a charlatan who promised a naïve young woman the earth and then deserted her or far more depraved and heartless than any other kind of a man, she could never know.

17

Kristjana was developing a veritable phobia of e-mail. Like most irrational fears it asked to be indulged, and she signed into her e-mail account, willing there to be a message from Benedict whilst still managing to dread the prospect. She began clicking on the list of unread messages, working through them in reverse date order.

My Darling,

Thank you for answering my e-mail finally. I still think you should go back to England. You've got a job and a life in London, please don't just turn your back on it. I know you didn't want me to go to Harvard but I only did it because it will help my career and I wanted to prepare properly for the future. Surely you can see that? I hope by now that you have had a little time to think things through and are perhaps feeling a bit better about everything. Please let me know how you are and what your plans are.
I love you.
Benedict

Dear Kris,

It's been three days. I know you don't have very good internet access where you are, so I'm hoping you just haven't had the chance to read your e-mails. Have you had any further thoughts on what you want to do? If you could just give me a date when you're planning on returning to London, it would give me a lot of peace of mind. You are planning on coming back, aren't you? Maybe I was too negative about everything, maybe you needed a bit of time out. Lots of people go abroad to find themselves for a few months and it doesn't do any harm, but I'd like to know that you're all right. I know how much you love Jerusalem, I have such happy memories of the stories you used to tell about your time there and how happy you were. I want you to be happy and I'm sure you are happy, but please just e-mail me and tell me you're safe. It would mean a lot to me if you did.
I love you.
Benedict

OK, I'm not going to keep pestering you. Either you're not reading your e-mails (I hope) or you're ignoring me. Either way, there hardly seems to be any point in continuing this. If you are reading your e-mails, Kris, for the last time PLEASE get in touch. You don't seem to realise how much worry you're causing.

I've been thinking about everything that's happened to you over the past months and I wonder if you really don't believe anybody cares about you. If that is how you are feeling, please please PLEASE believe me when I tell you that there are so many people who do but you don't always see it. Even if there was no one else to notice your absence, I love you, I will always love you. Please don't doubt it for a single second. I love you and I am waiting for you.

I have my e-mail account open all the time I am at my computer, praying I will receive some word from you but I am beginning to give up hope. If your feelings towards me have changed, you must at least do me the courtesy of telling me. It's very unkind to leave a man hanging on like this. I believe that we can have a happy future together. It you think otherwise, there is nothing further for me to say, except perhaps that there is so much suffering and unhappiness in the world, it would be a pity to add to it for no reason.

There, I'll stop right there. I love you, my darling, and I will always love you. I hope this e-mail finds you well and happy.

Your own,
Benedict

Kristjana blinked at the computer screen, but the words refused to snap back into focus. A good psychiatrist would no doubt have found a name for the aching, yawning sense of paralysis she was experiencing. It was a little like fear or grief, the dull feeling of gloom that hit her every time she thought about her life and the mess she was making of it. Kristjana felt almost muted, dampened like a musical instrument, so much so that she wondered whether she would be able to make any sound at all if she were pleading for her own life.

"You know, *habibti*, if he were my man I wouldn't be so cruel," said a voice at her side, causing her to swerve round. An attractive young woman in a *hijab* was peering over her shoulder at the messages on the screen, silently reading them. "Sorry, sorry, I didn't want to leave you crying. You want?"

"Thank you." Kristjana took the piece of baklava she was holding out to her. "*Shukran*."

"Why you here? You take holiday?"

Kristjana shook her head. "I work at a hospital. *Mustashfa Francewi*."

The woman gave a triumphant smile. "I knew it! You running away! Westerners working here always they are running from something!"

Kristjana felt unreasonably affronted by the woman's knowing laughter, not least because she was so obviously right. "I'm trying to help!"

"Don't be angry, don't be angry!" The woman was at her side again, placing a placatory arm round Kristjana's stiff shoulders. "But I am right, aren't I?"

"Yes." Kristjana looked back at the screen, where even Benedict's patience had finally begun to unravel, and she felt more paralysed than ever. She knew that so much might hang on the response she wrote, but doubted that anything she could possibly compose would make everything right again. "I don't know what to write," she declared to the complete stranger who had had the audacity to pry into her latest emotional crisis.

Another girly giggle. "Easy! How about, 'I'm sorry and I love you, my darling.'"

> And I will return to England soon, I promise. I never meant to cause you so much worry, you really don't deserve this loopy behaviour from me. I really am sorry. I can't get it out of my head that everyone— you, my family, my friends—would all have been so much happier if it wasn't for me. Concentrate on your work now. I am safe and in a strange way, I am happy, but I can't face England just yet. I know it sounds ridiculous, but I feel so lost.
>
> Please wait for me as you asked me to wait for you. I love you always and forever.
>
> Kris

A few minutes after pressing the "send" button, Kristjana stepped outside and let herself be overwhelmed by the throng of busy, noise-making, oblivious humanity. She felt lost and she liked being lost. She came to this country to be lost.

***

Joseph knew what it meant to feel lost and overwhelmed by sudden crowds of people, but in his case he could not escape or disappear. As the hospital ship docked, he became aware of the roar of many people when he had become gratefully accustomed to being left alone. Matthew Horton's death had taken away the only real company he had enjoyed on the voyage, and the unexpectedness of it had left him miserably shaken.

Sudden death in no-man's-land was hard enough to bear, but on that ship he had felt an irrational sense of safety before the night of the raid. A small part of him had envied Matthew Horton for not being a soldier, for having the chance to be safe and honourable at the same time; but there were no places of safety left, and death had come for Matthew Horton as it had come for so many men in uniform and as it might still come for him.

A crowd of well-wishers were standing at the dockside, and Joseph was puzzled to discover that they were not cheering or shouting as he had thought when he was still aboard. At the first sight of the sick soldiers being helped onto land, the people—many of them women with their children—had descended into silence and stood in sombre rows, watching as the men were carried into ambulances and driven away. Joseph peered out and saw little children throwing sweets and cigarettes at the wounded soldiers in front of him; many of the women, he noticed, were in tears as though they were attending a funeral procession, not the arrival of hundreds of men who had clung to life by their fingernails. He made his best effort to sit up and managed to lift his head high enough to get a better look, but he was overwhelmed by the eerie pall that seemed to have covered everyone, even the children. Beautiful children, he thought, beautiful olive-skinned children with huge inky-black eyes and oval faces like those of little Madonnas. But sad today because men like him had erupted into their lives and their innocence and made them unhappy.

"My word, they're so young!" he heard an elderly English woman declare to a companion. "What a dreadful pity."

Joseph leaned back and closed his eyes. He was not going to weep. He was hot and exhausted and his wounds simmered with pain, but it all was such a pity, such a dreadful *pity*. Oh no, he could not break down where he would be seen. Joseph squeezed his eyes tight shut, but he could still feel tears escaping and prayed they would be caught in his eyelashes so that no one would notice. How had he found himself alive and weeping at his own funeral? Should he not tell someone he was alive? Or perhaps he was not alive and everything that had passed since that terrible moment in no-man's-land had been a hideous demonic vision of some afterlife in which he had never truly believed. He was weeping. The *shame* of it! He could not even exhibit a little dignity after his own death.

"Poor boy," he heard a creaking voice say, he thought ages later. "Poor little boy." He opened his eyes and realised that they had stopped somewhere and the stronger among them (of which he was apparently one) were being carried out. An old woman, swathed in the faded black of long widowhood, held out a hand and traced a cross on his forehead. "God bless you, my son," she said. "It's all right. You are among friends now."

Joseph felt her hand against his head again, then she smiled and hurried on her way in a rustle of skirts. He looked about him and saw some of the walking wounded being helped away, some of them still trying to stand straight as they had learned from the parade ground. They appeared to be in some public place, and he suspected that they were in the capital city. He could hear English being spoken over a language that was unlike anything he had ever heard before; a strange, rich, singsong flow of sounds from dark, exotic faces that smiled warmly in his direction whenever he made eye contact. An elderly man with the deeply lined face of a biblical prophet came up to him and placed a cigarette in his hand. "Welcome to our beautiful country, young man," he said in perfect English before disappearing into the crowd again.

Joseph had barely drawn breath when a schoolboy with fiery red hair and freckles came bouncing up to him and handed him a paper bag with traces of chocolate already melting through. "You're a soldier!" he said in sparkling cut-glass tones that jangled against Joseph's nerves. "I wanted to see the war but my father said it won't last long enough."

"I wouldn't be so sure," said Joseph, but he was distracted by the sensation that he was being lowered into a stone oven. Dear God, he was so hot! What joker had thought it sensible to leave stretcher cases out in the sun to boil alive like this?

"Where did you get it? Your wound I mean?"

"I was shot," struggled Joseph. "Then there was an explosion and I couldn't move away. Shrapnel."

"I say! What's it like?"

"Loud" was the only word that sprang to mind, and he knew the poor child must think him an imbecile. Of course it was bloody *loud*. "Deafening, like being in the middle of a thunderstorm."

A man appeared behind the boy, his own red hair turning grey beneath his hat. "Timothy, do leave the poor chap alone." He glanced uneasily at Joseph. "I'm most dreadfully sorry, he wanted to see a hero."

Joseph blushed and hoped that in the heat he would simply look a little feverish. "I don't mind a bit," he lied, wishing to goodness that the child and his father and anyone with nothing better to do than disturb him would just disappear. "He's . . . he's only a child." The man nodded politely and made to leave when it occurred to Joseph to ask, "I'm sorry, sir, but where on earth am I? I . . . I think I dozed off in the ambulance. What are we waiting for? Where are we going?"

The man chuckled in a rather tiresome way and shook his head. "Dear me, they don't give away much, do they? It's all right, you'll be off to hospital in a little while, no doubt. They call this place the Nurse of the Mediterranean these days, hospitals popping up all over the place. Can you sit up at all?"

"Yes, with a little help."

"Well then, if you think you might survive the afternoon, they'll be taking you for tea first, I suspect, while they find beds for you all." The man gave a knowing smile and placed a hand on his young son's shoulder, as though he were quite relieved that his own children would never find themselves wounded on a battlefield. Or so he imagined. "Chin up, old chap, you'll be well looked after here."

"Those people, the people who greeted us—who were they?"

"Only well-wishers. They gather, pay their respects, then they go. Kind of them, don't you think?"

Then he was gone as well. Joseph reached into the paper bag and pulled out a sticky, misshapen chocolate and ate it simply to have something to do. So this was Malta, which Matthew Horton had spoken of so highly and not lived to see again. Joseph stared fixedly upwards at the blue cloudless square of sky above his head and hoped that if he stared long enough without blinking, the tears that were welling up in his eyes again would disappear without being noticed by the orderlies who had appeared to carry him away.

He was in Malta, being carried among a friendly crowd, with a cigarette in his hand and a sweet taste in his mouth. If not for the hushed, reverential introduction and that child, he could almost have believed that the war was over simply because it was over for him.

Joseph had slipped somehow from a hospital ship to a military funeral to something that felt a little like the world as it should be. If he had not been lying on a stretcher, it would all have felt so normal—absurdly so. He could see shops so like his own lining either side of the street; clean and shiny windows displaying books, pastries and sweetmeats, packets of cigarettes and matches, pipes, newspapers, boxes and bottles; painted wooden signs bearing proprietorial names he had never seen before and had no idea how to pronounce: Grech, Zammit, Nani, Azzopardi. The men in uniform who walked past him were fresh-faced and alert, backs ramrod straight, colonials who had not yet fought a battle in their lives. Men who had never seen death, never felt lice prickling along the seams of their clothes, never known hunger or fear, never marched asleep because it really was possible to be so exhausted that the mind blacked out whilst the body laboured on without rest. He was in a land of innocence.

An hour later, Joseph found himself settled in a chair in a clean, bright room filled with other wounded men, being poured a glorious cup of tea by a smiling English lady who cut an elegant figure swathed in lace.

"Thank you," he said, but he was filled with panic at the prospect of holding something as fragile and delicate as a teacup. He grasped the saucer but his hands shook so much that she did not risk letting it go in case he dropped it. "I'm awfully sorry."

The lady smiled a little more nervously, the way she might have smiled at a blundering child. "Don't worry, you poor man. Let me put it on the table for you."

Joseph waited until she had turned her attentions to another soldier, before lowering his head in shame. He had felt perpetually disorientated since the moment he had waved good-bye to his family, and this was yet another moment when he barely knew where he was. It was all so perfect. These dear ladies had put all their passion and affection and patriotic zeal into serving wounded soldiers they both pitied and revered. They were gentle and courteous, moving deftly among them to ensure that they had plenty to eat and drink. The tables heaved with cakes and little triangular sandwiches, lovingly prepared and so dainty that Joseph was almost afraid to reach out and take anything in case his hands began to shake again. It was all so bewildering, the cleanness, the elegance, the delicacy of it all. After army rations—dry hard biscuits, bully beef, stewed tea—the food tasted so sweet and soft that it hardly seemed real. He swallowed mouthfuls of white bread and sponge cake, his eyes lowered to avoid the smiles of these worthy ladies who imagined—as the well-wishers at the dockside had imagined—that they were ministering to heroes.

The shame of it all. Joseph was not a hero; he did not even aspire to be a hero. The second the bullet had entered between his ribs and left his body through his back, he had screamed like a silly child and only the infernal roar of the explosion that had almost finished him off silenced the ridiculous noise he had made. He was not a hero and he did not deserve any of this. He did not deserve to be alive when better men were dead, and in his cowardice he thought that he would be prepared to lose his wounded leg if it meant never going back to face the enemy artillery again. He wanted this safety, even in his embarrassment and shame; he wallowed in this perfect, precious, wholly artificial world without ugliness and bloodshed. He was savagely grateful for not being a hero who would that very moment be at the front—wounded or otherwise—because the best of men did not return.

18

It was the first night in many months that those dead men did not haunt Joseph's dreams. The exhaustion of travel and the many different, bewildering experiences had the effect of a powerful narcotic, and Joseph slept deeply for more hours than he could later recall, waking up pleasantly warm and groggy to the most heavenly sight a young man could possibly desire. A woman's rounded face, framed by the crisp white covering that marked her out as a nurse, hovered close to him as she stooped forward to straighten his bedclothes. She had the look of exotic innocence they all seemed to have here, the warm, autumnal skin tones; the ruddy lips and cheeks more perfect than the most skilfully painted face; the long, glossy black eyelashes framing almond-shaped eyes that seemed to have gazed upon the entire world and all its mysteries without being tainted by them. He told himself that she was the loveliest woman he had ever set eyes on. "Good morning," she said, with a quizzical Mona Lisa smile. "I hope you are feeling a little stronger today."

"You are English!" He exclaimed, bewildered by her impeccable English accent that simply did not fit with her appearance. "I thought you were a native."

Joseph worried immediately that he had insulted her but she giggled delightfully. "Now there's a mystery! May I take your temperature?"

During the minutes he lay with the glass thermometer in his mouth, grateful that he did not need to make conversation with her, he luxuriated in her presence. Joseph noted that she wore no wedding band and tried to guess her age. It was so hard to tell, the way they were dressed. She could have been anything from fifteen to thirty-five, but he suspected that she was very young, perhaps a little too young. Not that there was anything unusual about that. She took the thermometer from his mouth and peered at it; her every movement was elegant, deft, careful. "You have a fever," she said gravely. "Try to get some rest now. I will come and change your dressings later."

Joseph did feel hot, and during the rest of the morning he felt the steady encroachment of those telltale signs, the aching joints, the flushed, prickling skin. Sometime later, a pale, freckled-face nurse brought him water. "That nurse who came this morning," he said, but his hands were trembling again and he could not hold the glass. "What's her name? I forgot to ask her name."

The nurse chuckled. "I think you mean Lily," she said, pressing the cup to his lips. "All the men ask about her."

"Does she have a young man?" He asked between gulps.

"Certainly not, she's a very particular young lady. I'd mind your step if I were you."

Not that he were likely to cause anyone any trouble in the state he was in, thought the girl glumly, taking away the empty beaker and filling it again. She wished she had thought of a more appropriate comment, one that did not involve a reference to walking. One of the man's wounds had become infected, hence the fever that was overtaking him, and she knew, as he evidently did not, where it was likely to end. "Could you put in a good word for me, nurse?"

"Quiet now, get some rest."

But there was to be no quiet and no rest for Joseph. During his last moments of consciousness, he was aware that he was trembling, quite gently at first then so violently that he eventually had to be physically restrained from battering himself in his fit. He could feel that he was soaking wet, sweat pouring out of him until his night-clothes and sheets could have been wrung out, and yet he still felt as though he were burning alive. He remembered fevers like this from his childhood, his mother cooling his temples and the sound of her calm voice promising him that there really were no monsters waiting to devour him; that the sharp fangs and claws, the huge red glaring eyes were not really there in the room with him. When he could not be convinced she would play along instead. It was all right, she would say, there was nothing to fear. If there were monsters she would protect him; she was an Amazonian warrior and would stay at his side and fight them off. Joseph remembered her singing to him in his quieter moments when he was incapable of sitting up or even moving and the terrible time the doctor said in his hearing that they should prepare for the worst.

There was no one here to tell Joseph that the monsters were not real; and no one knew when he screamed so chillingly that he believed the world was shattering all around him. He was surrounded by dismembered bodies, faces rendered unrecognisable by explosions that had erased all those delicately chiselled features. A body was stretched out on barbed wire where the soldier had become ensnared a moment before he was riddled with bullets, his arms extended like those on a Baroque crucifix or a scarecrow. Helpless and ridiculous.

Joseph trailed his hand along the ground where he was lying, trying to remember where he was. All he could remember was the noise, a hellish explosion that God in his heaven must surely have heard even though he appeared to be deaf to the screams of the world in its death throes. Joseph began to realise that the explosion had left him with a ringing in his ears, and the screams he thought he could hear were clawing around in his own head. Worse than that, he could not move, he was trapped. On every side of him there was a muddy bank of earth; he must have fallen into the crater made by the explosion, and it felt so very like an open grave. If help did not come to him in the form of stretcher bearers and a rescue team, he would lie in this crater until either he was captured by enemy soldiers or he died the slow, terrible death soldiers feared more than a bullet, ravaged by thirst and pain as his life blood trickled away from him.

Joseph struggled to shift position and let his head flop to one side, only to find himself staring into a dead face only inches away from his own. If he could call it a face. The explosion that had left Joseph so dangerously wounded had killed the other man instantly. He must have taken the impact of the blast because his eyes had been blown out of their sockets and one side of his head looked as though it had been smashed by a hammer.

Joseph's head swam. He closed his eyes but the sight was still before him. He could feel himself shuddering with the effort of suppressing a scream. He wanted to open his mouth and scream loud enough for the whole world to hear, but he felt his mother's protecting presence at his side, willing him to be strong; he heard her voice saying over and over again: "Hush now, there's nothing there. Don't be afraid."

But the voice was not his mother's, and the hand pressing his burning forehead had never held him before. Joseph opened his eyes, and in a single lucid moment he saw that painfully young face framed in white like a sad angel hovering at his side and knew that she was keeping watch over him because she believed he was about to die. He summoned up all his remaining strength and reached up to grasp her wrist, which she evidently took as a sign that he did not want her to touch his head and began to move away. He held on to her arm as though she were the only person alive who could save him from the annihilation that was coming; she was an angel, she was stronger than death and hell and the spectres of his lost friends. He could feel darkness coming again and the sense that he was slipping away, but even as his eyes closed he was aware that she was holding his hand, whispering words in a language that was not his own.

19

"That's so romantic," Kristjana mused out loud, aware that it sounded unbearably girlish. "People always fall in love with their carers." Oh, that remark was most unfortunate. "Well, sometimes at least. I mean, young men do." Even worse. "No, no, age doesn't have anything to do with it. In stories at least, people always fall in love with their carers."

Leo took one bemused look at his own carer and burst out laughing. It would have been a roaring belly laugh once, Kristjana suspected, but in his weakening state, it came out as a rasping noise that would have been ugly to hear if it were not a sign of such obvious amusement. "Oh dear, oh dear," he managed to say at last, clutching his stomach as though trying to hold himself together. "You mustn't make me laugh like that, it's exhausting. Oh my dear, you are funny." He reached out for her hand. "It's all right, Kris, I think you are right. People always fall in love with the people who care for them. Don't look so scared."

"I'm not, I promise." Of course she was not scared of him, the poor man was so frail that he could not perform even the most basic functions for himself—eating, drinking, washing. A tube inserted through his nasal cavity fed him, another tube in his arm provided him with hydration and the drugs he required, yet another tube emptied his bladder, since even that most primitive act was impossible without assistance. It would not be long before he became unable to reach out and grasp her hand to reassure her. He might well lose the capacity for speech before he had finished his story. She was becoming scared of losing him, certainly, but hardly scared of him.

"There are all kinds of ways to fall in love, you know. I love you, Kristjana, but not the way my father loved my mother, full of the passion and fire of a young man who knew he would probably never grow old. I love you very differently to that."

Leo's voice cracked, then petered out. A terrible thought suddenly hit Kristjana. "Leo, you know the night of the storm? Was the person you lost a child?"

But he had turned away. "How did it feel to fall in love?" he asked quietly.

Kristjana shrugged. "Nice." Oh dear. "Wonderful. You ... well, you know, you start to notice a person, then you start enjoying their company. I suppose then you start trying to meet them."

"You young people are so," he pondered the word, "prosaic."

"Well really, what do you expect me to say? You start liking a person, then you ... you get all tingly when they come near you, then ... well, for goodness' sake, it all happens quite gradually! You know, it's quite nerve-racking to start with. Does he like me, doesn't he? Then you start relaxing with one another, then you know, one day you get a sign ..." This was ridiculous, she was positively stammering! How could it be so cringe-worthily difficult to talk about love to a man who had told her about bloody battles and abandoned little children and medical students drowning and every manner of human horror? Maybe her generation was "prosaic" after all, so oversexed and infantilised that they couldn't be expected to talk seriously about one of the commonest and most delightful of human afflictions—falling in love. "I never thought anyone could fall in love with me; I think a lot of girls think like that. I thought he would just want to be friends. Then one day, he took me on a long walk early in the morning when the whole of the town was fast asleep. We climbed a hill, the sun shone. Then we kissed and it was ... perfect. I never wanted the moment to pass."

"Do you still love him?"

"Yes. Of course I do."

"Have you told him?"

"Well, of course. I told him last time I e-mailed him!" The man had a talent for touching her raw nerves. "Why do you ask?"

The room was eerily silent when neither of them was speaking, apart from the gentle purr of the air conditioning and the hiss of Leo's breath as his lungs laboured like a broken accordion playing its final melody. "Well, it's just that I think my parents' courtship was not so different. Lovers are terribly conventional, nothing much changes. They get tingly feelings, as you put it, they long for one another's company. They kiss; they say 'I love you.' And every time it happens, lovers pride themselves that there is something special and unique about their particular love, their particular way of saying 'I love you.' Except that in my parents' case, they went through all the stages of falling in love very quickly, since there was so little time."

Once again, Kristjana felt the relief of being drawn away from her own world to a time of formal courtships and chaperones and ladies in starched, high-necked frocks on the hottest summer day—and a young man dangerously weakened by wounds and fever, reaching out instinctively to throw his arms around a girl's neck as she reached innocently over him.

***

"Well, it seems Private Radcliffe may fight another day after all," said Matron glibly, as she witnessed Liljana struggling desperately to extricate herself from his embrace. She waited until Liljana had staggered back, her face flame red from the sudden, unexpected closeness, and gave her a knowing look. "Not sure I should leave you on this ward for night duty by the look of things. For pity's sake, girl, you look like a beetroot!"

But Liljana was almost too startled and hot to reply. "I'm awfully sorry, I didn't ask him to do that."

"No harm done, I'm sure."

"I was trying to make him more comfortable ..."

"Put the little incident entirely out of your mind," Matron advised Liljana, though the advice came out sounding more like a brisk command. "There is nothing quite so attractive to a silly young man than a girl in uniform. No doubt he imagines himself desperately in love with every nurse who pays him attention."

Liljana needed no further instruction on the matter. Her logical mind told her that men in wartime—plagued by boredom and long months with only other men for company—naturally tended to express affection for any woman who came near them. She knew perfectly well she had no right to take it personally, but even reciting the thought to herself on a daily basis did little to dislodge the strange feeling that came over her in his presence.

Joseph was the first man she did not pity. That was how she knew that something beyond her control was drawing her to him. She did not want him to live because she pitied the poor boy for the years he would not enjoy or pitied his parents—whoever and wherever they were—for having to bear the grief of a beloved son lost. She simply wanted him alive. She found herself approaching his bed with trepidation every time she came on duty, in case it were empty or—more likely—filled by another patient.

Matron would no doubt have said that the poor girl was the one who was infatuated, drawn inexorably towards the first man who had taken notice of her, and she might well have been right, in the unfortunate, sour way frustrated older women so often are. Whatever Matron's thoughts were on the matter, however, she kept them to herself and failed to notice—during the long, wearisome week of night duties that followed—that Liljana seemed to keep drifting in one particular direction.

And Liljana told herself that there was nothing to notice, that she was doing nothing untoward and had nothing to hide, whilst at the same time she felt the overwhelming temptation to find ways to be close to him. Night shifts offered so many more opportunities because they were by their very nature quieter, involving little more than observation on her part and brief moments of attention. As Joseph slept, she would look at his peaceful face and take in its every detail: the gentle contours of his sunken cheeks, which must have been plump once; the light dusting of freckles over his nose; his thick, baby-soft hair growing a little too long during his long stay in hospital; the slight creases across his forehead, where age had written its signature on his otherwise boyish face. Perhaps it was that detail that drew her to him—the sense that he, like her, was a youth grown old before his time.

"'We that are young,'" mused Liljana out loud, struggling to remember the rest of the quote. "'We that are young ... shall never see so much, nor live so long.'"

"Speak for yourself, nurse, I'm not going anywhere!"

Liljana found herself confronted by two wide, mischievous eyes, which blinked with the effort of trying to focus on an unexpected sight. "I thought you were sound asleep!"

Joseph's smile broadened. "I'll tell you a secret. I often lie with my eyes closed pretending to sleep so you won't walk away. You always disappear when I start opening my eyes."

Liljana felt herself blushing like a schoolgirl who had been caught smuggling contraband toffees. "I think that's beastly."

"You do talk posh." Joseph noticed that she was seated at his bed-side with her hand—deliberately, he suspected—resting against the edge of his bed, and he took the invitation to reach for it. "You're not really cross are you? You're always saying poetry to yourself. What was that one?"

Liljana felt herself relaxing a little as the subject moved in what she thought was a safe direction. "Shakespeare, but he's wrong. The old have not borne most, and we shall see far more than them, though I think the last part is right. Strange," she hesitated, pondering the thought, "it's the first time Mr Shakespeare has let me down. Who could have thought there might be tragedy in the world greater than *King Lear*?"

Joseph had no idea what she was talking about. He had left school apace at the earliest possible opportunity, safe in the knowledge that he could find gainful employment in his father's shop as long as he could read, write and perform halfway decent mental arithmetic. He could have listened to her all day, but he did not want her to think him ignorant and pretended to have a dizzy spell. "I'm feeling a little … strange," he wheezed, rolling his head listlessly from side to side. "I wonder … please …"

The ruse worked perfectly. In a split second she was a nurse again, hurrying to ease his misery with a cool cloth to his brow and a short warning that he really must make an effort to drink more since it was so warm and the fever had not yet left him. Honour was restored.

"I ate my elbow this morning," said Emily, as they sat in the Upper Barrakka Gardens, enjoying a much anticipated day out.

"Yes," answered Lily, gazing out at the view of the harbour.

They had come out early to avoid the heat of the day and should have been enjoying the hearty picnic breakfast Emily had prepared, with the idea of perhaps shopping at one of Valletta's bustling markets later on. Emily was in need of a new frock, and since her sewing skills had never developed beyond eccentrically shaped pin cushions and half-finished samplers, Liljana had promised to make it for her if she could choose the fabric. At least, this had been the plan, but since Liljana had barely said a word since they had sat down, Emily was beginning to wonder whether they should just give up and go home. She was used to Liljana's melancholy silences and had learned to accommodate them over the years, but this was not melancholy. "Lily, who is he?"

Liljana looked blankly at her friend. "What are you talking about?"

"Oh come on, old girl, you don't honestly think I haven't guessed?"

"Who's who?"

"Lily!"

"Oh dear, is it very obvious?"

Emily burst into shrieking giggles, causing a number of caustic glances in her direction from passersby. "Oh Lily, you are funny! You used to be so good at hiding everything. You might have a sign around your neck saying, 'I'm in love with a soldier!'"

"I didn't say he was a soldier." Lily looked suddenly crestfallen. "Well, I suppose it would have to be, wouldn't it? And I didn't say I was in love."

Emily moved a little closer and put a hand on Liljana's arm. "It's all right, Lily, there need not be any cause for shame. You *have* fallen in love, haven't you?"

"How should I know?" Liljana had that look of cold anguish on her face Emily recognised so well, that stood in place of tears in any other girl. "This is the first time in so long I have wished I had a mother to talk to, but even if mine were alive it wouldn't help. She never fell in love."

"You don't know that. Perhaps she loved your father." But Liljana's happy reverie had evaporated, and Emily was horribly aware of being the cause—as usual. "It's all right, Lily," she promised, "it's a marvellous thing to fall in love. Nothing to worry about."

"It feels so strange. I cannot get my head around it. He arrived at the hospital only ten days ago and has been dreadfully ill, and I am afraid of losing him."

Emily, who had never been the sort of soul to plumb the depths of human feeling, laughed lightly. "Gosh, it's ever so romantic, Lily! I never thought you had it in you to be swept off your feet like that!"

"Don't! It's irrational! It's unseemly!"

"Oh come on, Lily, don't spoil it! When I fall in love it shall be love at first sight too. Well, it will have to be since the men are hardly hanging around, are they?"

But Emily's hearty banter did nothing to lighten the mood, and Emily soon gave up trying. One of the blessings of youth is being largely unaware of being very young or, at least, of being too young.

It did not occur to Emily as she sat watching Liljana with her arms hugging her knees, that if it had not been for the war, the two of them might still be safely tucked away in some educational establishment— school or finishing school or perhaps even university for Lily because she was so very clever and Mr Hampton had had ambitions for her. Nor did it occur to either of them that history would never hold a place for two girls coming of age at a time when millions would never reach their majority. "It's all right, my darling," said Emily finally. "I'll look after you."

20

Kristjana was beginning to suspect that there was a mad romantic in her after all. That, at least, was what Leo must have been thinking before he dozed off for his afternoon nap. His naps were getting longer, taking up more of the day as though he needed to fit his wakefulness around his rest, not the other way around. The morning routine exhausted him: the washing and changing, the checking of IV fluids since he no longer took fluids orally, the recording of vital signs.

Leo never said a word as Kristjana washed him, and she suspected that he still felt a residual embarrassment about her closeness to him, when all that passed through her mind as the flannel glanced carefully over his taut flesh, was how thin he was becoming. She felt more and more bones protruding discreetly under her hand, and for the first time, she was beginning to understand the meaning of the words "wasting away". All in all, it was a relief when Leo was clean and dry and she had slipped a fresh cotton hospital gown over him, which he always took as the cue to start talking.

Kristjana could not get over how unafraid he seemed to be about the fact that he was dying. For a young person who had often pondered the apparent pointlessness of life, she was morbidly frightened of it ending and sat at Leo's side during his many naps wondering how he could bear to fall asleep when he might quite possibly never wake up. And he was so exhausted, sleeping more and more frequently, drifting who knew where.

> *We are such stuff*
> *As dreams are made on; and our little life*
> *Is rounded with a sleep.*

During his precious moments of consciousness, Leo was giving her snapshots of a story. Perhaps that was exactly the way stories should be told, in tiny fragments. That was, after all, the way human beings remembered: a conversation here; a fleeting moment there; the sight of an iced cake covered in candles; a harsh word heard echoing over and over again across the years; the tiny, insignificant details of a favourite room; a familiar face, its every nuance and contour burned into the mind, smiling, scowling, weeping, sneering. With Leo's ever more fleeting moments of wakefulness, Kristjana found herself a witness to an altercation in a reeking sluice room, a promise made between lifelong friends on a quiet morning in wartime Malta, the scribbling of secret letters left inside books or under pillows, the giddy, agony-ecstasy of the first act of falling in love.

"Look, it was a love affair that was never going to end well," said Leo sulkily when Kristjana pestered him for details. She told herself she was not a walking gender stereotype because she wanted to see Liljana going through the well-worn adventure of a youthful love affair. But Leo seemed to prefer remembering her as a child, as though he felt safer in the relative peace of her rural education, when there was still the possibility that everything might have turned out differently.

"All the world loves a lover," quipped Kristjana, but Leo positively scowled at her.

"There were thousands and thousands of broken hearts scattered across Europe in those days," he retorted. "One day, she went on duty and found him gone. His bed was stripped and he was nowhere to be found. Then the matron told her that he had been moved to another ward since his condition had improved and he was out of danger. Then the two of them did what they all did. They found ways to meet: she got herself transferred to his ward by some sleight of hand, no doubt; they talked; he wrote her long letters telling her she was the most beautiful girl in the whole world and he loved her more than any man had ever loved a woman. I suspect he had a go at writing her poems to that effect."

"You talk as though you're reading a shopping list!" exclaimed Kristjana, horrified at the uncharacteristically sarcastic tone he had employed to rattle off the beautiful moments of his parents' union. He almost sounded angry with them for daring to believe they could fall in love, could build a happy life together, could defy the wrath of the entire world that had brought them together without meaning to and would part them with equally indifferent cruelty. He might almost wish he had never come into the world at all. "'Tis better to have loved and lost than never to have loved at all.' That's Tennyson."

He responded with a smirk. "It is foolish to have loved and lost for fear of having loved at all. That's one of my pearls of wisdom."

"I haven't lost," she said a little too quickly, but his expression had already begun to look apologetic. "I haven't lost."

Kristjana reassured herself all the way down the Neblus Road, past the American Colony Hotel, past the absurdly out-of-place Anglican Cathedral, past the tradesmen vying with teenage soldiers at the entrance to Damascus Gate. She was still reassuring herself as she sat in the lobby of the Al-Arab Hostel, munching her way through a truly appalling portion of *shawarma* she had brought with her to supplement the hospital diet that was slowly wearing her down.

"Ten minutes?" asked Noor from behind the counter, giving her a knowing grin. "Or shall we make it twenty just to save time?"

"Can you give me a special price for fifteen?"

"You supposed to bargain over the price not the minutes!"

But Kristjana was at the computer again and felt a certain fluttering of the chest as she logged into her e-mail account and scanned the list of names and subject headings cluttering up her in-box. She told herself she had no right to feel affronted, but all the same she looked over and over again to make absolutely sure, and she did feel affronted. Benedict had not written, and she could not even hide behind the comfort of a former age when a girl could tell herself that the letter must have got lost in the post. She knew that if he had written her an e-mail and pressed the *send* button, it would have arrived. He had not written.

Kristjana swallowed a rising sense of panic and told herself again that she had no business expecting anything different, since he was only doing in much modified form what she had done to him. She had not spared him a thought when she had failed to get in touch with him; she had never imagined him sitting at his computer in the hopeful anticipation of an e-mail that seldom ever arrived. "It is foolish to have loved and lost for fear of having loved at all," Leo had said. Was he simply projecting his mother's fear onto her or was that something else they had in common? The fear of surrender, because falling in love was a form of surrender and there was a certain kind of woman who could not face being that vulnerable.

Kristjana exhaled slowly, letting herself be distracted by the omnipresent whirr of ancient electric fans and the tap, tap, tapping of other people communicating with their friends. Her fingers reached towards the tri-alphabet keyboard as though they had taken on a mind of their own, but she knew that if she did not break the silence now there would be no other chance to do so.

Dear Benedict,

I haven't heard from you. I suppose I've no business feeling put out, given the way I've behaved, but I would love to hear from you. Life is quite quiet here, I am still looking after the same patient, but not sure how long he has left now. I don't know why but I can't bear to think of him slipping away, I feel as though I have known him for years. I hope your work is going well. I love you. You do know that, don't you? I love you and I hope we will be together again before too long.
    Lots of love,
    Kris x

She waited a moment to be sure the message had definitely gone, shut down her account and stood up. "You only been five minutes!" she heard an incredulous voice announce from some faraway place. "You want your money back?"

Kristjana shrugged as she walked to the door. "Save it for next time," she suggested, though she found it hard to imagine coming that way again. As she began the walk home, Kristjana felt a cloud of gloom enveloping her like the caress of an old friend. She knew she had no right to wallow in self-pity so she descended into self-hatred instead and staggered under the weight of a torrent of abuse that would have no doubt been deemed a hate crime if she had directed it at anyone else. *Capricious, fickle, ill-tempered, irascible, useless, evil, infinitely hateable parasite!* Even her care for Leo seemed to have little to commend it under the circumstances. She wasn't caring for him, she was using him to fill in the empty hours of her own wasting life. She was a time-travelling parasite, attaching herself to another life, another time, another tragedy as though Leo's past could act as life support for her future.

When she arrived at the hospital, Kristjana went straight to her room to freshen up and to change into her uniform, but she found herself sitting by the window instead, staring glassily down at the convent garden. She could see a solitary white figure some way off, stooping to tend a dry, tired flower bed, but with her back to

Kristjana it was difficult to guess which sister she was. Had those dear women in white chosen to be alone? She had always assumed that women who entered convents must have fled tragic love affairs or a powerful dissatisfaction with the world; could any young woman actually *choose* to lead a single life?

The white figure stood up and turned towards the hospital building, glancing up at Kristjana's window as though she had sensed she was being watched. Kristjana tried to look as though she had been staring into space, but Sister Pauline gave an impish smile and waved up at her before tapping her wristwatch to indicate the time. It wasn't so much that she could not understand a woman choosing a life like that, Kristjana pondered glumly, she just could not imagine anyone having the nerve to stand alone.

* * *

Liljana would not have understood a habited woman in a convent garden any more than Kristjana did, but one thing she did have was nerve; and there was nothing quite so pleasurably risky as a clandestine assignation. During the weeks Joseph was too ill to leave the hospital, Liljana spent her time off reading to him and pretending not to notice when he slipped a discreet note in between the leaves of the book for her to read later. When he became a little stronger, Joseph was allowed to sit in a shady spot on the roof for some fresh air, which he cheerfully squandered by smoking a chain of cheap cigarettes. A snapshot. One of Leo's many little snapshots. Two impossibly young people, sitting together on a flat, walled, limestone roof—Joseph trying to hide the residual pain and the nagging discomfort of hot, itchy dressings and Liljana positioned very carefully to hide the sight of their clasped hands. Sunlight dapples their faces, and it is almost possible to dream, as they dreamed, that they would look back on it all from the happy vantage point of old age.

And Joseph dreamed. For the first time since many of his friends had perished, he began to imagine a time after the war when he would no longer be a soldier. They had been warned to brace themselves for four or five more years of war, but it might not come to that and here it already seemed as though it *were* all over. Everywhere Joseph looked, he saw the scarred and wounded recovering after a battle long ended, surrounded by the tantalising comings and goings of civilian life. He had been told it was possible to hear gunfire from far distant battlefields if the wind blew in the right direction, but he had never heard any such thing.

"Lily?" he asked one afternoon as she sat at his side, knitting. "Where would you like to make your home if you could choose anywhere? Would it be here or in England?"

Liljana pretended to be preoccupied with a stitch she had dropped. Joseph found it most endearing that Liljana was so infinitely practical, capable of putting her mind to virtually anything, but did not seem able to master what appeared to his male gaze to be a quite straightforward art. She was constantly stopping to pick up the stitches she had inadvertently dropped, only to get to the end of the row of knitting and discover two or three new ones she had picked up along the way, ruining what should have been a straight edge. He was not even sure precisely what the creation was supposed to be and suspected he would have to ask his mother to knit their children jumpers when winter came.

A winter's evening in that little Cambridge house—that would be truly perfect. A quiet hour with his mother sitting by the fire knitting a tiny jacket for a new baby and Liljana seated by the lamp, reading aloud. Joseph always imagined her with a book in one hand, but he was only just beginning to imagine her in such a setting. "What do you think, my love? Where is your heart?"

"My heart is not bound by time and space," Liljana said mysteriously, unsettling him until she glanced up and he realised she was not speaking entirely seriously. "Where is yours?"

"Well I suppose ..." But Joseph was lost for an answer yet again, and she had completely shattered the domestic idyll he had been conjuring up. He tried to travel back to the safety of his parents' house, but he was sweltering on a hospital roof with Liljana's Madonna face gazing up at him as though she held the secrets of the universe hidden in the pupils of her eyes. "I'm not sure, I think ... that is ..." She was too ethereal for a world of clanking tills and cheeky customers and dusty bags of sugar and flour; he was not even convinced he could risk taking her anywhere near his family.

"Penny for your thoughts?"

"My heart is here," he said truthfully. "It's here."

"Well then," she said, as though a decision had been made, "I think here is as good a place as any to make a home."

***

"I have sometimes wondered what sort of a life they would have had together if he had lived," remarked Leo, staring up at the ceiling. "He must always have known that it would be very difficult for them to make a happy home, not that it seemed to trouble them much at the time."

"If two people love one another … my boyfriend and I are completely different in almost everything."

"Class meant a good deal more in those days," said Leo. "I think it still does. The fact is, they were both from very ordinary backgrounds—he was a tradesman, she had been a domestic servant—but her education turned her into a lady. Even if he had been happy to have a clever wife, his family would not have seen it that way. Her accent, her manners, her name, everything about her would have unnerved them for being too well-to-do or too foreign. They would have adored her then rejected her."

"You are getting so gloomy!" Kristjana could not understand why he was so determined to poor cold water over everything, but it had become a persistent theme. "They were in love; they would have made it work."

"They were little children!" he retorted. "They were neither of them yet *twenty*! They couldn't possibly have known what they really wanted. If there hadn't been a war to throw them together for such a short time, that little love affair would have fizzled out within months and they would both had looked back on it when they were older as a joyous silliness."

"You're a curmudgeon."

"Hmm?"

"A grumpy old man."

"It's called experience."

"What the old call their mistakes."

Leo raised an eyebrow. "And the young don't make mistakes? You're not making a mistake?"

"Why don't you want to tell me how it happened? How you happened, I mean."

The supercilious glance did not waver. "How do you think it happened? Something I need to tell you about human reproduction, is there?"

162

Kristjana waited for him to continue, but he closed his eyes and she suspected he was pretending to have fallen asleep. "I'm sorry, Leo, I've upset you, haven't you?"

"I'm not upset, but I am getting rather tired if you don't mind."

"Of course. Sorry."

"Good night."

"Sweet dreams."

21

Joseph sat in a small side chapel in Saint John's Cathedral and pondered a statue before him. It was yet another depiction of the Madonna and Child, a little sentimental for his taste and generic: the radiant-faced young woman in blue Renaissance garb, glancing piously up to heaven; a baby Jesus immortalised at about ten months old, the hands open as though prefiguring the crucifixion, his fingers raised in a gesture Joseph suspected meant something to the papists who worshipped here day after day. He was not a religious man, and he had had most of his latent childhood piety beaten out of him by an overzealous pastor by the time he was eight; but he felt drawn to the cathedral if for nothing else than a peaceful place out of the sun to meet Liljana. He needed somewhere quiet to have a conversation with her that would not arouse any suspicion.

In the main body of the Church, there was some service or other going on. Joseph could hear the melancholy tones of the Latin chants and found them reassuringly foreign. He had a mild dislike of the English hymns he had learned as a child. They should have been beautiful, but he could still feel his palms smarting whenever he heard words like "Love divine all loves excelling" or "My song is love unknown", which always seemed to have been chosen for assembly on the morning he was in particularly serious trouble. These sounds and sights could not hurt him, not because they were superior in beauty but simply because they were nothing to do with him. Everything around him was so gloriously, gaudily un-English: the vast, sumptuous altars, decorated with silver candlesticks and strange shining objects he did not recognise; the swathes of silk everywhere; the walls lined with endless little objects; Maltese crosses, any kind of crosses; the statues and icons that should have appalled him; the marble floors; the terrifyingly graphic crucifixes depicting a man suffering death by the slowest and cruellest of tortures. He smiled bitterly to think that there had been a time he would have thought the Christ of Mediterranean artwork disgracefully tasteless. But that had been when he had fondly imagined that there were limits to how seriously a human being could hurt another.

Joseph had come to the church a few minutes early, partly out of boredom and partly because he wanted to settle his mind before Liljana arrived. His nerves were ragged after a turbulent night, during which he had dreamed repeatedly about his first glimpse of the war, seen as his ship arrived at the Gallipoli peninsula to an explosive reception. The nightmare had assaulted his senses so completely that Joseph had felt as though he were there body and soul. He groaned under the useless weight of a pack filled with every object a soldier could not possibly need—biscuits, tea and empty sandbags as though they would ever have the chance to build their own defences. The awkwardly slung rifle he would not have had the presence of mind to fire even if the opportunity had arisen. There was the same bizarre reassurance of being crammed so close to other soldiers that moving at any speed was impossible.

Joseph saw men slipping below the surface of the water, their metal-capped boots sliding and sinking into the shingle beneath them, unable to shed their load in time. He saw bodies washed up on the shore and a boat ahead of him as it suffered a direct hit and was immediately blown into the air like some hideous volcano blasting torn human limbs into the water. He smelled cordite and burned flesh and blood, felt the odours stinging the back of this throat. Every inner voice told him he had seen enough already, more than the fragile human mind could possibly take in, and he lowered his eyes, only to glimpse a partially destroyed human hand floating past him, the uncommon presence of a wedding band still shining with newness on one finger. And all this before they had even reached dry land. The beach awaited them, a paradise of golden sand and steep, dramatic cliffs. Except hidden away among those cliffs were machine guns ready to shower them with death.

Joseph had woken up screaming and screamed until a nurse appeared at his side, enquiring as to whether he needed something for the pain.

He felt a presence in the pew behind him and turned his head slightly to see Liljana kneeling so as to be as close to him as possible. "What is it, my darling?" she asked softly. "You look as though you've seen a ghost."

"I wonder whether I shall ever see anything else," he said, to no one in particular. "Until they send me back and I become one."

"Oh, perhaps you won't need to!" answered Liljana, placing her hands on the back of his pew as though in prayer. He leaned his head to one side and touched her fingers with his cheek. She felt the rough texture of his skin against her knuckles and shuddered. "They may not send you back, you may not fully recover."

It was a ludicrous argument, a ludicrous conversation. In any other situation a nurse so hopefully telling a patient, or a lover telling her sweetheart, that he might face a lifetime of ill-health would have been perverse, but in other situations the alternative was rather more palatable. "My love, it's only a matter of time," he answered as though there were something she could do about it. "I'm recovering, I can feel my old strength coming back. There is a shortage of men, no one's enlisting anymore, they're not stupid, and so many men have been killed. Thousands of them." He closed his eyes. He could see them going down, row upon row of them like grass before the blade of a scythe—vital, moving, feeling, thinking men one moment, butchered cadavers the next. Who could have known there were so many men alive to be killed like that? "As soon as I am cleared for service, I shall be gone. I've started dreaming about it again, almost to prepare myself."

"Don't."

But it was too late. Joseph's shoulders had begun to shudder, and not for the first time he could do nothing but break down. He covered his face, but he knew that the sound of him struggling to catch his breath gave him away. Dear God, this was a second childhood, the loss of every means of self-control he had ever known. He could smell blood everywhere, hear the incessantly clean, regular clatter of the guns, and see—oh God !—he was under attack from all sides. A man reached out to him like some avenging angel, screaming at him to stop, but he ran on, staggered on, not doing the man the courtesy of so much as looking back to see if he were still alive.

"It might not happen, my love, please!" It was so many years since she had been forced to watch a loved one suffer that she too did not understand what was happening to her. Liljana buried her head in his shaking arm, whispering, "It might not happen, it might not happen. I won't let it happen! I won't let you go!"

"Don't hate me, don't hate me for being a coward."

They sat together in that side chapel for the rest of the afternoon, wasting precious time together, quailing before a future they knew they could not control. And around them, images and tableaux of suffering expressed everything that they could not, everything that was fragile and painful and pitiful about human existence, with its fleeting joys and life-shattering passions. And hope, but neither of them could have recognised it because neither had noticed that the ceremony taking place just yards away from them was a Requiem. The priest and the altar and the coffin and all the mourners filled the cathedral with waves and ripples of black, but Liljana and Joseph, trapped in their own grief, saw neither the black cascading around them nor the tiny threads of gold woven into the mourning clothes.

And was that why Leo could not bear to think of how he came to be? Because it was thanks to that misery that Leo first entered the cosmos as a single, microscopic cell? Did all children of wartime feel the same sense that even the ecstasy of lovemaking had to have been a little tainted by the gloom and fear that pervaded everything else?

"People take risks they would never normally take," Leo had said to Kristjana on more than one occasion. "When there is so much danger and nobody thinks there will be a future, consequences are not so important. People act on impulse. Especially youngsters."

Kristjana could not imagine Liljana acting on impulse, but how else could Leo have come to be? How did all those sad, demure little tableaux, those moments upon which Kristjana had so unkindly eavesdropped, culminate in an event so wildly, ecstatically out of character? Kristjana and Leo had watched the happy months of safety trickling away as Leo's frail life trickled away: those snatches of conversation, those moments of merriment, those entwined hands, those unspoken desires, those muddled prayers Liljana offered up every time Joseph went before a medical board to have his fitness for service determined.

And somewhere, tangled in that blur of ill-defined memories Leo could not articulate, Liljana herself watched as Joseph began to show signs of recovery she could not deny. He began walking with Liljana's support—haltingly at first, then unaided but with a visible limp. As his stride became straighter and more powerful, she hoped against all vain hope that he would still be deemed permanently unfit for service. Liljana did not have a fanciful bone in her body, yet she wanted so badly to imagine him telling her that the war was all over for him and they could marry and find some corner of the world to hide in. She could almost will herself to run from the certainty that of the three people in the whole of her life she had loved enough for it to hurt, he would be the second to be taken away from her.

A group of children were playing funerals. They had brought a Union flag with them and what looked like an old crate or palette and were coaxing the lightest among them—a small boy aged around five or six—to lie down in it. There was a certain amount of heaving and groaning as the other boys struggled to lift the funeral bier off the ground, and the self-appointed leader of the whole charade draped the flag over the still-protesting body, commanding the fatality in Maltese to shut his mouth. Then, to the strained amusement of the convalescing soldiers enjoying the sun in the Argotti Gardens, the procession moved solemnly among them to the discordant whine of Chopin's funeral march.

"How can they do that?" demanded Joseph, before forcing a cigarette between his teeth and striking a light. He drew in a long breath as slowly as he could until the end of the cigarette was glowing comfortably before taking it out of his mouth again. "I caught a group of them gunning one another down in the street the other day. Could've given them the back of my hand."

"They're only children, they can turn anything into a game," said Liljana, quietly. "Poor little things, they see those military funerals so often and all they ever hear about is the war. It's hardly surprising it's all they play at these days."

"They don't need your pity," Joseph retorted. "They don't have to do the damned fighting. Pity the poor souls in the real coffins, or the ones who never get the privilege of being put in a box." He covered his eyes with the finger and thumb of one hand.

"Darling, *please.*"

"I'm sorry."

They sat together with Emily perched a discreet distance from them, close enough to have a good view of them, but slightly out of earshot. In the time since Joseph had been deemed well enough to leave the hospital, they had employed the services of Emily to join them on all of their outings so as to maintain the necessary aura of respectability. Emily Sheppard was, it turned out, the world's most perfectly designed chaperone: straight-laced, respectable, discreet and easily prevailed upon to get lost at the appropriate moment. When she sensed that Joseph was desperate to speak with Liljana alone, she found an excuse to slip away for a few minutes in search of refreshment for them all.

"Please don't be sad, my love," he ventured, when he had barely found the energy to say a word that afternoon. "We knew it would have to happen. You've looked after me so well."

The truth was that since he had been cleared for active service, he had felt so wretched it had been as much as his life was worth not to let it show and he knew it did show. He had acted out the moment in his mind over and over again, and yet he had still felt taken aback when it came to it. As soon as he had been cheerfully told—as though he ought to be delighted at the news—that he was well enough to rejoin his regiment, he had been aware of preparations being made to carry him away from Liljana and the sanctuary of Malta. The helplessness he had felt so consistently since his regiment had first set sail had returned again, the sense of being a wholly insignificant detail like a counter on a draughts board, to be shunted about from square to square like so many other insignificant, indistinguishable, infinitely dispensable counters.

"I hoped we might have had a little longer. At least a little longer before they sent you away."

"I know, but I suppose we should be grateful for the time we have had."

This will all feel like a dream before long, he thought, *all of it. The war will be real and this will seem as though it never happened*. "It has happened," he said out loud.

"What has?"

He knew Emily might return at any moment and that he could not delay. "Lily, you will wait for me, won't you?"

"Of course," she answered, with a quiet determination that would have unsettled Joseph if he had not come to know Liljana so well. "You know I will wait for you."

"I want to marry you, Lily, when it's all over. We ... we don't have to go back to England, I'll stay here with you if you like."

"You silly boy!" She placed a finger on his lips to silence him. It was all so ridiculous; he was talking as though the only thing that could possibly divide them was a dispute over where they lived. "I have never had a home, Jo, I do not care where we live if we can only be together."

He itched to kiss her, but he could see Emily slipping into view out of the corner of his eye and held back. "There's something else," he said quickly and so quietly Liljana strained to hear. "I don't want to offend you, please don't be insulted, but ... well, I want you to spend the night with me."

She looked askance at him. "Are you mad?"

"Not like that, not like that. I mean ..." He was suddenly an awkward boy again, blundering his way through a situation a soldier should have taken in his stride. "I don't want to be alone ... on the last night, I mean. I won't sleep thinking about what's coming, and I ... well, I can't bear to be away from you if I don't have to be. I just want to be with you, that's all. To ... to talk with you."

His fingers curled around her hand. She felt the terrible, persistent throbbing in her chest she had felt ever since Joseph had told her the day he would be departing. "No one will believe we merely talked."

"No one has to know."

"Someone is bound to notice."

"Not if we are careful. We've been careful enough so far."

***

There was a house somewhere in Valletta that Leo had never dared to visit and would rather not speak about. "Some things are just private," he said, with a prim tone that did not suit him. "He persuaded an Englishman he had made friends with to let them stay at his house, and the man made himself scarce for the night. Well, you're a big girl, you can guess what happened."

"Do you suppose he meant it to turn out that way?"

"How am I supposed to know?" Anger again, appearing out of nowhere only to subside as fast as it emerged. "Look, you will no doubt think me a naïve old man, but part of me thinks he truly did not intend to do anything wrong that night. He was a frightened boy and he wanted her near him. Think how horrid it must have been, like awaiting your execution, you wouldn't want to be alone. But perhaps it was inevitable under the circumstances that things got a little out of hand."

A little out of hand. Two terrified young people facing the prospect of an eternal parting, a thought impossible for an old man like Leo to understand, let alone a boy and a girl barely at the point of adulthood. They were not so much lovers as two small animals huddling together from the torrential rain that would otherwise sweep them to their deaths. Perhaps Liljana's mother would have told her never to get herself into such a compromising situation, but there had been so little time for her mother to tell her anything and what she had told her had made so little sense that Liljana could never have trusted her. But they would all have said that—even Emily, who so rarely stood in her way—and yet all she could have thought about as they stepped into that deserted house was that every moment was precious and could not be wasted.

Leo could not relate what happened behind the closed doors of that house; it was a moment his mother never shared, and he had told Kristjana to use her imagination—so she used it. Kristjana spent the hours Leo slept imagining Liljana's final hours with Joseph as though painting a picture with the faintest of pencil lines to guide her.

She painted Liljana snuggled in Joseph's arms, feeling the heat of his body and the sense, more powerful than anything else, that they fitted so perfectly together, as though his arm had been meant to carry the weight of her head against it and his hand was that precise shape and size so that it spanned the length of her face from temple to jaw perfectly. There had been many partings in Liljana's life, but never could she have felt this indescribable, yawning emptiness that made her want to scream and scream at the top of her voice simply to distract herself from the feeling that she was dying.

"Don't! Oh please don't!" begged Joseph, when he felt tears touching his fingers. He drew her face towards his until their foreheads almost touched. "I love you, my darling. My darling, darling girl, I can't bear to do this to you. I won't go!"

He began kissing her face and neck with the desperation of a man staring into his own grave. His hand rested on the button of her collar. "You know you have to go!" she sobbed. "You do not have a choice!"

"I will not leave you!" He began unbuttoning her blouse and she did nothing to stop him. "I'll find some place to hide where they'll never find us."

"This is madness, you know you'll go!" She felt so dizzy that she was forced to close her eyes. She felt the forbidden, alien sensation of his bare hands pressing against her naked back and those interminable layers of clothing falling away from her, and there was a warning somewhere to go no further. She could still appeal to his honour and sense of duty; she too still believed in something called honour herself. His mouth pressed against hers and she trembled with fear before that too was replaced by an emotion she did not understand, and she knew she would not resist. She felt him holding the back of her neck and the overwhelming pressure of his body covering her. Never had she felt so loved, so wanted, so *light* with love.

"This is a sin."

"Don't."

They were falling together, spinning out of control, falling like dreamers who know somehow that they must be sleeping and long for the dawn never to come and shatter the world.

Knowing that it must.

When Liljana woke up, Joseph was standing close to her, fully dressed in his uniform, his kit bag packed and ready at his side. "I didn't want to disturb you," he said, reaching down to kiss her cheek. "You looked so lovely fast asleep."

She sat bolt upright, horrified. The searing light of day poured into the room, throwing Joseph into shadow. "I'm sorry! Wait for me!"

She made to get out of bed, but he stopped her gently. "No. Please don't see me off, I don't I think I could bear it now. Anyway, it is too dangerous. What if we are seen leaving the house together?" He got on his knees and held her in his arms, feeling her body jerking and trembling with emotion. "I will be one of the survivors, I promise. I will come back to you and we will be together. Always, I swear. Always and forever."

He separated from her as quickly as he could, picked up his belongings and hurried from the room without a backward glance. Liljana watched the door closing with an ugly, jarring creak and felt her head swimming again, not with ecstasy or even fear, but with the horror of being alone. She glanced down at the bed sheets and saw the telltale stains of blood, all that was left now of the night's encounter, and she threw herself down. With her face buried in the pillow, she let out a long, desperate scream of rage until her voice broke and tears overcame her again.

IV

22

Leo's face did not flicker as Kristjana announced her plan, but then it did not need to. She could feel the chill creeping across the room as he lay in his bed, pondering what she had suggested. "You'll have trouble finding it," he said finally, "there are hundreds of little white gravestones in that place."

"I'll find it somehow or other," she promised. "If you can try and cast your mind back. You said you'd visited your father's grave before. I don't need the exact location, if you can just remember more or less which area it was."

Leo could not make his indifference more evident. "If you don't mind my saying so, it's a rather odd way for you to be spending your day off. It will be sweltering hot, you'll be out there in the sun for hours and you still might not find it."

"Would you like me to say a prayer for you?"

Leo smiled and indicated his prayer book. "Take it with you and say the prayers for the dead. Don't take flowers, nobody does that in this climate. You can tell me all about your adventure afterwards."

Travelling in the back of the sweltering minibus, Kristjana told herself it was not morbid curiosity driving her to give up a precious day off to travel to one of the most miserable places in the entire West Bank, in search of the grave of a man to whom she was not related and had never known. The desire to remember the dead is buried so deep in the human psyche, it crosses cultures and creeds, as though mankind harbours a collective fear that their own lives will be forgotten if they themselves forget the lives of others. "You get off here," announced the driver, glancing over his shoulder at his passengers. There were eight of them in total, all foreigners with their own macabre reasons for venturing away from the Golden City for the day.

"I thought you said you'd take me all the way to the cemetery?" Kristjana protested, hesitating to get out with the others. "I've no idea where it is!"

"I can't go through the checkpoint, *habibti*," he said, gesturing towards the heavily fortified guard post, manned by a small group of nervous-looking teenage soldiers. "Get out, go to that building over there and they will let you through. There will be another van waiting on the other side. If I were you, I will hold up my British passport in front of me for everyone to see. You look far too like us."

Kristjana managed a smile to match the driver's grin but felt an uncomfortable churning of the stomach as she staggered out into the white-hot outside world, arriving inside the building just in time to see a row erupting between the men on duty and the man she had sat next to throughout the journey. He was a British Asian called Sahir, and they seemed convinced he was a Palestinian with a stolen passport, a situation not helped by the fact that they were all hot, fed up and evidently spoiling for a fight. A Canadian traveller started trying to mediate, only to inflame the situation further. "Passport!" called a voice from behind the growing mayhem, and Kristjana realised the order was being addressed to her.

She avoided making eye contact with anyone as she walked across the border, waving her small maroon passport with its gold embossed emblem of the lion and the unicorn. The soldiers she passed were young men doing their national service, the same age as many of the soldiers buried in the cemetery she was trying to locate. If she had had the courage, Kristjana would have turned and asked them how it felt, whether they felt that Edwardian pride or at least that sense of duty, the belief, instilled since infancy, that they were part of some great cause deserving of their heroism and perhaps their blood. Or did they feel, as Joseph Radcliffe surely felt as he stepped aboard that ship, the bitter, overpowering cocktail of rage and confusion and fear that marked out the reluctant fighter for an obscure cause. Fear more than anything else.

The second minibus was waiting as promised, dusty, slightly battered at one side from what looked like a minor traffic accident. Kristjana had slipped through first and found herself hanging back, anxious about getting in on her own in case she had made a mistake. A grizzled head poked out of the driver's window, amid a small burst of acrid cigarette smoke. "You getting in or what?"

"Coming." *Pull yourself together*, commanded a cross voice in her head, but her own subconscious always sounded harsher than Benedict's chiding tone ever did. *Who on earth would ever abduct you? The ransom you were worth wouldn't cover the cost of detaining you.* "I want to go to the war cemetery," she told the driver as she climbed inside. "The people at the Al-Arab hostel said you could take me."

"Yes, yes, no problem." He stubbed out his cigarette and threw it out of the window before reaching into his pocket to produce another. He had evidently run out and pulled out his hand shaking with disappointment. "Why you want to go there?"

"I need to find the grave of . . . a relative."

"It's a big cemetery. Very big cemetery. You know where it is?"

"Roughly."

"We only staying there five minutes. I have to take you to the flag shop."

Kristjana took a packet of cigarettes out of her handbag and offered him one. She was not a smoker but being able to produce good quality cigarettes at opportune moments had served her well before. "Why don't you take a couple?" She could hear the rest of the group starting to clamber in, but the promise of impending nicotine did the trick.

"OK, my friend, no problem. I drop you there and pick you up on the way back. Hmm?"

"That would be perfect."

During the journey to the cemetery, Kristjana pondered the ethics of bribing a man with a drug to which he was addicted, but he was as good as his word and dropped her exactly where she wanted to be. "You sure about this?" he asked.

"Absolutely sure. *Shukran.*"

In Flanders fields the poppies blow
Between the crosses, row on row.

War cemeteries had a tendency to look the same in any country. There were no poppies growing in Gaza, but the rest was depressingly familiar; the rows and rows and rows of gravestones as neat and tidy and regular as the soldiers were once, before they marched unresisting into the mire of the Great War's many bloodbaths. Mons, the Marne, Neuve-Chapelle, Ypres, the Somme, Tannenberg, Vimy Ridge, Verdun, Gallipoli. Like most British-educated schoolchildren, Kristjana had studied them all. She remembered the names printed in her school textbook, written down in her GCSE history notes, spoken with a faintly reverent tone by Mrs Parkes as she wrote down the number of fatalities and other details on the whiteboard in red marker.

It had never quite come to life then, not for her anyway, because she told herself that it was not her war and it was not her heritage. She could pity the doomed youth of Britain, Canada, Australia, America, India, Germany, France, Russia, Africa, and she could pity them all from the safe distance of eighty years and a nationality whose name was not intrinsically connected with that conflict the way it was with the next. But no one emerged from the Great War unharmed, and she stood now in a cemetery in Gaza, searching for the final resting place of a man whose life she had observed through the stories of another dying man, whose love she had witnessed, whose child she had nursed though Joseph himself had never held him in his arms.

"I am looking for the grave of Joseph Radcliffe."

The caretaker, a sturdy, rugged-looking man in his sixties, blinked at her in the sunlight. "There are thousands, Madam."

"He was in the Sixty-Fourth East Anglian Regiment. English."

"Ah. This way. Follow me."

"Thanks."

He walked among the gravestones with the ease of a gamekeeper treading a well-worn path through woods he had protected all his life. When three small children jumped out from behind a row of gravestones, he chatted to them casually and was evidently aware that they had been hiding there all the time. "My grandchildren," he explained. "Not offended, are you? They're only kids."

"Of course not."

No, she was not offended exactly. Unsettled perhaps. They were beautiful-looking children, aged between around four and eight, two boys and a girl with tight black plaits and the cheeky smile of a female already accustomed to getting her own way. "It's almost apocalyptic," she told the world in general.

"Eh?"

"Nothing, I was just thinking ..." but she could not find the words. "I was just thinking, you know, little children playing in a cemetery ..."

"I knew I remembered that name," declared the caretaker with evident excitement, picking up his pace so that Kristjana struggled to catch up with him. "There was something strange about it."

"Really?" This was too good to be true.

"Yes. Here it is."

Kristjana came to a standstill next to her guide and squinted in the sunlight. It was so bright and searing that for a moment, she could not read the words engraved on the stone. Then she realised that she had wasted her time. "It's not the right Joseph Radcliffe. He died of wounds."

"I'm sorry, Madam, but certainly it is the right stone."

"But he died of wounds."

There were some stories that were simply too squalid to tell. There were stories from that most disgraceful, that most disgusting of wars, too shameful to be granted a place in the collective memory. It was a story that Leo did not know because Liljana had never known. It was the story of Joseph Radcliffe's sorry death, alone and without honour. Joseph, who had always known that he was not a hero but had never thought of doing anything other than what was demanded of him until something snapped his nerves.

> *You can't believe that British troops 'retire'*
> *When hell's last horror breaks them, and they run.*

Was it the brutality of the war that broke him, or the blessed peace of his happy months in Malta that rendered it all so utterly futile? Was that what had happened? That glimpse into a world beyond his theatre of war—the men and women and children going about their daily business, walking along sunny streets to school or church or the market; the colonial women sipping tea; the local men arguing in their red-blooded language. Might it be that Joseph's paper-thin idealism was not broken by artillery fire, but was stifled by the haze of everyday life that made such a mockery of the hell he had so blithely entered once? And her, a body untarnished, undamaged, so lovely and so perfect he ached for her with every passing moment that took him away from her.

No one could ever answer the question because even if Joseph had been given the chance to make a written account of his motives, it was unlikely that he would have found the words and arguments to express them. The rest of Joseph's story passed in a miasma of doubt and confusion. He was one of hundreds of men whose last days were concealed, lied about and wilfully forgotten by a War Office determined to convince an increasingly weary public that there was still such a thing as chivalry in a world reeling from the horrors of mechanised slaughter. The most that could be surmised was that—only weeks after rejoining his regiment—Joseph decided he had simply had enough.

He could have argued at his court martial that he was not in his right mind, but it was to be many years before the true consequences of shell shock were known about or at least admitted; he could have argued that chronic sleep deprivation had left him confused and incapable, but thousands of men were shattered with a weariness that only death could relieve and did not do as Joseph Radcliffe had done. But like those who did walk away, with no leave of absence, no plan, no money, he was put on trial for his life with little in the way of defence and sentenced to be executed by firing squad.

It was likely that Joseph had imagined he could find his way back to Liljana somehow and she would hide and protect him. Even after he had been arrested and condemned, the thought must have lingered that Liljana would come to his side and plead his case, that she would know of his peril even though there was no chance he could get a message to her in time. She was the angel who had held his hand when fever was threatening to overpower him; he knew it was her touch, her presence, the sound of her Latin prayers that had called him back from the dead and could do so again.

"Can I do anything for you?" asked the guard. After the merciless outrage of the court martial, Joseph's cell felt positively friendly, and the guard, a young man little older than he was, behaved as though guarding him were a painful duty he would have advanced on the enemy to avoid. "I couldn't help noticing that letter you were writing. Shall I see it safely delivered?"

"I wrote it some time ago," Joseph explained. Ever since his arrest he had been unable to speak in more than a whisper, and the guard strained to hear him. "I wrote it on the boat here in case I was killed. I was only writing the address."

"Would you like to write another one?" asked the guard, "I can get you fresh paper?"

"She will never know it ended this way," he said. "I mean her not to know. Let her think I was worthy of her."

"Very well, old chap. I shall see that it's delivered."

"You won't need to. She'll come for it herself."

The guard looked at Joseph in alarm. He did not appear mad, at least not in the way the guard would have imagined a madman would look. Tired, yes, wan, dishevelled, distracted, but he took the man's behaviour to be more a sign of resignation than anything else. "How about another cigarette?"

Through a haze of smoke, Joseph saw Liljana's face as he had first seen it and felt his eyes watering. "Where is Lily? Why doesn't she come? There is so little time, why will she not come?"

"How could she, old man?" The guard had seen condemned men do the most appalling things—weep, rage, scream hysterically for their mothers though he had never thought they believed their mothers would really come to them. "She doesn't know where you are."

Joseph blinked away tears. Somewhere, more miles away than he could count, across desert and sea, Liljana lay in her bed, a place where he had so recently known the ecstasy of her embraces, and she slept unawares. She did not know that as she slept, her lover was spending his last night on this earth awake and alone. "I have been calling for her since I first walked away," he said. "I know she will come. She is on her way to me; she would never leave me alone."

But the hours slipped away, wretched hours worse than the night before a battle where somewhere there was the tiniest morsel of hope that life need not end there. Wretched hours without her, without her presence. He might not have cared about what was coming as soon as the dawn rose if she could only be there with him, if she could only hurry and hold him, press her face against his, say something, anything; he knew she would think of the right thing to say. But she did not come.

"If it helps at all," volunteered the guard, "it's not such a bad way to go. Quick and painless. You've been hurt worse before."

But Joseph was not afraid of pain. The guard was right, he had suffered worse before; he had known what it meant to scream with all his strength in the most terrible agony a human being could inflict upon another; he had been through the wretched torment of having dressings changed and carbolic acid poured into open wounds. He knew a bullet through the heart or head would not hurt him, but he did not care. Pain was what had brought him to Liljana; he could bear pain again if he could be sure it would mean finding himself back in that hospital bed with her presence at his side. But to go wherever death took a man meant to be taken away from her.

"She will come," he said, but the words choked in his throat and he found himself weeping again. "Sweet Jesus, why does she not come? How many hours are left? What time is it?"

"For pity's sake man, she will never come!" shouted the guard, beginning to panic. "How could she possibly come? How would she know where to come?"

"She will come!" shrieked Joseph, and the guard could barely make out the words he was saying, all he could see was a crazed man, tears still tracing patterns down his contorted face, stamping his feet like a child hiding fear behind rage. "I called for her! You do not understand, I *called* for her!"

"Pull yourself together!" But even shouting was not enough and the guard slapped him in the face in sheer desperation.

It worked. Joseph staggered back, plunged instantly into silence. A moment later, he has curled up in a corner, his arms wrapped around his knees, sobbing quietly as he awaited Liljana's arrival, praying over and over again that she would hurry.

Two hours later, Joseph was hauled to his feet and marched out of the cell in the direction of a quiet piece of wasteland. The sky was tainted with blood all around him—why did it have to be dawn? Why was it necessary to murder him as the sun rose to greet him, as though to taunt him with the promise of a new day he could never enjoy. "Why does she not come? Wait! Please wait, I know she will arrive soon."

"Be quiet."

A blindfold was placed over his eyes and he felt himself being pushed against a rough, cool surface which he thought must be the side of a deserted building. "Wait, please wait until she comes. I need to see her. Only . . . only for a minute." He began shouting her name over and over again, but he could still hear the shouting of orders and the repeated clicks as the instruments of his own death were prepared. Through the dark folds of the blindfold, he could see the shadows of men standing before him and knew that only she could stop them, but he could not see her. His mind was so clouded he could not conjure up a picture of her face to comfort him and called her name once again. "Liljana. Oh please, my darling. *Please.*" It was too late. She had abandoned him.

***

"He was not executed," said Kristjana, looking fixedly at the words etched into the tombstone. "His son came to visit this grave years ago. He told me it said, 'Died of wounds.' There must be another Joseph Radcliffe, it's not an unusual name. There must be others."

"Why you don't come out of the sun?" asked the caretaker, "you don't look well."

"He wouldn't have lied to me. He definitely said, 'Died of wounds.'"

"Madam, they change the stone. You can see it looks more recent than the rest. Some relation come just a few years ago, a very old man. He said he looked at the papers of the ... you know, the trial."

"Court martial."

"Yes, yes, and found out the British shoot him because he ran. He made trouble about it, said they have to tell the truth, and they change the stone."

Kristjana looked at it again. He was right: it looked quite new, the lettering clean and deep where the stone had yet to be worn down by the elements. And there it read as clear as daylight: "Joseph Radcliffe. Shot at dawn. A volunteer in the service of his country and a loyal son of England."

She could feel tears sliding down her face, a response so powerful she could not remember breaking down, just the awareness that she was standing at a deserter's graveside and could not stop crying. There had been many tears and she knew there would be more, but she could not imagine a more bitter moment than this and was not even sure whose loneliness was the more poignant—poor, frightened Joseph Radcliffe being dragged to his ignominious little death, or Leo, the bastard son who never knew his father's family and never made himself known to them, who never even knew that a man to whom he was related had sought out and changed Joseph's epitaph.

Back in the van, both the guide and the other passengers gave Kristjana a wide berth as she stared fixedly out of the window. Leo would not die the lonely death his father suffered, Kristjana told herself. She would not allow him to die alone and uncomforted, but she also doubted she would ever find a way to tell him of her discovery.

Before heading up the Neblus Road to the hospital, Kristjana sought out one of the many Catholic churches and slipped a small quantity of shekels into the hand of a Franciscan priest, along with a scrap of paper containing the name of the dead man for whom the Mass was to be offered. If Joseph Radcliffe was not a hero, then he was at least a kindred spirit. They had both run away, possibly whilst suffering a temporary madness, and for all her confusion, Kristjana knew she would want somebody to offer Mass for her one day.

23

"You're very quiet," said Leo, fifteen minutes after Kristjana's arrival for the morning shift. She had wished him a lacklustre good morning, changed his blood-stained sheets with assistance from a grumbling Sura and had just opened the shutters to let in some light.

"No I'm not."

"I told you not to go to the cemetery. You're far too easily upset."

"I wanted to go. Ow!"

"Did you trap your fingers? You're distracted."

Kristjana had trapped her fingers in the wretched hinges of the wretched shutter and she *was* distracted and quiet and depressed. "Give me a minute and I'll sit with you." The words popped out of her mouth like a rebuke. "I need to take your vital signs."

He smiled. "Very well." She placed a hand on his wrist and pressed her fingers against his steady pulse. "She heard him calling to her across the sea," he said.

"Shush. Oh, I've lost count now."

"She woke up in the night to the sound of him calling her name. It must have been the last word to pass his lips before he died. Spooky, isn't it?"

"I don't believe it."

"You're scared. I felt your hand tremble before you let go. I'll tell you another thing . . ."

It was no good. Leo's pulse, temperature and blood pressure charts sat abandoned on his bedside table, awaiting the wrath of the oncologist, but Kristjana knew she would never get her morning duties done as he drew her away once again like some latter day Homer trapped within the lines of his own epic poem. With the weight of her unshared knowledge bearing down on her, Kristjana found herself hovering in the corridor of another hospital not so unlike her own, in the doorway of a doctor's office where Liljana was engaged in an argument Kristjana did not want to hear. She could not bear to look at her face. "Leo, I can't."

***

"I need to go on leave," Liljana insisted, having barely given Dr Hampton time to rise to his feet. "I need to go out to him, he's in trouble."

"Sit down, nurse," commanded Dr Hampton, indicating a chair. "Sit down and calm yourself."

"I would rather stand," she answered, breathlessly. "I need to find him. He called for me."

"Will you please sit down?" Dr Hampton had never seen Liljana in an excitable state before, and he felt faintly disorientated. She had burst into his office before he could invite her to enter and stood before him, out of breath, her face flushed, her hair uncombed and unpinned. If he had not thought that she had been struck by some tragedy, he might have reprimanded her for having the nerve to appear before him in such a condition. "What do you mean he called for you? Have you received a telegram?"

"No, he called my name in the night. I heard him in my dreams."

"Sit down this minute!" He took her arm and assisted her into the chair. She had turned instantaneously from a troubled nurse to an all too typical medical case, and he felt himself relaxing. "The strain is evidently beginning to show, my dear, we had better organise some leave for you."

"Absolutely, that's exactly what I need," she babbled, taking his hand. "Could you arrange it for me? I shall certainly make up the time when I return, I simply need to—"

"Indefinite leave starting today." He shrugged her off and sat down at his desk. "Now, there is an excellent little ... little place I would like you to go for a few weeks to get some peace and quiet—"

"But I need to find Joseph's regiment!" she burst out. "Do you not understand? I may already be too late!"

Dr Hampton looked pityingly across the room at her. "Lily, I'm afraid you are unwell," he said, as gently as he could. "It happens to the best of people sometimes."

"I am not," she said immediately, rising to her feet, but she felt faint. Ever since she had woken up in a state of panic, she had been

186

plagued by the sound of Joseph calling her name over and over again. Not even calling, his voice had had an almost animal quality to it as though he were shrieking her name whilst fighting a losing battle with some terror too horrible to contemplate. "Do you think me mad?"

"Lily, this is hardly the behaviour of a sane woman."

"I am not mad, I have never been mad!"

"Your mother—"

"Have I ever given you reason to believe I was mad?"

She had never given him any reason whatsoever, Dr Hampton had to admit; but he also knew that madness could strike without warning, and he could hardly ignore the evidence of his own eyes. "I cannot say I have, Lily," he said finally, "but you must surely realise that what you are suggesting is absolutely out of the question?" She lowered her head, which he took as a sign that he was winning her over. "If—and only *if*—your young man has come to grief, there is nothing you can possibly do about it. It may already be too late."

Too late. The most miserable words in any language. Liljana rose to her feet. "Forgive me for wasting your time, Dr Hampton," she said with cold dignity, "if you will excuse me ..."

She made for the door. "Wait a moment, please," said Dr Hampton, raising a hand like a policeman. "I would like you to take some leave."

"That will be quite unnecessary."

"I'll be the judge of that, my girl. You can start today."

The letter arrived a fortnight later and Liljana was so distracted with excitement she could barely tear open the envelope. She had never had a lover at the front before but had come to realise through her acquaintance with other nurses, that letters provided the only brief respite from the anxiety that covered every other waking moment. When a soldier was away there were so many different ways in which he could die even if he were not caught up in some bloody battle, and a letter was like the sound of the man's voice promising that he was still there, far away and in terrible danger, but alive. The sight of Joseph's round, childlike handwriting brought his invisible shade into the room with her. Liljana could almost feel him sitting beside her on her bed as she sat and read:

My Darling,

I hoped you would never have to read this letter and I want you to be strong now as I know you are. I am writing this letter on board the ship that is taking me far away from you, back to a war you helped me to forget. I realised when we parted that if I am killed you will never be told. My family will be sent a telegram but they do not know about you, which is why I am writing this letter and will carry it with me so that if anything happens, it will be found with instructions to send it to your hospital.

That is why I said at the start that I hoped you would never read it because if you are, it means that I am dead. I cannot bear to think of you waiting for me when the war is over, thinking I had abandoned you or forgotten my promise to return.

I love you, my darling, you can never know how much. I know we were together such a little time, but I wanted more than anything to marry you and give you the happy home you have never had. I am so sorry it will never be. Please find somebody else. You should never have been alone, you have so much love to give and deserve a good husband. I want so badly for you to be happy and to be loved, even if it is in the arms of another man.

I want to keep writing forever. I can see your face, smiling the way you did the first time I opened my eyes and knew it was all going to be all right. I loved you from the moment I first saw you. I am so sorry, so very sorry my darling. Perhaps it would have been better for you if I had died in my sick bed, I never meant to hurt you. If there is such a place as heaven and I can get there, I promise I will watch over you and keep you safe until we meet again.

Your humble servant,

Joseph

Liljana was aware of the darkness in the room and glanced up at the inky skies on the other side of the glass. For a moment, she could have been a child again, standing at another window, feeling nothing except the cold numbness of a shock too terrible to endure. But she felt something this time, a tugging pain in her chest like the dull throb of a bruise soon after the blow has been dealt. Her hands were so cold that she felt paralysed, but she could not bear to let go of the letter as though Joseph's extinguished life were somehow bound up in it. Winter was coming, she told herself, that was all, the rainy season with its ominous skies and sudden violent downpours, but all she felt was that the world could weep for those she loved even in arid, sun-drenched Malta. The world could weep and she could weep. She felt tears shuddering down her face and sank to the ground with the weight of the whole, wretched, grieving world bearing down on her shoulders. Night had come to claim her again.

24

Liljana spent much of the remaining day slipping in and out of consciousness. She remembered tiny details—the sound of shouting when someone discovered her, the murmur of distant voices, the feeling that she was being carried. The unsettling rumble of movement all around her. She tried repeatedly to communicate but seemed to have been locked into a trance that left her unable to move or speak or even think clearly. When her mind finally snapped into focus, she was aware of lying in a bed, held down by tightly tucked bedclothes as though her nurses had thought she might make a break for it when she awoke.

Dr Hampton was standing at her side and she suspected he had been waiting for her to come round for quite some time. "Where on earth am I?" she asked haltingly.

"You are in a convent, enjoying the ministrations of a kindly group of nuns," he said in a mildly sardonic tone that was somewhat unlike him. "When I told you to take some leave, I meant you to leave the hospital, but I suppose you did not have anywhere else to go. When Emily returned to her room after her night duty this morning, she found you in a dead faint."

"I see."

"She also found your letter. I am very sorry, Lily."

"I was right that he was calling me!" she wailed, and she could feel tears gathering around her eyes again. "I heard him."

"Lily, it would have been too soon ..." He trailed off, knowing that it would never be the right moment to have an argument with a distraught young woman about whether or not her lover had mysteriously communicated with her from the grave. "It was not only the shock that made you faint, was it?"

"It would have been better if he'd died at the hospital," she said, listlessly. "At least then I could have been with him. Who knows how alone he was when he was killed?" In her mind, the picture was rapidly forming of Joseph dying, not alone at all, but charging into enemy fire shoulder-to-shoulder with his friends, but even then she knew he would have felt alone without her. He must have called for her as he climbed the ladder and emerged, perhaps only for a brief moment, over the lip of the trench. That was why the sound had been so like an animal shriek in her dreams because he would have had to shout over the noise of the ensuing battle, perhaps he had even shouted her name as he had been fatally wounded.

"Lily," said Dr Hampton, clicking his fingers in front of her face. "You knew you were with child, did you not?"

Deathly pale when she first awoke, her face turned white blotched with scarlet as her body tried to blush but appeared unable to find enough blood to colour her shame. "Impossible," she whispered.

"Lily, I'm not stupid, I have suspected this for a while. At first I put your lethargy down to your young man going back to fight. I thought you were simply a little melancholy in his absence, but I knew there was more to it than that."

"It cannot be. I would be sick, I would be sick in the mornings."

"Not always. Come now, are you going to tell me you had not noticed the changes in your own body?"

He knew of course that she had not. The fear of pregnancy, the shame of conceiving a child out of wedlock when Liljana herself had been the result of an illicit liaison, was so intense that Dr Hampton knew she would not have entertained the idea even if every possible symptom had been screaming at her for weeks. She would have chosen not to notice her failure to menstruate, the dizzy spells, the fatigue, the slow tightening of her clothing as her waist and breasts thickened. But in spite of it all, deep down in some hidden recess of her mind there would have been a growing sense of terror that she would sooner or later have to face the nightmare she had created for herself. "I do not show yet," she said lamely.

"There are other signs," Dr Hampton explained. "Everything about a woman changes when she is carrying a child; the way she moves, the way she looks. Even her skin tones change a little." He was interrupted by the sight of Liljana breaking down. She had already cried so much she had no strength left to retain any self-control whatsoever and sobbed into a corner of the bed sheets with miserable abandon. Dr Hampton watched the woman weeping in front of him. Hardly a woman, she was little more than a child but like so many members of her generation, she had already lost more in the first flourishing of her youth than her elders had lost by the time they had reached middle age. In all their encounters, Liljana had always seemed to him a tragic creature: the small child sitting on the doorstep because her mother had been taken away; the bruised victim of a wrongful accusation; the lonely, silent figure at the dockside with no loved one to wave her off; the bewildered girl standing outside Mount Carmel Hospital, struggling to make sense of the loss of a parent she had struggled so hard to love; and now, a woman like thousands of others, grieving when she should have been courting, carrying yet another war baby who faced an even more uncertain future. "Oh Lily, you silly girl!" he cried out, because rage was so much easier to express than grief and he *was* grieving. "You silly girl! Why did you not stay in England? Why did you not stay away when you had the chance?"

In spite of her determination not to do so, Liljana was calming down, and Dr Hampton did not have long to wait before she was able to say, "He promised he would come back for me."

Dr Hampton placed a hand over his forehead. "Lily, what have you done? I thought a girl with your intelligence, with your *decorum* . . . what on earth are you laughing at?"

Liljana's tears had effortlessly turned into bitter laughter. "You speak to me of decorum? Do you truly believe that there is such a thing any longer, with the world killing itself? Look at all those wrecked bodies! All those boys who come to us to die because the human race is so much better at wounding than healing anything . . ."

"Lily, please do not presume to lecture me. I am a good deal older than you, and I have seen war before. I do not need you to tell me anything about the propensity of human beings to wound one another. And yes, I do believe that there is such a thing as decorum. In time of war, the temptations are much greater but one still has a choice. You could have done the right thing."

Liljana turned her head to face the wall. Laughter and tears had disappeared. "It's too late now. What am I going to do?"

"I'm so sorry, Lily," said Dr Hampton, pulling up a chair by her bedside, and she was relieved to hear his tone becoming more familiar. "This is no time for recriminations. I will ask that you be discharged due to ill health, then no one need know the real reason. It is not a lie, you are in no condition to work."

"What about the baby?"

"I am coming to that. I have had a word with the mother superior here. There is no need to be concerned, she is a discreet woman and has seen such things before. She said that there is another convent in Gozo, where they could take in the child."

"No," Liljana said.

"I would not dismiss the possibility so quickly, if I were you. You have very few possibilities."

"I will think of something."

"If you are worried about leaving the child, you do not have to. She said you could stay with them, earn your keep—"

"Be a good servant."

"Lily, will you please see reason? They are offering you a home! How else will you ever provide for a child? You have no family, you have no one to turn to."

"No one to catch you if you fall."

"What?"

"Your brother told me that years ago when my mother died and I couldn't pull myself together. He said I was not like the others, I was all alone."

Dr Hampton sighed. "Well, it's a little harsh to say, but it is true."

Liljana stared into space. She tried to imagine Joseph standing at the end of her bed but found, to her horror, that she could not recollect his face. It was as though they had been standing together in the same room and someone had put out the light. There was darkness all around her. "'When I consider how my light is spent,'" she whispered dreamily.

"Lily, stop it!" demanded Dr Hampton. "Have you not considered that you may be forced to give up the child after it is born, whether you wish to or not?"

Liljana forced herself to sit up, dismissing Dr Hampton's proffered hand with an angry wave. At least she was compos mentis again, he thought, but he was still unsettled by her behaviour and could not be sure what she would do next. "I will leave the country," she said, with cold rage that somehow fitted her better than wild displays of grief. "Little Malta seems to have taken everything else that ever mattered to me. I will not lose this child."

"And how precisely do you propose to do that?"

"I have a little money saved."

"To pay your passage back to England? To support yourself in the meantime? And when you have had your baby, how do you intend to provide for him?"

Liljana had descended into silence again, which he would have thought positively sulky coming from anyone else. "I want you to do something for me, Dr Hampton."

He hesitated, but only for a moment. "What is it?"

"It's all right, I wasn't going to touch you for money. I want you to take me to see Mr Burnett."

Dr Hampton backed away. "Are you mad? Why on earth do you want to involve George Burnett in this disaster you've created?"

"Because he has lots of money," she answered brutally, "and he has helped me before."

"You cannot just appear in his life again after all these years and demand money from him! Have you no shame?"

"Oh yes, I do have shame, but I have very little money, and as you have been kind enough to tell me I have very few places to turn."

Dr Hampton groaned in the wearisome knowledge that he would do exactly what she wanted. Part of him quietly wished that some other person had crossed that child's path all those years ago.

Liljana wondered, as she sat in that familiar drawing room, whether she would ever stop feeling ashamed. She was unsettled by everything, most of all by the fact that she was sitting in that room at all, having a tea tray placed at her side by a servant she at least did not recognise. She did not know that Dr Hampton had carefully arranged to take her to see George Burnett when his wife was away so that she would not have the horror of that woman lording it over her. Not that Sue Burnett needed to be there in person, Liljana felt her condescending presence all the same and her hand trembled a little as she poured milk into the gold-rimmed teacup.

She had been sitting alone for over twenty minutes whilst Dr Hampton and George Burnett talked about her in the study. She might have felt indignant that so many of the important moments in her life had been decided by others, but she was almost relieved not to have to listen to them or worse, to have to defend her disgraceful position. If she had not been so anxious about the future, she might have let her mind linger a little on the past, she might have felt grief at the absence of Reno and Mrs Debono, but the thought of Joseph and the tiny baby growing inside her blocked out everything else.

The door began to open and she instinctively rose to her feet. "Please sit down," said Dr Hampton as soon as he saw her. "A lady does not stand."

Liljana blushed at the faux pas and sat down again. "I'm afraid she has hardly grown into a lady by the sound of it," responded George Burnett unkindly. His physical appearance had barely changed with the years, Liljana noted, except that his hair had become a little greyer and he sat down on the sofa opposite her as though it were a relief to be off his feet. Dr Hampton did not sit down and instead stood at her side, though he seemed unable to look at her.

"I have explained the situation to Mr Burnett," said Dr Hampton. *Evidently*, thought Liljana, noting her benefactor's expression. To her horror, he looked disappointed rather than angry.

"I am very sorry to hear about your situation, Lily. I had hoped you would do rather better with your education than this."

He might as well have slapped her face. "Look here, Burnett, I think we know the score," Dr Hampton put in. "There is no easy way to say this, but what she really needs is money. She needs to get out of the island, she needs help to provide for her child before she can begin providing for him herself. She is a trained nurse, she is— as you say—well educated, but in her current state she cannot look after herself."

"No amount of money will unravel this mess. I have already told you my opinion of the matter."

Liljana could feel the suppressed rage in the air, and she suspected they had already had a blazing row in her absence. She turned to look at Dr Hampton and noticed an expression she had never seen before. The muscles of his face were taut with anger, and she felt her pulse racing, imagining that he was angry with her. "Absolutely out of the question," said Dr Hampton tersely. "You know I will not countenance such an idea."

"You know how to do it, you're a doctor," George Burnett went on, getting to his feet. "Furthermore, you are one of the few doctors I would trust. I know you would do it safely."

"I repeat: absolutely out of the question. You will not involve me in the killing of an innocent."

Liljana suddenly realised what they had been arguing about and leaped to her feet, slightly too quickly. Dr Hampton helped her back into the chair before she could fall, not realising how vulnerable she felt sitting down with the two of them standing over her. "You cannot be so cruel!" she burst out. "It's a sin!"

"I did not ask your opinion!" George Burnett raised a hand instinctively. He had no intention of striking her, but Dr Hampton clearly thought otherwise and stepped between them, protesting, "For God's sake man, think of her condition!" George Burnett backed away, mortified. "The deed is done now. Please show a little respect, she's not a servant."

"No, she's a beggar."

Liljana covered her face with her hands. There had been a time when she had been used to gratuitous insults, but her education had taught her self-respect. She listened to the two men arguing again and almost wished she had agreed to go into a convent if it could have shielded her from this outrage.

"You have no business talking about her like that!"

"Well, what else is she doing if she is touching me for money? What of the money I spent sending her to school? If she has this child she'll go straight back to the gutter into which she was born, she'll be *ruined*!"

"What about the child?"

"What about it? Some poor little bastard half-caste? A fine figure he'll cut in the world!" George Burnett spun round in time to see Liljana heading purposefully for the door. "And where do you think you're going, young woman?"

Liljana hesitated but found it impossible to speak and placed her hand on the door knob. "Good day," she finally managed, in little more than a whisper. "I should not have come to you."

"You are not going anywhere!" barked George Burnett, yanking her by the wrist so aggressively that she cried out. "Sit down!"

"Be careful!" demanded Dr Hampton.

"Kindly wait outside, I need to speak with Lily alone." Dr Hampton refused to move. "For pity's sake, what sort of a man do you take me for? You needn't fear for her safety."

Dr Hampton sighed and stepped out into the hall, leaving Liljana feeling as though a protector had just disappeared. She trembled as he nudged her back into her chair. "I should not have come to you," she said finally. "Forgive me, but I wish to leave."

"There now, I'm sorry I was so harsh," he said a little sheepishly, but she noted that his manner had softened almost as soon as Dr Hampton had left the room. "I should not have insulted you."

"I suppose you had a right to say those things."

George Burnett sat down in the chair directly facing her and scrutinised her very carefully before continuing. "You know, Lily, I did not send you to England because I felt guilty about my wife's rash actions all those years ago. This may surprise you, but I did it because I believed that you deserved better than what life had thrown at you. So did Dr Hampton."

This was worse, oh this was worse than his contempt, worse than his anger. "I'm sorry," she mumbled, but she could not bear to look at him. Her mother had said she would never come to any good, and these two men—heaven knew why—had thought differently; now it was not George Burnett's disappointed face she feared to look at, it was her mother's, glancing accusingly at her from beyond the grave. "I am truly sorry. I meant to do better than this."

"It's all right, Lily, you must not reproach yourself now, it is too late for that." He reached forward and took her hand, hesitating to see whether she would pull it away from him. She didn't. "Lily, the best of people make mistakes but society does not forgive easily. I will not have you ridiculed and hurt the way you were when you were a child. I may never have told you this, but I knew about you before you came to my house."

Liljana flinched. She had been blissfully free of any link with her past during her years in England, and she felt threatened by anything that connected her with it. "How could you have known?"

"It's a small country, people talk. I saw you once with your mother on Kingsway. You were dressed in some absurd costume in that stifling heat, and she was shouting at you at the top of her voice, causing a terrible commotion."

"Don't." She could remember that particular outrage as though it had just happened. It had been during that excruciating phase when her mother had decided that Liljana ought to have been a boy and was forcing her to dress that way. She had changed her mind within about three weeks, but at the time it had seemed an eternity of mockery and spittle in the street, yet more of the same treatment at school accompanied by rage from teachers who imagined it was her idea. When George Burnett saw her, she had just been thrown out of a shop on account of her appearance and given in to a rare outburst of emotion. The sight of Liljana's tears had caused her mother to fly into a temper, and she was forced to endure an outburst of maternal disgust on top of the background noise of derisive laughter.

"What I most remember about you was your dignity. Your eyes were red, but you walked on with your head held high as though none of that mockery and hate could touch you."

"I was used to it."

"You do not have to get used to it again," he said gently. "These problems can be dealt with, even in a country such as this." She tried to draw away from him but he placed just enough pressure on her to force her to stay still. "I am going to help you whether you want to be helped or not. You are too young to understand what it will mean if you have this child. I will give you the money tonight, and you will finish this business as quickly as you can."

He let go, much to her relief and stood up, passing Dr Hampton as he walked out of the room in the direction of his study. Dr Hampton immediately hurried into the room. "Lily, are you all right? What's going on?" He took her by the hand and pushed back her sleeve a couple of inches to reveal a red shadow across her wrist where George Burnett had squeezed with the full force of his strength to prevent her running out of the room. "Did he hurt you?"

"Of course I didn't hurt her, Hampton," said Burnett from the doorway. "We have just been having a little conversation about the matter. Two more minutes please."

Dr Hampton glanced in Liljana's direction, but she indicated that she was happy for him to go and he left looking a little crestfallen, as though he had hoped she would throw herself at him, desperate to be rescued. "I wouldn't tell Dr Hampton about this," said George Burnett, pulling a handful of notes from his pocket. "He is a good chap, but not a man of the world. Here, take it." She did not move. "Hold out your hands."

In the end, he grabbed one of her hands, forced open the closed fingers and rammed the money into her palm, holding her hand closed until he was sure she would not throw it back at him. "I cannot do this," she said lamely.

198

"You have no choice. In the end, you will be grateful that I gave you a way out."

***

Leo lay with his eyes closed, but Kristjana had grown accustomed to this habit of his and could sense that he was still awake. "Don't worry, they said things like that about me before I was born," she said, though she was not sure why she was volunteering the information.

"Really?"

"Yes. Bastard, mistake. It doesn't matter."

"It mattered to my mother and it mattered to me," he stated quietly, "and it clearly matters to you. It sets the tone for a person's life when someone didn't want them before they were even born."

"Your mother wanted you."

"Oh yes." He smiled. "Oh yes she did. She was quite a devious lady in some ways. She took that man's money—quite a lot of money she said, because he wanted her to go to a doctor who would do it properly—and then she walked out of his life without any intention of doing as she was told."

"She went to England." He looked up at her quizzically. "Sorry, it said on your medical notes that you were born in England. Did she use the money to go back there?"

He nodded. "She went to her friend Emily and told her everything. They concocted a plan. My mother used the money to pay her passage back to England and to buy two things—a cheap ring and black cloth from which she made a frock. Emily wrote to her family and told them that poor Lily had been widowed just weeks after her wedding and was with child, knowing that they would welcome her with open arms."

"It must have been hard for her to lie like that."

"Certainly it was, but not as hard as losing a child would have been. Mothers will do anything—absolutely anything to protect a child."

Another lonely boat trip then, but at least this time there was Emily to see her off with promises that she would return as soon as ever she could. "Don't despair, Lily, it will all work out, I swear."

"I'm sorry," was all Lily could find to say. "I'm so sorry I've put you to so much trouble!" Emily threw her arms around her old

199

friend. "You have never been any trouble, you silly thing! I have covered for you before, I can do it again." She broke off and looked at Lily's calm face, aware that she was the one who was on the verge of tears—but there was nothing very new about that. "As soon as I have sorted out matters here, I will come to England and look after you. Just make sure you get home safely."

"I shall ask the torpedoes very nicely to go elsewhere," said Liljana wryly, but neither dared say anything else on the matter. Both women knew that travel by sea was a dangerous undertaking but that every solution to Liljana's predicament lay across that stretch of treacherous sea. "Don't worry about me."

Liljana boarded the ship, swathed in black, with the same quiet, sad composure Dr Hampton remembered from her last departure. He too was there to see her off, though he stood some distance away and watched her board without making his presence known to her. Not that she would have noticed: since the first raw grief of Joseph's death had passed, she had been overtaken by the old, familiar silence of her childhood and stared blindly at the dock, oblivious to every sight and sense.

Somehow Liljana knew she would never return to Malta again, but the thought was too momentous to ponder as the ship steamed away and she was dragged into the blank abyss of the sea. She would never see Malta again, she would never see Joseph again. Liljana placed a hand over her abdomen and caught sight of the fake wedding band on her finger. She remembered a promise she had been made years ago that she would not always have to be alone and might have a home and family of her own one day, but the words only sounded cruel now. As cruel as hope.

25

"Have you written to your young man?" asked Leo all of a sudden. He had been part of the way through telling Kristjana about his mother's return to England and the Sheppard family's desperate attempts to cheer her up when they were themselves beset with grief, when he had lost the thread completely. "You have, haven't you?"

"Yes, but he hasn't written back yet. No reason why he should, I've treated him abominably."

"You should kiss and make up."

"With him at Harvard and me here? A little logistically complex."

Leo squeezed her hand with a strength she had not realised he still had. "Life is so much better lived in company. I always regretted never marrying and having children. I was afraid to die alone, but here you are." Leo unnerved Kristjana when he got personal. She found herself fidgeting, but he refused to let go. "There are many lonely people in this world who never wanted to be. My mother was left alone because her sweetheart died in battle ..." That grave flashed through Kristjana's mind, causing her to flinch. "No, don't be like that, you need to hear it. It was bad luck, the world she was living in, but I chose to be alone and you are choosing to be alone."

Kristjana wriggled free and stepped back. "Did you really choose? I thought there was someone, you called for her during that storm ..."

She could almost see the energy trickling out of him. "That was different," he whispered. "Quite different."

"I'm sorry." Too late, his eyes had closed and this time there was not the slightest flicker of movement from him to reassure her that he was awake. "Do you want to sleep?"

"Yes please, I shouldn't have excited myself like that. It hits me all at once."

"Sweet dreams then."

"Good night."

***

Liljana was alone, but she was alone in a country full of lonely women. The streets were marked out by young girls in black, mourning their lovers and husbands, and older women in black whose sons would never be the comfort of their old age. Throughout the remaining months of her pregnancy it seemed to her that the world was as it had been when her mother had died—all the colour sucked out as though she had stepped into a photograph—and she moved among the monochrome buildings and people with cold, melancholic indifference. One of the benefits of having grown up was that there was no one to tell her to pull herself together or to suggest a beating might bring her to her senses. She was left alone and she wanted nothing more than to be left alone.

She stayed with the Sheppards for the duration of her pregnancy and spent much of her time in her room, partly because she had nothing left to say to anyone and partly because she felt shamed by the pity her false existence induced in them. As the months advanced, she was joined by Emily, who gave her some solace, especially when she became ill and anaemic, confined to bed for days at a time. Emily sat at her bedside, as she had once sat with her in the school infirmary, talking incessantly about anything that entered her mind or reading to her from her favourite books in the hope that it would bring her back to life.

"Poor little mite," said Mrs Sheppard one morning, shortly before noon. "I hate to think of her hiding from us. We're virtually family; she knows she is not imposing."

"She knows," promised Emily, carefully hiding the morning paper someone had been thoughtless enough to leave lying about. "She told me only the other day how safe she feels here. A haven, she called it."

"I'm glad we can keep someone safe," said Mrs Sheppard wearily.

"Don't, Mama."

Emily's mother had always been of a solemn disposition, but Harry's horrific injury had aged her, all the more so because many of her friends had lost sons; she almost felt she had to be grateful that her beloved son was trapped in a hospital, maimed for life and as yet unable to speak, because virtually every friend he had ever known was dead and he ought by rights to have followed them.

"You'll feel better when Harry is allowed home," said Emily, sitting down beside her mother and placing a hand over hers. "He will come home soon, at least we know he will. And Dicky will come home. And ..." Why couldn't she say it with any conviction? "And Lily's baby will be here soon. Think of that! A lovely bonny baby ..."

Mrs Sheppard sat up, startled. "Has anyone looked in on Lily today? I haven't seen her at all."

"I looked in early to see if she wanted breakfast, but she was curled up in bed, saying she didn't feel able to get up just yet."

"I must ask the doctor to come and take another look at her. The baby could come at any time, and if she's too weak ..." She glanced sidelong at Emily. "Go and tell her I'm calling the doctor."

"Hadn't I better ask if she wants—"

"No, she'll be too polite to say yes. I am going to call him now. Tell her he is on his way."

Emily shrugged and made her way out of the room, musing that her mother's sudden desire to fuss over Lily was a better response to her own anxieties than sitting in her chair brooding. She climbed the stairs and knocked gently at Liljana's door, but there was no response. She knocked again, then opened the door a crack and listened for sounds that her friend was awake. Emily heard what sounded like a strangled moan and hurried inside. At the sight of her friend she uttered a scream that could be heard in the street.

Liljana sat hunched over the side of her bed, her hair and nightdress stuck to her profusely sweating body, the wet, torn shreds of a muslin cloth in one hand. "How long have you been like this?" Emily demanded, but she was distracted by the sound of running footsteps as every other person in the house hurried in the direction of her scream. She turned to the maid who had reached the top of the stairs first. "Fetch the doctor! Run!"

"There may not be time for the doctor," said Mrs Sheppard, pushing past her to Liljana's side, "I can smell blood. Emmy, can you deliver a baby?"

"Soldiers do not normally give birth," Emily answered, tartly. "Oh Lily, darling, why did you not call for us? How long have you been labouring?"

But Liljana began slamming her hands against the wall; then as the contraction gathered momentum, she threw herself bodily against it like an animal trying to break out of a cage. "Help me get her into bed," commanded Mrs Sheppard. "We should never have left her alone so long. I knew something was wrong."

But Mrs Sheppard's self-reproach was nothing to the wrath of the doctor when he arrived shortly afterwards, out of breath from hurrying down the street. "This young woman has been labouring for hours," he roared at them, "perhaps since early last night! Are you honestly telling me nobody noticed?"

"She's such a quiet little thing, she didn't want to make a fuss," Emily tried to explain, but the sort of behaviour she had come to expect from her friend after all these years sounded implausible expressed to another. "The bleeding has only just started."

"Where is her husband?" He was a young man with a terse, condescending manner that set Emily's already ragged nerves on edge.

"Dead."

His face softened. "I see. Is she a relative?"

"In a manner of speaking."

"Come with me then."

He stepped aside to let her back into the room, where Liljana was lying in her bed, rocking to and fro. She had refused to allow the window to be opened in case she was heard, and the room was unbearably hot. "Fetch more water," he ordered, removing his jacket, "and some clean towels."

Emily was standing in the doorway when Liljana was rocked by another contraction and began gulping with the effort of remaining silent. It reminded her horribly of some of the wounded soldiers she had attended, who convulsed with spasms of pain on and on for days, writhing and shuddering with the final struggle to submit to death when it finally came. Something about the white cloth protruding from her friend's mouth made her think of gas victims frothing at the mouth as their lungs collapsed. "Doctor, is she going to die?"

"That rather depends on the lady, I suspect," he answered glibly. "Hurry along now please."

Liljana could not remember whether it was night or day. She could scarcely remember where she was or who it was who kept stepping in and out of the room. She had witnessed so much agony since she had begun nursing but never had known it herself, and she could not believe how quickly it had taken her over. She seemed to be trapped in a dugout with the solid stone walls bearing down on her, threatening to crush her at every explosion, whilst all around her there were invisible creatures striking her spine with steel-capped boots until she could no longer bear it and staggered about the room, tearing at herself with her own fingernails.

It was a judgement. Somewhere in her near-madness, Liljana thought that this must be a punishment for that night of forbidden intimacy or some purgatorial ordeal for the suffering she had caused as she ministered to those poor dying boys at the hospital. With each wave of torture she remembered another writhing face: the lad they had held down screaming as she dropped ethanol into wounds deep enough to reveal bone beneath the jagged flesh; the man dragged from a burning building whose body was so badly burned that her gentlest touch had been met by blood-curdling shrieks ...

"Pull yourself together!" shouted the doctor, clicking his fingers in front of her eyes. "Stop babbling! You are ready to deliver, but you must do as I tell you!"

Someone seemed to be pressing a searing hot poker against the base of her spine; she shuddered, moaned, then felt the doctor tearing the cloth out of her mouth to stop her choking on her own vomit. She slumped back, exhausted. Soon she felt the horror of yet another spasm in its early stages, the pain mounting with every passing second until, in the absence of the cloth, she opened her mouth and screamed at the top of her voice. The doctor slapped a hand over her mouth. "Don't waste your energy making that noise! Push!"

"She's too weak, she's been labouring too long!" cried Emily, placing on Liljana's forehead a damp cloth, which was immediately shrugged away.

Liljana felt her body urging her to push the baby out, but the pain subsided before she had found the strength to exert herself. The doctor was shouting, but he seemed to be separated from her by a glass window and she could only just hear him. "I cannot do it," she managed to say.

"You will push when I tell you!"

Emily was kneeling at her side, holding her head. "Please try, Lily. Please. You are losing blood. I know it hurts, but you must deliver now." She could see the slow trickle of blood seeping into the white bedclothes, the red circle expanding around her friend like the hideous vision of a life slipping away from her. Like Liljana she had seen so many young lives cut short, but this was one she could not bear to lose. "Lily, for heaven's sake, you cannot leave this child without a mother! You cannot be so cruel!"

Emily felt her friend bracing against her and heard the thin, strangled sound of Liljana trying, trying with every scrap of strength she had left, to bring her baby into the world before the effort killed her. For seven long minutes that ticked by like the ages of man, Emily watched her fighting like a wildcat, straining, twisting and bleeding, until finally, she heard the weak but unmistakable squawk of a birth cry. The doctor busied himself cutting the umbilical cord and wrapping the baby in a towel, whilst Emily helped Liljana deliver the afterbirth, praying that the bleeding would stop now that the infant was delivered.

Liljana had no strength left and lay in precisely the position she had collapsed into with her final exertion. She was aware of movement all around her and the sound of a baby crying, which sent a shudder through her body. "Please," she croaked, but her throat was dry. "My baby."

"Mrs Radcliffe, you have a son," said the doctor, placing the wriggling bundle into her arms; but she was too weak to hold him, and in the end he had to place the baby beside Liljana so that she could be close to him.

Liljana stared sleepily at the purple head close to hers, with its miniature features and eyes screwed tightly shut. "My son," she said and let her eyelids droop. She smelled the soft, sweet smell of his newborn flesh and slipped into an exhausted trance, where she dreamed fleetingly that Joseph was standing at her side holding their baby and then walking away as she called and called for him to return.

26

Rest and sleep and dreams. A tiny baby slept peacefully by her side; warm, fragrant, his soft, round head nestled against her breast. Every night Liljana would wake from some tormented dream to the blissful peace of her room and the rhythm of her baby's breathing or the first whimpers as he began to stir. It seemed to her that Mr Hampton's promise that she would not be alone had come true after all with this tiny, trusting companion in her arms, whom she told herself would never leave her. Liljana imagined him by her side through all the ages of her life, this blessed child whom she could love and nurture without the heartache that her love would be unrequited. Leo, her son, her lion cub, with his perfectly formed face and eyes so huge and grave they might have witnessed the rise and fall of every worldly empire.

During the weeks that followed, Liljana's strength began slowly to return under the careful ministrations of her friends. The Sheppard family's faithful nanny was brought out of her sleepy retirement to attend the infant, but Liljana refused to surrender him to the arms of any other woman, even one as trusted as Nanny Barlow. In the end, Nanny had a bed made up for her in a corner of Liljana's room so that she could watch over them and take charge of the more strenuous duties Liljana could not yet perform. Nanny joked a little wistfully that she had two children in her charge and it would not do to let them out of her sight for long.

Liljana did not mind. She felt loved and she felt free to love in this house where a grey-haired woman insisted upon tucking her up at night and kissing her and the baby before she retired. It reminded her of the love she had taken for granted from Mrs Debono until she had been parted from her, but there were to be no partings now. There had to be some fixed points in a person's life, and this house and its good residents, the tiny baby born into this haven, these were Liljana's fixed points and they would not be taken from her.

Liljana could even believe she would recover. By the time Leo was two months old, she was well enough to walk around the house, carrying him in her arms, and to take short walks around the park with Emily in attendance. And inevitably, they all began to discuss what she should do when she was well again.

"You know, you could stay here if you wanted, Lily," promised Emily. They were sitting on a park bench as Liljana had become a little short of breath. "My mother is quite in love with the baby. Well, you must have noticed. You're no trouble at all."

Liljana distracted herself glancing into the perambulator to take a look at Leo, who was obligingly fast asleep. "I cannot possibly live off your family's generosity forever, Emmy. You have all been so kind."

"Nonsense! You are so quiet, we would hardly know you were in the house at all. It's good for mother, anyway. Takes her mind off ... things."

"Your brother will be discharged from hospital soon. He will need all your attention. It would not be fair ..."

Emily gave her a nudge. "There is always my other plan."

Liljana smiled. "You have yet to persuade your mother."

"I need to find the right moment."

Emily harboured the dream of the two of them renting a little place of their own. There was still plenty of nursing work, and she fancied that they could take it in turns to go out to work while the other minded the little one. Her mother would certainly be against the idea, but she was convinced—with characteristic misplaced confidence—that she could talk her into it somehow. They need not go far away, after all, and they had travelled as far as Malta without coming to any mischief. That was not true, of course, but they had both lived to fight another day.

It was on one such afternoon that Emily and Liljana came home from a stroll to be greeted by Mrs Sheppard at the door in an unusually agitated state. "Lily, my dear," she began, helping her inside as though she could not close the front door quickly enough. "Let me take the little one for you, there's—well, there is someone here to see you."

Liljana was not sure whom she expected to find waiting for her in the drawing room, but she could not hide her surprise—and mild disappointment—when she opened the door and found Dr Hampton rising nervously to his feet. She glanced over her shoulder immediately and noted that nobody had followed her into the room. "Good heavens!" was all that she could find to say. "Dr Hampton, I had no idea you were in England."

"I have only recently arrived," he answered quickly, "and I ... I wanted to see how you were."

"You are most kind." They stood awkwardly regarding one another.

"You look pale."

"I am quite well," she said, with a half smile. "It is so very kind of you to come and visit me."

"I have been terribly worried about you, Lily, ever since you left. I do wish you had told me where you were going."

"I thought I had caused you enough trouble. You knew I would come here, didn't you?"

"Emily told me. I'm afraid I was rather worried you may have come to harm. May I ... I trust I may sit down?"

"Of course." She sat down herself to put him out of his misery and indicated a chair to him.

"I asked her to tell me everything," he said, "in the strictest confidence you understand. Please don't think she let you down, I assured her I simply wanted to know that you were safe."

"You did not seriously imagine I would have done what Mr Burnett wanted, did you?" Liljana checked herself. Her tone sounded angry, which she had not intended, but Liljana felt stung that her friend had sneaked on her and not thought it necessary to let her know about it.

"I thought it highly unlikely, but there is no knowing what a girl might do if she finds herself in difficulties. You have grown up to be a very brave woman, Lily. I want you to know that I admire you very much for that. I have always admired that quality in you." Lily would have blushed if she had had enough blood in her. Instead, she simply lowered her head. She heard him clearing his throat. "Mrs Sheppard tells me you have been very unwell since the birth."

"It was a difficult birth, but I have been well looked after here. I am quite recovered now."

Dr Hampton smiled but seemed to have run out of polite conversation, and an uncomfortable silence descended. Liljana could hear the sound of her baby gurgling in the next room and felt an almost unbearable urge to get up and run after him. Instead, the sound offered Dr Hampton a lifeline. "Mrs Sheppard told me it was a boy. What name did you give him?"

"Leo."

"Was that his father's name?"

"No. His other name is Joseph, but Leo seemed right. I want him to grow up to be a hero like his father."

"I have no doubt he will. Look here, Lily ..." He passed a hand over his temples as though he had a raging headache. "You ... you have probably guessed that I did not come all the way to England to pay you a friendly call. There is something I would like to ask you, if you will allow me?"

"Of course."

"Have you given any thought to how you will provide for your child?"

"I think about it all the time," said Liljana quietly. "I hope to return to nursing when I have regained my strength. Sadly, there are still many casualties arriving at our hospitals."

"There are indeed. Nevertheless, it will be a struggle to work those long hours when you have a child to raise."

"I shall manage well enough!" she snapped, then felt mortally ashamed for being so sharp with him. Her nerves were on edge. "That is, it is kind of you to think of me, but I do not intend to live off the goodwill of these people forever if that is what you imagine. Thank God, I have the means to provide for my child, even if it will be very hard. After all, I have only myself to thank for my position."

"You misunderstand me, my dear," he began, looking to all intents and purposes as though he wished he had never started the conversation. "I know you are more than capable, I have always known that. What I mean is ..." He sighed, then smiled sheepishly. "Oh dear, I have been rehearsing this moment since I stepped aboard the boat. I'm afraid you must think me a blithering idiot."

She giggled. "Not you, Dr Hampton. Mad perhaps. Now what on earth are you trying to tell me?"

He stood up and walked towards her, reaching out to take her hand. She responded without thinking. "I know that this will come as a surprise to you, but I would be grateful if you would consider what I have to say. I would be ... I would deem it a very great honour if you would consent to become my wife."

She looked up at him as though stunned by an unexpected blow to the back of the head. Her hand slipped limply from his. "But you are old enough to be my father!"

"I know, God help me. But such unions are hardly unknown."

"But ... but! I do not even know your Christian name!"

It was his turn to look surprised. "It's Albert, if it helps."

To Dr Hampton's relief, her look of restrained panic slowly softened into a smile. Then she threw her head into her hands and burst out laughing. "Oh you are such a darling!" she declared finally, lifting herself up to look at him. "But I know you are trying to rescue me again."

"No, no. It's not only that." He got on his knees so that he could be at eye level with her, but it looked too much like a formal proposal and he had to ignore her flinching as he took her hands. "It's true that I do want to look after you—is that so bad? I cannot bear to think of you wearing out your life slaving to put food on the table. I have always wanted to look after you, but there is so much more to it than that." He closed his eyes. He was not a man given to expressing powerful emotions or opinions, but he sensed that a great deal might hang on what he felt able to say to her. "I know I can never be to you what Joseph was, but I do love you and I believe I could make you happy." He plucked up the courage to look at her again and felt certain he was having no effect on her whatsoever. He tried again. "It is a pity to be alone. We ... well, we live in such a lonely world, so lonely and so uncertain. I have always thought that life is more happily lived in company."

Liljana stared at an undefined point across the room, so blankly that Dr Hampton could never have guessed what was going through her mind if he had had the imagination to try. "I have never considered this," she said. "I hardly know what to say to you."

"It's all right," he said, standing up with an evident sense of relief. "Please do not give me an answer now. I know you have much to think about, but please consider my proposal. You deserve a husband and your son deserves a father."

With that, he was gone. The family waited twenty minutes after his departure for Liljana to call for them or step out of the room but she failed to emerge. Finally, still bearing the guilt of leaving her alone when she was in labour, Emily tiptoed gingerly through the door to find her friend staring at the same patch of wallpaper, as though her life depended upon unravelling some riddle woven into it.

27

"Not afraid, are you?" he asked, reaching out to take her hand.

"Certainly not," answered Liljana, with a terse tone that gave away her nerves. "Are you sure we should not have brought a lantern? I cannot see a thing!" She had never been afraid of the dark, but never had she been in such a remote place in the middle of the night before, and she took her husband's hand gratefully.

"I know it sounds a bit mad, but it's easier this way. Bright lights trick the eyes somewhat. In a minute, your eyes will grow accustomed to the darkness and you will start to make things out. Best to keep moving though, it's colder than you think."

"When you said you wanted to bring me to the Lake District for a walking holiday," said Liljana, stepping gingerly over the stony path he was leading her along, "I rather supposed you meant us to go walking in daylight."

"It's all right, no more night-time excursions after this one, I promise. You'll see why we had to walk Skiddaw at night when we reach the top." Bertie squeezed her hand and was relieved when she returned the gesture. "You know, in some ways it is less tiring walking up a steep hill in the dark. One cannot see how far away the summit is!"

Liljana giggled. "Or how far the drop is before one steps into it."

"Don't worry, you shan't fall, it is very safe. I chose Skiddaw because there are no nasty crags or sudden drops, just smooth, friendly slopes. She's a gentle old fell, older than the Ice Age."

"Really?" Liljana suspected Bertie was talking simply to relax her, but if he was it did the trick. There was a soporific quality to his voice, something about the soft, mellow tone he had developed over the years to reassure nervous patients that always set her at ease. She focused her attention on the sensation of her walking boots scuffing against the rocks that protruded from the ever-steepening path and the rhythm of her breathing as it became more laboured with the effort of climbing uphill.

"Centuries old. While all the fells around her were being moulded by the glaciers, she stood there and watched it all. There's Derwent Water!"

She glanced down to her left and saw the lake far below them, lit up in the moonlight of a crisp, clear night sky. "Thank you for bringing me here," she said. "What an old romantic you are!"

"Certainly old," Bertie answered, pausing so that they could enjoy the view a little longer and he could discreetly catch his breath. "I have always felt very blessed to have grown up somewhere as beautiful as the Lake District. That's why I wanted to bring you here, as soon as Leo was weaned and you could bear to part with him. I wanted you to see how lovely it is."

"I'm glad."

They walked on, Bertie keeping a steady pace, his feet stepping carefully along the path with the confidence of a man who has been this way many times before; Liliana walking more erratically, seldom raising her eyes from the path before her in case she missed some hidden danger. As they rose ever higher, Liljana began to feel as though they were crossing some barren desert, with the shapes of dark, unyielding rocks all around them and the sudden swathes of cloud they passed through from time to time. Or they were at the top of the world, walking through mist and darkness together, the last man and woman alive on a silent planet.

The rest is silence.

"You're shivering, my dear, are you cold?"

"I do hope the baby is all right without me," she said and then regretted it. Somewhere in her mind there was the thought that Bertie might see Leo as a rival in spite of his promises otherwise and would rather she did not mention him here when he had made such efforts to gain her undivided attention.

Bertie sighed. "I'm sure he's being pampered quite enough by your dear friend Emily," he said. "You mustn't worry."

"I'm sorry."

"It's perfectly natural." He pointed ahead of them. "You see that faint light above us? It's the first sign of the morning coming. We have about half an hour to reach the summit."

They quickened their pace, but by now Liljana's nerves had been drowned out by the exhilaration of being so close to the top. They no longer held hands in case either of them took a tumble and needed to reach out quickly to catch themselves. After a lengthy scramble, during which they were temporarily forced onto their hands and knees, they emerged onto the flat. Liljana was not sure what she had expected, but suddenly there was nowhere else to climb and they had reached the place they had been making for throughout the night when every sensible Englishman had been tucked up fast asleep.

Bertie took off his knapsack and set up camp in the shelter of a large boulder, then he took out a flask of tea whilst Liljana wrapped herself up in a rug he had brought for the purpose. He settled down beside her and handed her an enamel mug of what turned out to be the most revolting, lukewarm tea she had ever sampled. She found herself smiling. In the pale, reluctant light, they sat together huddled up in a coarse army surplus rug, sharing terrible tea, and she was aware—as only those who have been overcome by grief can be aware—of being happy. She pressed her head against the soft fibres of his jacket and closed her eyes, overcome by weariness.

" 'Surprised by joy'."

Bertie glanced down at her sleepy face. "I beg your pardon?"

"Nothing, darling, I was just trying to remember something. 'Surprised by joy—impatient as the Wind'."

"William Wordsworth. 'Love, faithful love, recalled thee to my mind /—But how could I forget thee?' "

"Yes, that's right."

"He might have written it here."

Liljana's body was relaxed and still with sleep, and he held her a little closer. She had a face that looked as though it might have been painted, her lips and cheeks reddened by the cold air. Her hair was concealed behind a thick woolen hat that drew attention to the clean, finely sculpted contours of her jawline. Bertie let the minutes pass, resisting the temptation to close his own eyes. He was a watchman guarding her from the perils of the wilderness as she slept. He too was quite content.

"Wake up, my dear, you mustn't sleep now."

Liljana was not sure how long her eyes had been closed, but she was aware of Bertie glancing down at her, his hand gently stroking her cheek, whilst behind his head, the sky had erupted into a carnival of light and colour. "What time is it?"

"Morning. Up you get, I want to show you something."

She struggled to her feet, shivering and aching all over, and let Bertie guide her in the direction of the sunrise. She blinked, dazzled by the sudden intrusion of light and found her eyes watering with the sheer intensity of it. During the quiet moments Liljana had slept, the dawn had crept up on her, and she stood now, dazed with the last vestiges of sleep, surrounded by a new day awakening all around. The green, rugged hills lay glistening like the virgin lands of some unconquered paradise; above her head and beneath her feet there were swirls of pink and orange cloud, pierced through in places by the peaks of encroaching fells. And light. Light so radiant she could have believed that there had never been another morning, that there had never been a world to set ablaze before.

Liljana felt Bertie's arm around her shoulder and turned to embrace him. "There you see," he said, luxuriating in the blissful thought that for the first time since their marriage, she had reached out for him not for comfort or out of a muddled sense that she ought to, but because she could not help herself. "It was worth a walk through the darkness to see the sun rise from here, wasn't it?"

Liljana had stopped shivering and noticed their shadows dancing in the wild grass beside them, so close that they no longer seemed to belong to different people. "I shall walk with you through the darkness again one day," she said quietly, "and however it ends, I know I will still be happy."

***

"I can't believe she actually said *yes*?"

Leo looked nonplussed. "Of course she said yes, it was an excellent proposal for a girl who had got herself into trouble."

"But!" Kristjana was seldom lost for words, but she simply could not find the words to describe how utterly appalled she was. "But he was old enough to be her father!"

"Yes, she noticed that."

"But he was ... he was *old*."

"Twenty-year age gap. Sorry Kris, would you mind raising the bed a little? I'm getting a bit sick of glancing at that crack in the ceiling."

Kristjana suspected he was just distracting her as usual, but the ruse failed. Even with that wretched whiny noise as the head of the bed rose to a slant, she thought of the idyllic life Liljana could have enjoyed with her friend Emily, taking it in turns to raise her dear little boy, the independence, the adventure. "Is that a little more comfortable?"

"Much better, thank you." He looked at her from his elevated position. "You're disgusted, aren't you?"

"Yes."

"You think he was a pervert, don't you?"

"I would never use that word." But she was on a back-footer already. "But what about Emily?"

"Emily wanted her to do it, she would have got married herself if the right fellow had turned up. You young people are such bigots! If my mother had set up with anyone else, you would be going out of your way to say how splendid it was."

"But that's different! If people love one another ..."

"How do you know they didn't love one another?"

"But I just, I can't quite imagine having that kind of relationship with a middle-aged man."

"You mean sex?"

Kristjana always knew her face was turning the colour of a stewed beetroot when Leo started sniggering. "Yes."

"One never really enquires about one's parents' bedroom arrangements," he said, with a philosophical air, "but they did give me a much-loved baby brother, so I suppose they sorted out that side of things."

"Is he still alive?"

"Charlie? No, he had a heart attack fifteen years ago."

"I'm sorry."

"A quick and painless end to a happy life. The ambulance lady said it was the best way to go. Nothing to be sorry about." Except that Leo had been burdened with being the last survivor and Kristjana was feeling sorry for him. "Listen, my dear, you're distracting me. They loved one another. Perhaps it took her a while but ... it wasn't so strange for a young woman of that generation to marry an older man if she was going to marry at all—so many of the young men were lost, and it would not have been at all easy for my mother to face the future alone. Things were so different then."

"I suppose they were."

Leo reached out for her. Kristjana had noticed that the weaker he became, the more he seemed to crave closeness—even just a hand to hold—like a child seeking the reassurance that he is not alone in the middle of the night. She suspected his sight was failing. "They were happy," he protested, pressing her hand to his face, and he looked so sad she loathed herself for being so childish about it all. As far as he was concerned, Dr Albert Hampton was his father. Not the hero he still dreamed about, but the man who carried him and played with him and provided a home for him and reprimanded him and loved him. And *loved* him. "You crave adventure because nothing truly terrible has ever happened to your generation."

"Well …" *Ouch! Now who's being a bigot?* she wanted to ask but couldn't. The only decent thing she could do now was to shut her mouth.

"They had both had excitement they never wanted …" He trailed off, pausing for what seemed like an eternity as though he had lost his train of thought. "I do wish sometimes that I could go back just for a single day to all of that. You wouldn't despise it if you have seen it."

"I don't despise it," she promised, but she was not even a good liar. "Please, I don't. I don't mean to anyway. I'm sure it was wonderful." His eyes had closed again, and she could not avoid noticing the tiny drops of moisture gathered beneath the arc of his eyelashes. "I'm sorry. I'm so stupid! Why don't you tell me about it?"

Kristjana had reduced a man to tears and hardly knew how it had happened, only that it was all her fault and her attempts at distracting him sounded so clumsy they only made the situation a thousand times worse. "I don't despise it," she insisted. "I suppose it just all feels so distant."

A line from some dead author she had read at school whispered across the room, across time as Leo recited:

The past is a foreign country; they do things differently there.

"The strange thing is," Leo continued, swallowing hard the way men do when they are trying to pull themselves together, "I try not to think too hard about those days because I loved them so much. It hurts much more to remember happy memories than tragic ones;

that's why we're all so obsessed with misery. For you, the only torture is boredom."

"I'm not bored!" Kristjana almost wailed, but she knew she was transparent at the best of times. She opened Leo's box of memories and searched through the photographs, taking out what was obviously a wedding print. "There! So that's what he looked like. You know, he's not bad-looking."

"Well recovered, my dear," answered Leo, reaching out for the picture. "He could be quite dapper when he tried."

"Absolutely."

The bride was unbearably young, as though she were hanging on the arm of her father as they waited at the back of the church to process down the aisle—and she did not even look like a proper bride. There was no flowing white satin, no lace veil coyly framing her face. Liljana's dress looked attractive and formal, but the grey shade suggested lilac or rose. Her hair was prettily pinned beneath a charming hat, and she clasped a single rose tied with ribbon. They both managed a half smile into the camera, but both looked a little awkward as though the photographer had intruded into the privacy of this quiet, unlikely wedding.

"Women wore their best frock in those days, not necessarily white," Leo explained, sensing Kristjana's confusion, "and well, in those days white meant something. She did have a child, after all."

"I see."

It was no use. Kristjana could not bear the idea of being dragged headlong into the tedium of interwar domesticity Leo so craved to remember. After lives that between them had seen the atrocities of the Boer War and the Great War—the bloody infancy of the twentieth century that should have held such promise—after the sad, understated tragedy of Liljana's lonely childhood, her exile and heartbreak, that ill-fated love affair that did not even have the privilege of being unique, somehow it seemed wrong that it could all melt away into the sleepy, colourless world whose borders were the four red brick walls of a well-to-do suburban dwelling.

Part of her wondered whether she feared to enter into this particular memory because it was the first time Leo was taking her to a place that was his once and she knew it might hurt him, but Kristjana could not abandon him now and found herself walking with Leo down a street in Greater London, between the two neat rows of

Victorian terraced houses that made up the forest of chimneys and bay windows and tiled porches and metal garden gates in which Leo and Charlie grew up.

To any resident of modern Britain, it felt quite familiar and could easily have been the same road in which Kristjana rented a room, apart from the fashions displayed by passersby and the absence of traffic congestion. There were cars in evidence, but Kristjana was thrown by the lack of traffic noise, that perpetual rumble and whir of engines and tyres along tarmac-covered roads, so much a part of modern life that she only noticed it in absence. Yet the road was far from silent. Above their heads, a confused twitter of bird-song distracted Kristjana's attention, and she looked up to feel the soft sunlight of an early summer afternoon touching her face. "Is it summer?"

"It is always summer when I remember my childhood," said Leo, pointing at a group of boys playing ahead. "Sunny summer after-noons or freezing cold winter mornings with the garden covered in snow. The dull rainy days have vanished without a trace."

The boys were playing some complicated game involving a tatty leather football, oblivious to the presence of observers. There were six of them, all dressed in the same prep school uniform—grey shorts, blazer, cap. The school colours were green and yellow as evidenced by the stripes on their belts and ties and by the piping on their caps and blazers. Two of them stood out, obviously brothers aged around ten and eight, sharing the hallmarks of having a Latin parent—dark brown hair poking out beneath their caps, skin tones three or four shades darker than that of their companions and the huge, soulful mandorla eyes of their mother.

A man Kristjana recognised as Dr Hampton strolled into view from around the corner of the street. He was dressed in the grey, high-buttoned suit and fedora hat of a professional man with conser-vative tastes, a little formally even for the time, carrying the leather bag without which doctors in popular memory could not exist. He paused at the sight of the boys rushing around in front of him, throw-ing them a glance of mild disapproval. A second later, however, he appeared to have resigned himself and gave a low whistle that was clearly intended to avoid the need to shout.

Two dark heads looked round in his direction before running up to greet him. "Hello, you chaps! Had a good day?"

They immediately began bombarding him with information, competing for his attention all the way to the front gate, when it seemed to dawn on them that they would not be allowed out again if they stepped across that threshold. "May we have another ten minutes?" asked the older of the two, hanging back. "*Please*? We're about to win."

"You are always about to win when I appear," laughed Bertie. "Inside now, if you please. I'm sure you have better things to do than kick that old football about."

"Pl —"

"Come along, Lion, I won't have you late for dinner."

Kristjana and Leo drew a little closer and watched as Liljana opened the door, but Leo was overwhelmed by the clarity of the memory and hung back, letting the door close in his face with the sound of happy conversation disappearing behind the red-painted wood. Kristjana tiptoed instead towards the bay window to the right of the door and peered inside at the dining room, where a rectangular table covered in a white tablecloth had been laid out for a family meal. She saw Liljana, walking gracefully in and out bearing plates and covered dishes whilst her boys disappeared to wash their hands. She was a mature young woman but looked like a girl dressed up as a matron who would have perfected the role of housewife if only she could have made it look a little more natural. She had shed the starched, constricting uniform of her nursing days for a loose-fitting polka dot frock and white pinny, but she still wore her hair long as though she had been unable to persuade her husband to let her cut her hair short like the other women.

The boys rushed in and plonked themselves in their chairs, fidgeting unbearably like two baby birds jumping up and down with their mouths wide open. Perhaps the past was not so unfamiliar after all. The clothes they wore and the food on the table were different. The accidentals—the lighting, the décor, the colloquialisms—all belonged to the past, but families still sat around the table to enjoy an evening meal; and Kristjana found herself whispering along with the words Bertie recited so solemnly before they began:

> Bless us, O Lord, and these thy gifts,
> which we are about to receive from thy bounty,
> through Christ our Lord. Amen.

Against her better judgement, Kristjana found herself slipping into a peaceful reverie, watching these four people sitting in apparent harmony, eating with alacrity whilst Bertie read aloud from *A Tale of Two Cities*. She could whisper along with some of those words as well: "It was the best of times, it was the worst of times ..." The best of times. Her hand reached out to touch the glass pane, but she was suddenly aware of Leo's head resting on her shoulder, sobbing quietly like a little boy. He did not offer an explanation and he did not need to. They sat in his wretched hospital room as they always had, with the acrid smell of disinfectant and the harsh, unforgiving bleeping and blinking of machines blotting out the memory of a perfect moment lost long ago.

"I'm sorry, Leo, I'm sorry." Kristjana was not even sure why she was apologising, except that she felt certain there was some way she could help him but could not think what it could be. "You're homesick, aren't you? Would you like me to get you something? Something that reminds you of home? Perhaps I could cook you something ..." It was nonsense. Even if she could rustle up a steak and kidney pudding or whatever it was he remembered eating during his 1920s childhood, he could barely swallow the nutritional shakes she gave him by the spoonful every four hours.

"It's all gone," he whispered, "all of it. The house, the street. There's no one left to call me Lion any more, they're all dead."

Kristjana stroked his hair and prayed he could not feel the tremor of her own emotion. His fate awaited her and any human being who outlived his loved ones: to be lost in a hinterland without links to the past, without familiarity, where everything that was once taken for granted—a noisy, affectionate household, a hearty meal, a good-night kiss, the intricacies and trivialities of everyday life—would become the stuff of dreams. "Who called you Lion?" she asked, as Leo's tears began to subside. He did not answer. "Who called you that? Was it a family nickname?"

"'Lion cub' is how it started. My mother came up with it, then everyone called me that." He lay still whilst she dabbed his face with tissue, and Kristjana suspected he was a little embarrassed. "It was supposed to be ironic because I was always rather quiet as a child. I wasn't even a fighter when everyone else was a soldier."

"You became a doctor like your ... like Bertie?"

"Yes. I used to hide in his study and leaf through his medical books."

Another snapshot. Kristjana could see him in one of those generic little studies with their musty books and heavy furniture, which children of past eras were supposed to dread entering, but which appeared to have held no fears for Leo. Or perhaps he simply remembered it that way. "Did he mind?"

"Not much. He never minded anything much." His eyes had closed again; the fit of crying had left him exhausted. "I think the worst I ever got was a tap on the wrist and, 'Clear off, sonny.' The only times I ever saw him angry was when someone insulted my mother."

"Oh? Did that happen often?"

"Oh no, but he always said a wife was . . . I can't remember." The effort of speaking and remembering was getting the better of him again. Kristjana pulled the bed sheet up over his shoulders, folding back the green coverlet—so convenient for disguising blood stains—and got up to pull the shutters across. She noticed with a quick glance at her watch, that she was tucking him up to sleep earlier and earlier.

"Our Lady in his house?" she suggested. The corners of his mouth twitched, but even a smile was too much of an effort all of a sudden. "Sweet dreams."

"Good night."

Kristjana lingered at the door, watching him sleeping and tried unsuccessfully to block out the thought that he might not wake up.

28

Liljana sank back in her armchair, looking carefully over a newly pinned hem she had meant to finish that evening. It was early December, and a fire roared in the grate, dragging her attention to the warm, irregular spikes of flame creeping across one of the logs. The boys had requisitioned the dining table to finish their homework, and part of her thought she ought to check on them; but they were beyond the age of needing her help now, and she knew it was best not to interfere. For the first time in many evenings, she felt at a loose end and wallowed in the pleasant pointlessness of daydreaming. She was aware of feeling comfortable and warm after a busy day and good food, of having an unquestionable sense of belonging.

This was Liljana's home. In the nearly thirteen years since Bertie had brought her to this house, she had felt herself growing into it in a strange sort of way, letting it claim her as part of its elegant English furniture until she had taken on its identity of mild, understated charm. Liljana had become attached to the house as the one domain she had ever inhabited that was hers and that offered no threat and no bad memories, inhabited as it was by two boys and a man who had been good to her. Boys. They were very nearly men, especially Leo, who stood at that uncertain age of not-yet-manhood, torn between childhood safety and all the daunting promise of adult life.

Bertie had indulged her plea not to send the boys to boarding school even though it went against his own plans for them, but she suspected that her husband still felt a little awkward about imposing his will on a boy who was not his own. Boarding schools made no sense to Liljana for children from a happy home, and nothing he had had to say on the matter about tradition and his own experience had persuaded her to part with them. "They need toughening up," he had said weakly. "You keep them far too comfortable." But she could think only of the boys she had nursed all those years ago, who had cried for their homes and their mothers as they lay dying, and how she had longed to be able to protect them.

"I want them to be comfortable," she had said. "God knows they have their whole lives to be toughened up by the world."

"It won't happen again, my dear, you mustn't be so fearful. The world has changed, thank God."

Liljana became aware of "The Blue Danube" playing and glanced up where Bertie had tiptoed inside and put on a gramophone record. "Good evening, my darling," he said, stepping quietly towards her. He reached down and helped her out of her chair. "Penny for your thoughts?"

"I'm sorry, I didn't hear the door," she said, resting her head on his chest. "I must have dozed off."

"No, you were sad," he replied, putting his arms around her waist and lifting her off the ground. "I was watching you, you were sad. We can't have that now, can we?"

"Not sad, I promise."

He kissed her forehead. "Wistful then."

"Perhaps." She snuggled into his arms and let him dance her gently around the room to the quick, dignified rhythm of the Viennese waltz. "I'm happy now."

"Good."

They turned in broad circles, blissfully unaware that Leo and Charlie were standing in the doorway, watching them dance in mild amusement. As the music died, the boys slipped unnoticed back to their work, leaving their parents to collapse dizzily onto the sofa. "I feel my great age doing that, you know."

"Me too. I found a grey hair this morning." She could feel Bertie's chest rising and falling a little more slowly every minute until he had finally caught his breath. "Should you like your supper now?"

"No, let's just sit for a minute." She sat up and glanced at him warily. "No, I'm all right; I just want to spend a little time with you, that's all."

She sat back with evident suspicion. "All right then. There's no great hurry. It's still quite early and the boys are using the table."

They sat in silence, Liljana staring into the flames again and Bertie stroking her arm as though to reassure her that he really had meant he just wanted to sit with her. "Has something happened?" she asked, minutes later.

"No, no. I was just a little worried about you, that's all. You have been rather distracted over the past few days." He could feel her beginning to fidget, confirming his suspicions immediately. "Why don't you tell me what's wrong?"

He could always see through her. Liljana's guarded, inscrutable demeanour worked well with everyone else, but she could always sense Bertie noting the slightest changes in her tone of voice or even the way she moved. It was the hazard of having married a man who had known her as a child. She broke away from him and stood up. She walked a stone's throw away and turned to face him. "You will not be angry, will you? It's nothing really, but I do wish awfully you hadn't asked."

Bertie sighed. He had few complaints to make about his wife. She had been a loyal, welcoming presence at his side for enough years now that he could not remember a time without her companionship. He had never once heard her complain or make a scene about anything, even on that terrible occasion when he had arrived home to find her lying in bed, listless and ashen faced, with the doctor at her side explaining to her that she had suffered another miscarriage. She had been chillingly silent on the matter for days, and he had only realised how devastated she had been when he had got up in the night to find the bathroom door locked and the sound of stifled female weeping on the other side of the door. Even now, the first sound of a personal question had caused her to flee his arms and stand in such a way that her face was cast in shadow in case she betrayed any emotion. He did wish she could trust him a little more. "Come on now, my darling, you know I'm never angry with you. Why don't you come and sit down again?"

"There's no need to fuss," she said, sitting gingerly next to him again. "I have been a little under the weather, that's all."

He kissed her cheek. "My love, I hope you will not think it remiss of me, but I ... well ... I was looking for something the other day and came across an old letter of yours. It was the one Joseph wrote to you—"

"I'm sorry, I never meant to take it out!" she protested, struggling to get up—but he held on to her as though he expected her to do something rash if he let her go. "I was ... I was sorting through some old papers and found it ..."

"It's all right, it's all right. Please don't fight me! I was afraid it had upset you, nothing more."

They had barely spoken that man's name since the war, and it had turned Liljana into a panic-stricken wreck, shaking so violently her teeth chattered with the effort. "Please don't!" he begged her. Dear God, anyone would think he routinely beat seven bells out of her from the way she was behaving. "I am not going to hurt you; I've been worried about you. *Shssh.* There now." He rocked her to and fro as though lulling her back to sleep after a bad dream, feeling the pulse in her neck slow down. "I am not jealous of a dead man, Lily. You had every right to keep his letters."

He awaited her response, but Liljana glanced downwards, unnervingly silent.

"I mean it, Lily, you mustn't be afraid to tell me anything."

Liljana laughed lightly. "I have never thought you'd hurt me, you silly man," she said. "I was afraid of hurting you. It seems ungrateful even to mention Joseph to you somehow."

"Look at me." Bertie touched Liljana's cheek to encourage her, but he could sense her own reluctance as she turned to look at him. "I told you years ago that the past is your own business and I meant it. Many women did what you did and did not deal honourably with the consequences. I know you loved him and if he had survived the war, I'm sure you would have had a happy marriage. But he's gone, Lily."

Another interminable time passed as he waited for her to answer. Bertie felt the weight of her weariness pressing on him and the blurred sounds around him of crackling flames and ticking seconds and somewhere far away, the low murmur of his sons talking as they pretended to work. When he finally heard her voice, it seemed to come from the end of a long tunnel. "It is such a long time since I have thought of him," said the voice uncertainly. "Sometimes I feel guilty for letting him go too easily. There are so many women who lost their loved ones during the war who never married because they loved their dead husbands and sweethearts so much. I sometimes wonder whether I was worthy of him or I would not have made a new life for myself."

Bertie held her as close as he dared. "Oh no, my love. If that's what's eating you up, you must not let it. You had the child to think of..."

She sat up sharply, causing him to shrink back in surprise. "Do you truly believe I only married you for the sake of the child?" she demanded, with the closest to anger she could manage. "I wanted to marry, I'm not some ..." she wanted to say the word "whore", but was too delicate to say it. "I wanted to marry you. I know my own mind well enough not to have done something so foolish as to marry a man I could never love. Please never think that of me."

It was Bertie's turn to relax. "It's all right, I didn't mean it like that. But you mustn't worry. I never knew your young man, but I am sure he would never have wanted you to be alone. No one likes to imagine his beloved in the arms of another, but if one really loves, one must desire them to find love again."

"I know, I know ..." They had had this conversation before, and every time Bertie had said the words, Liljana had suspected he had rehearsed them in his mind many times. "It's all right, my love."

"I know he would be happy that you are not alone."

"You do know I'm happy, don't you?" she asked quietly. Anyone else would have passed her off as a poor liar from her hushed tones, but Bertie recognised every nuance of her voice and knew she meant it. "You always make me happy. I only kept Joseph's letters because I want Leo to have them one day. I hid them away in my keepsake box, but I was tidying the bureau and out they came, then I couldn't bring myself to put them back. The worst thing is, you remember all those terribly wounded men, boys really? All those mothers' sons in hospitals in Malta."

"Of course. It would be hard to forget them." *Impossible*, came the thought, and he was a man who had personally attended the tortured victims of two bloody wars. It was years since he had allowed himself to daydream because he would inevitably find himself facing a gallery of his former patients: shot, burned, gassed young men, some without limbs, without faces. And as the years passed he found it increasingly difficult to remember which memories belonged to which war, save for the details of some of their injuries.

"It is not known how he died," she continued. "I only know that he did. I can never know whether it was in some bloody battle or a raid or an accident. I keep praying it was quick, but perhaps he died as those lads did, screaming the place down, and I wasn't there." She could feel tears rising in her throat, but the memory was too powerful to stop. "I keep thinking, What if he took days to die? What if he was frightened? Would there have been anyone there to comfort him? He was not a Catholic, but I would have liked to know that maybe there was a priest or somebody to give him consolation at the end. I'll never even know where he's buried, if he has a grave anywhere. So many of them just disappeared, blown to pieces in the mud ..."

Bertie held her as her body trembled and shook. "Darling, try not to think about it. I know it's hard, but however he died at least you can be sure he is at peace now. Whatever else he did, he was a hero at the end and gave his life for his country. There must be a place in heaven for him and all those who were lost."

"There will be more. I know there will be more."

"Hush."

"In my darker moments, I think the end-times must surely be coming. Then there will be nobody left to remember; and all I can think of is, that someone has to remain to remember. Somebody has to live. The young must be allowed to grow old."

"They will, they will. Come on now, it's not like you to be morbid."

Bertie stared at the flickering flames as they danced about to keep his loved ones snug and warm, little knowing the waking nightmare emerging before his wife's eyes as she stared into the same fire. She watched in silence as flames tore across a young man's body as he ran through a wilderness of craters and wire. She saw plumes of smoke billowing from the ruins of a bombed building whilst men crawled across the rubble on their hands and knees to escape before the entire edifice collapsed. And she saw the young man again, stared at the lingering features of his face before the fire erased them forever. "I am afraid," she said.

29

Leo had barely stirred all day as Kristjana kept a lonely watch over him, willing him to wake up for just a few minutes and talk to her, but he slept on, slipping through the dreamworlds of his life into which she could not intrude. Looking at the photographs of Joseph and Liljana, she could not make up her mind whom Leo resembled, but it was impossible to know how close a likeness even a photograph really was and Leo swore the picture of his mother did not do her justice. It was certainly not an unflattering photograph, snapped in the garden on a warm day, judging by the pretty summer frock she wore. The person behind the camera—Bertie, probably—had caught her giving a surprisingly impish smile that did not fit well with Leo's telling of her story. It left Kristjana wondering how much about Liljana she would never know because he never knew, whether there was a tiny hint of a rebel in that serious, sensible girl, who betrayed very little of her real self even to those she loved.

Kristjana felt drawn to her, She imagined them talking, not as an old lady and a young woman but as contemporaries sitting down and having a cup of tea, putting the world to rights.

Kristjana saw herself asking her many questions. Lily, you did love Bertie, didn't you? But did he stir your heart? Did he set the blood roaring in your veins? And what did you really dream, during those long humdrum days when your husband was working and your boys were at school and you busied yourself with the tedium of domestic chores my generation so despises? Did you think of Joseph, not dying some terrible death but alive and powerful, walking by your side along some dusty Maltese street? Perhaps you thought of Malta during those cold winters when all the colours disappeared and you had to bury yourself in blankets to fight off the chill of the early morning. Did you yearn for your motherland the way I have yearned for it, my kindred Maltese spirit? Did you desire to hear someone speaking that language, to feel the heat of the sun kissing your face, to catch a glimpse of those perfect skies?

The more Kristjana thought about it, the more obvious it became that Bertie Hampton would have taken Liljana back to Malta if she had wanted to go, because Malta had been his home for years when they married. For whatever reason, she had chosen to live a life of exile in Britain, and Bertie Hampton had been happy to come home.

"You are brooding," said a familiar voice at Kristjana's side. It was Leo's; he had been watching her for heaven knew how long. "I took that photograph of her the summer the war broke out. I think it was the last time she ever smiled."

"She took it badly then?"

"Naturally. The older ones had seen it all before; they knew exactly where things were going, and she had seen it coming for years."

"Perhaps it just seems that way because of the way we remember things. It seems so obvious now that the twenties and thirties were the calm before the storm, but no one knew it at the time."

"She did," he insisted. "She said there was no such thing as a war to end all wars. Her own people had suffered so much violence and seen so much bloodshed that she did not believe there could be peace when there was such hatred in the world." There were tears in his eyes again, but he showed no sign of breaking down. "We used to nickname her Cassandra because she was so gloomy about the future. You know the legend of Cassandra, don't you?"

"I certainly do. It's a Greek myth. Cassandra was granted both a blessing and a curse ..."

"Indeed. The blessing of the gift of prophecy and the curse of never being believed. But I think that's a bit of a nonsense really; even if no one believes you, having the gift of prophecy must be a blessing and a curse anyway. Who on earth would want to know their own future?"

"She was wrong about the important things, wasn't she? You both survived the war; you said your brother lived to an old age."

"Oh yes, she was convinced that there would be another war and we would be parted forever. She used to creep into our bedroom at night when she thought we were both fast asleep and sing the prayer of the guardian angels over us, to protect us from harm."

"Don't Leo."

"I'm so ..." He closed his eyes but was too weary to control himself, and tears trickled sideways into his hair with barely a sound coming from his mouth. Kristjana took his hand but noticed that he did not have the energy to curl his fingers around hers any longer and his skin felt cold and dry. "She was so very wonderful," he whispered, "so very ... we were embarrassed by all the attention she gave us. I want ..."

"Leo, let me call the doctor."

"No. I want her."

"Leo ..." Did men really call for their mothers at that age? Kristjana fell to her knees at his side, uncertain what to do. Before she had met Leo, she was not even sure she had seen a man cry before. "Leo, it's all right. You're safe. I'll look after you."

"I want her to watch over me again. It's madness, but in every disaster of my life I have wanted her to be at my side. Even when I was a child I hoped I'd die first so I could never die alone."

Kristjana had a nasty feeling Bernadette and the other ward sisters would not approve, but she did the only thing she could think of doing to calm him down and cradled his head in her arms. "I've already promised you, Leo, I won't let you die alone. I'm not going to leave this room."

"You can't be here every second, it's not good for you. You're young, you shouldn't be in this room at all."

For the sake of her tattered dignity, Kristjana hoped no one would enter the room at that precise second. Their shared heritage had given her a link to Leo's past, and she knew the way to reach him. She closed his eyes as though closing the eyes of a dead man and started to sing as quietly as possible, hoping that the long years of her own exile had not sullied her accent too much.

> Lanca gejja u ohra sejra
> Minn tas-Sliema ghal Marsamxett.
> Il Kaptan bil-pipa f-halqu
> Jidderiegi l-bastiment.

***

"That's strange, I can't remember any more." Liljana slipped into silence, her lips opening and shutting as she tried to remember the rest of the verse but the thread of memory had evidently broken and she could not recall the next line. "I used to know it so well."

Leo had not found himself in this place for decades. Usually, when he heard the sound of a woman singing a cappella, the prompt would take him back to the drawing room of his childhood home and all the sights and smells of the early evening—his father's fruity pipe smoke, the tap, tap, tap of Charlie's fidgeting heels dancing against the wooden floor; his mother's pensive face, radiant in the candlelight as though she were far away from the rest of them. Leo would feel himself wallowing in that rose-coloured vision of serenity with his father's voice ringing out in its soporific tones: "The second Joyful Mystery, the Visitation. Our Father who art in heaven . . ." Even the inflections of his voice were comfortably predictable, the emphasis on "our" as though he were gently claiming ownership of the Almighty, the precise manner in which he announced each mystery as though he were addressing a room of sleepy students. But his mother was the one who sang, since Bertie had claims to being tone deaf. She sang virtually all the time under her breath as she went about her business, but only during the family Rosary did she ever sing aloud.

Apart from that wild day of summer rain. Liljana had sung for them then, which was why he remembered it, because the atypical always sears itself into memory. It was his last family holiday before entering medical school, which perhaps gave it more significance. Looking back through the telescope of so many years, it might have been a metaphor for the state of foreboding with which every citizen of Europe was living at the time. Yet it had been nothing more than a stormy summer day. Leo recalled again the walk along the beach they had attempted, he and Charlie leading the way with those ominous grey clouds crowding out every scrap of sky and the feeling that their clothes stuck to them and weighed them down. Then the heavens opened and dropped rain on their heads in sheets of tepid water, soaking them to the skin in minutes. "Why don't we just jump into the sea?" demanded Charlie, pulling Leo in the direction of the dishwater waves.

Leo walked through a tunnel of sounds and smells: the stale, acrid seaweed, the hypnotic hiss of rain against sand, the purr of churning water getting further and further away as the tide slipped out, leaving behind endless, turgid tracts of sand dotted with shells and limpets and clumps of green and brown threads. Leo stopped in his tracks and looked back at his parents as they slowly caught up. They looked determined if a little absurd, clothing hanging over them, sopping wet, hair plastered to their heads in thick, unkempt ripples, rainwater like tears coursing down their cheeks. As ever, Bertie had his arm around his wife's shoulder as though protecting her from the savage elements that were slowing drowning him, but she had other ideas and shrugged him off lightly as she turned to talk to him.

"This is madness, let's find shelter."

"I'm not sure where, my dear, we're quite some way from the town."

Liljana turned and began walking towards the wall of rock to her right. It looked smooth and sheer, but either she had noticed a gap or her instincts had told her there must be some little space for them somewhere. The men followed her without question as she walked along the cliffside, trailing her hand along the dripping stone as though searching for a secret door. Then quite suddenly she disappeared into thin air.

Leo dashed after her and found a narrow opening in the rock that expanded into a shallow cave, dim but mercifully dry. "Come on then!" she called brightly from where she had sat down, her back pressed against the inner wall. "I knew there would be somewhere for us to hide."

The four of them huddled up as far from the entrance as possible, feeling the childlike excitement of being hidden away in a secret den. "What a marvel you are!" mused Bertie, cradling Liljana in his arms. "This is really quite cosy."

"I have always been good at finding hiding places," she said with what was almost mirth. "The rain will not be long. It feels like Malta during the rainy season. Lots of sound and fury, then the storm's all over very quickly."

But this was not Malta, and the storm did not pass quite as quickly as Liljana had imagined. As the minutes passed and the rain showed no signs of relenting, she brought out biscuits and dried fruit. They sat and ate like beleaguered Arctic explorers, with the rain drumming against the wall of the cave, the noise magnified many times. As minutes turned to hours, they huddled together for warmth and sang campfire songs to distract their attention as the novelty of sheltering gave way to restlessness and finally a growing sense of anxiety that the tide might come in or darkness fall if they did not make a break for it.

"Don't worry," promised Bertie, who had got up to look outside, "the tide won't come in for hours and it is still very early. It seems late because of the weather."

"Any sign of it clearing up?"

"I think the rain's easing up a little. Give it a while longer."

It was some time after that, when Bertie was installed again between Liljana and Leo that Charlie pointed out that Lily was the only one who hadn't sung yet. "That's because I don't know any songs worth singing," she claimed, "apart from hymns, and I'm not sure this is the moment for 'Save us for still the tempest raves.'"

There was a patter of laughter. "Sing something from Malta," suggested Charlie, "you never have before."

"Charlie!"

Charlie blushed, aware of having ruined a happy moment. The atmosphere altered from convivial to stonily silent almost immediately. Malta was not a family taboo, but an unwritten rule had been established years ago that anything to do with Lily's past was null and void. "Sorry, I just thought it might be nice ..."

"It doesn't matter, it doesn't matter," said Lily desperately. "I'd ... I would like to do that ... why ... why ever not? Now let me think ..." She floundered desperately for something to sing, some words she could remember from a language she had not spoken since before Leo was born. "Here we are."

> Lanca gejja u ohra sejra
> Minn tas-Sliema ghal Marsamxett.
> Il Kaptan bil-pipa f-halqu
> Jidderiegi l-bastiment.

Leo watched as his mother sang in snatches, pausing every three or four lines, then more frequently as she struggled—or so he thought—to remember the words of a song learned in childhood. It was only when she stopped altogether and pressed her head against Bertie's arm as though she were trying to stay awake that Leo realised she was holding back tears.

30

Night overtook them all. There were no memorable photographs taken in sunny gardens during the August of 1939 or at least, none that Leo cared to keep. Another war came and another generation was doomed to be stolen from the face of the earth. Leo was exempted from military service since he was shortly to qualify as a doctor and his skills would be needed to mend those who could be saved. Charlie, on the other hand, had no such good fortune and received his call-up papers along with every other young able-bodied male in the country.

On the morning he left, the rest of the household was up early to see him off, except for Lily, who had not been to bed at all. She had waited until she was sure the boys were asleep; then—as she had done so many times before—she had tiptoed into their room and sat between their beds like a loyal sentry at a deserted outpost, praying over and over again with growing desperation that Charlie would come back or that he would not have to go at all.

Liljana's watch was disturbed only by the distant sound of a church clock chiming away the hours—midnight, one, two, three—until she cursed the bells for snatching away those precious hours of silent contemplation. With her eyes long accustomed to the darkness, she could see his sleeping head poking out from under the covers, the line of his thick, tawny brown hair. Charlie had been blonde as a toddler, with a strawberry cream complexion that threw his brown eyes into stunning relief. "He'll leave a string of broken hearts behind him when he grows," Mrs Bell their neighbour had said, as he had pottered around her kitchen armed with one of her freshly baked biscuits. "My word, those eyes!"

"Don't cry, Mother," whispered Charlie, eyes open and watching. "Please don't."

"I'm not," she promised, but she was startled at the thought of being seen in a place she had no right to be. "I was just ... I ... well I'm not."

"You are," he said, reaching out to take her hand. "Inside you are. I can feel it."

"Go back to sleep, my darling. You need to rest and it will be morning soon."

"I don't feel very tired." He held her hand under his head as he settled himself back into bed. "It's all right, I don't want morning to come either."

But morning insisted upon coming, and when it did, what should have been a moment of intense emotion was strangely understated. The great disasters of life can never provoke enough emotion to do them justice, and anyone would have thought that Charlie was going away for a few days' holiday but for the sombre atmosphere and the lack of conversation. Charlie and Leo embraced; Bertie attempted to shake Charlie by the hand but in the end could not resist embracing him too; Lily distracted herself with the details of the picnic she had packed for Charlie, trying to dispel the thought that he looked quite ridiculous in a military uniform, like a little boy who had had to settle for the fancy dress costume no one else wanted. Then she gave in and threw her arms around him. She stroked his hair, marvelling that she had to stand on tiptoe now to reach him and was only saved from breaking down when he put his arms around her waist and lifted her off her feet.

Laughter all around. Laughter without merriment.

"God bless you, my son," said Liljana, in an accent she had not spoken with for years, "wherever he sends you."

Charlie kissed the top of her head. "There will be good times again, Ma, I promise."

Liljana watched her son as he walked away, his retreating steps crowded out by Bertie and Leo standing in the doorway. She took irrational exception to them stealing her last glimpse of Charlie and fled upstairs, feeling her defences crumbling with every unsteady step. When Bertie went in search of Lily some minutes later, he was appalled to find her huddled up on the bedroom floor, sobbing as though she had just witnessed her son being murdered. Bertie knelt down beside her and tried to lift her but she turned on him, drumming her fists against his chest in such desperate, miserable rage that he did not have the heart to restrain her and braced himself until exhaustion began to take her over and he could restrain her without the risk of hurting her. "It's all right, calm down," he said, "you're breathing too quickly. Calm yourself, it's all right. It's all right. You're safe and Charlie is safe."

"I shall never see him again!" she wailed, "I shall never welcome him into this house again!"

"You do not know that. You mustn't give up hope now."

"I knew it! When he kissed me goodbye, I knew I would never see him again."

Bertie had so seldom seen his wife break down that he was at a loss to know how to handle her; in the end he took the coward's way out and persuaded her to take a sedative, hoping that she would sleep it off. As Liljana began to doze, he undressed her and slipped her night-dress over her head, reassuring her all the time that she simply needed to rest. Bertie brushed her hair away to fasten the buttons at the nape of her neck and winced at the sight of two tiny faded scars, the only real reminders to him that Liljana was the angry, stoically silent child he had attended once. "I am sorry, my darling," he said, turning her over so that he could kiss her moist, impassive face. "I know this hurts terribly, I am so sorry. I never meant it to happen this way."

"He's my son! He's *mine!* How can anyone order him away from me like this?"

"I know, I know. Hush."

"I shall never see him, I shall never, never ..."

"Shush. Don't."

Liljana was asleep, leaving Bertie feeling guiltily grateful for her silence and wearily aware of having let her down.

For three days, Liljana refused to leave her room and lay listlessly in her bed, unable to get up, dress or eat. Bertie tried his level best to bring her out of her depression. He sat at her bedside and tried to engage her attention, but she would not so much as acknowledge his presence, and it was hard for even a patient man to bear that chill, unwelcoming silence for long. He brought her, her favourite food only to bring it back down to the kitchen untouched.

"Well, I know what I would do if she were my wife," a dour acquaintance at his hospital said, when Bertie made the mistake of consulting him on the matter, "I'd have no patience with this female self-indulgence whatsoever. There is a war on."

But Bertie could never have raised a hand against a woman, par-ticularly not his own wife, and he felt sickened by the very idea. On the evening of the third day, he sat at Liljana's bedside and read

237

to her all evening from *A Tale of Two Cities* in the hope that the words of her favourite author might bring her back to the land of the living:

> It was the best of times, it was the worst of times, it was the age of wisdom, it was the age of foolishness, it was the epoch of belief, it was the epoch of incredulity, it was the season of Light, it was the season of Darkness, it was the spring of hope, it was the winter of despair, we had everything before us, we had nothing before us, we were all going direct to heaven, we were all going direct the other way

But as he put out the light and settled himself to an uneasy sleep, Bertie wondered whether he truly had lost his wife this time and whether her mother's madness had come to claim her as he had always feared it would.

Then the following morning, as Bertie and Leo sat eating a gloomy breakfast, Liljana appeared before them, washed, dressed and looking every bit as though nothing untoward had happened to her. "Good morning," she said, taking her place at the table. "Did you both sleep well?"

"Good morning, my darling," answered Bertie, as calmly as he could manage. "Leo, fetch your mother some breakfast."

Leo stifled his astonishment by hurrying to the kitchen to fetch more toast. "I want to help with the war effort," she said. "Charlie is fighting; you and Leo are busy at the hospital. I should be putting my nursing skills to better use. Do you suppose you could find me a position?"

"I am sure that could be arranged."

Bertie watched Liljana eating delicately, showing no indication of the ravenous hunger she ought to be feeling, and he heaved a vast sigh of relief. He told himself as he walked to work that he should never have doubted the quiet strength of a woman who had struggled through so many losses and disasters without descending into madness and that he had always known she would return to him. But Bertie had doubted. For a few terrible days he had been forced to imagine a life without Liljana's presence, and he knew he would be even more protective of her now. There was no harm in such feelings, he reassured himself, wars made everyone a little more determined to protect their own and he was no different.

Leo had only woken up for an hour the previous afternoon. As the cancer took over his body he required ever more powerful pain medications, and they had the inevitable effect of making him sleepy. Even when he slept, Kristjana liked to sit with him and read out loud or tell him stories of her own because she could not be sure how deeply unconscious he was and knew he feared to be alone. Bernadette, on the other hand, was becoming impatient and had taken to giving Kristjana duties that took her away from him.

As Leo slipped in and out of consciousness, he still needed a considerable amount of attention, and Kristjana took as long as possible with the routine of changing his bed linen, bathing and dressing him and giving him his morning shave. "That's a waste of time," one of the nurses protested, but Leo had never had a beard and Kristjana failed to see why he should have to put up with one now. Besides, he had a tendency to wake up at the touch of the razor gliding carefully across his cheek, and Kristjana could be sure of his company for a few minutes at least until she had finished the business of moisturising his face and combing his hair.

"You are like her," he said, reaching up to touch her hand. "Strong like her."

"I'm an appalling coward," Kristjana answered and there was no false modesty there. "I'm so squeamish I have to look away when they change your venflon."

"She thought she was a coward too. Strong people always feel weak. Who was it?"

"Who was what?"

"The person you knew who had a breakdown. You were far too upset when I mentioned it all those days ago. Who was it?"

"My mother. But it was a long time ago and she got better. There are things they can do now."

"I thought so, it shows. You can get better too you know."

"I'm not mentally ill," stated Kristjana, trying not to look quite so much like a scalded cat. "I just get sad sometimes. We Latins are a tragic lot."

"You've been hurt by life. You wouldn't be here if you hadn't been."

"Not as much as my parents, not as much as my grandparents . . ."

"I think that's called survivor guilt."

"I've heard that term once or twice before."

"Sorry to rub it in. But you know, most people run from the past. You are running from the future."

No, Kristjana was not running from the future, he was wrong. She was hiding from it in his past because it was his life not hers and other people's suffering was so much easier to bear. He was closer when he spoke of survivor guilt, though Kristjana would have called it a Simon of Cyrene Complex, the sense of always having had somebody else's cross laid upon her shoulders when the real victim became too exhausted and broken to bear it any longer. And now she was feeling sorry for herself. Better to be a coward hiding in the long lost streets of wartime London than commit that most un-English crime of self-pity.

As Leo slipped into dream, Kristjana willed herself to slip into memory again. She hardly needed him as a guide. The Second World War had been the subject of so many books, films, documentaries, stage plays, concerts, commemorations, symphonies, paintings, poems, exhibitions. It had been analysed on every possible level from every angle, not a corner of that six-year global hell left unglimpsed, so that for her generation it was almost as real as their own lives. Almost. She found herself walking down the street where Leo grew up, but a street scarred by three years of war this time; there were no children playing in the road, they had all been evacuated to the safety of the countryside. A house at the end of the street lay in ruins, hit by a stray bomb; here and there she could see the hallmarks of that era—a barrage balloon floating ominously on the horizon; the fluttery white scars against the sky where pilots had grappled and fought to the bloody end; women with that unflattering turban-style headgear, their bare legs painted to look as though they were wearing stockings. Strange that it should feel familiar at all, since this was not even Kristjana's war heritage. Her people were bombed and starved in faraway Malta, but only the accidentals were different—a burned-out building is a burned-out building whether built in red brick or limestone; the sound of the air raid siren was unmistakable even if the exclamations of the people running for cover were made in a different language. Fear was never lost in translation.

And Liljana was the spark that brought it all to life because Kristjana could claim her as a blood sister, born in the same tiny island, speaking a language nobody could ever place. Kristjana stopped within view of Liljana's house and watched her kissing her husband and son good-bye before she returned inside to clear away the empty plates and slipped out of sight for a moment. As Kristjana neared the house, she could hear the gentle clatter of a kitchen being put to rights and the breathy, untrained but quite pleasing tones of a woman's voice singing along to the tinny, wireless set:

I'll find you in the morning sun
And when the night is new.
I'll be looking at the moon
But I'll be seeing you.

Through the window, she saw Liljana taking off her pinny and stepping into that homely room where Kristjana had watched her dance with her husband and daydream by the fire. Liljana was still singing to herself, her mood sprightly and relaxed as she enjoyed a much needed day off. In her hand was a letter from an old friend she must have waited all morning to open. She settled herself in a chair and opened the envelope, unfolding a crisp, cream-coloured page covered in the familiar, florid hand of her beloved childhood friend Emily Sheppard.

These were the moments Leo never saw for himself but that he pieced together afterwards from the clues she left behind and had rehearsed over and over in his mind. Kristjana saw her face draining of colour as the letter fluttered to the ground like a sad autumn leaf. This was the same Liljana she had come to admire so much and understand so little. The face that had glanced impassively at her headmaster years before as she was told about her mother's death, stared directly out the window—an older, wearier, thinner face with the same inscrutable look of a woman whose first lesson in life had been the art of concealment. Kristjana knew what Liljana had read, because she had read the very same letter taken from Leo's box of mementos. She knew it began with the words:

My dearest, dearest Lily,

I have terrible news, so terrible I can scarcely find the words to tell you. Please prepare yourself. Mother is dead. She was killed in an air raid three days ago whilst I was at the hospital.

Lily must have stared into space for over an hour, paralysed by the knowledge that her friend's family home, in which she had so often found refuge, where she had given birth to her own beloved son, had received a direct hit and been razed to the ground, taking old Mrs Sheppard with it because she could never bear to leave when the siren shrieked its warning. Those sturdy Victorian walls had seemed so safe to her.

The wireless played unnoticed in the corner, a sad, elegiac song marking off the static minutes until Liljana stood up and walked upstairs as though in a trance, to her bureau and box of keepsakes She searched for and found a photograph of a merry family group, posing in a sunlit garden with the promise of tea in the shade once the photographer had left.

Liljana's eyes flicked from the row of faces—faded, monochrome—smiling at her from beyond the grave, and Emily's letter, whose tortured lines jumped out at her like the last, confused cries of a dying woman: "Everything is gone, Lily. Everything and everyone I have ever known. Everything that made life make sense." Somewhere—at the end of a long tunnel, it seemed—the air raid siren began its ominous wail, but Liljana was being drawn far away from the dangers of the moment, and it did not occur to her to move. The letter continued, "I used to envy you your suffering and your loneliness when we were children because it made you different and interesting. You were like the sad, mysterious princess of fairy stories and my life was so frightfully ordinary. Now I wonder how you bore it, how I am to bear it."

"Two smiling faces among the dead," said Liljana out loud, placing the photograph back in her box. She noticed a small silver crucifix she had thrown aside years ago when her mother died, and she took it out almost out of curiosity. *If I take my wings early in the morning,...* She could not remember the rest of the psalm and jumped in surprise at the patter of tears falling onto the wooden desk in front of her. Liljana was vaguely aware of the encroaching rumble of the air raid closing in around her, but she sat where she was. She was falling into the catatonic state grief had always provoked in her, and everything—the shriek of the bombers and their rain of death, her own tears—could not touch her or provoke her to run to the end of the garden and the safety of the Anderson shelter.

In her mind, Liljana *was* moving. She was walking quietly into the past, and her son many years into the future would have understood the anguish that was claiming her for that foreign country of long ago to which she could never return; to the holidays of her childhood and the walks in the park and the women in their starched lace collars taking the air and the clip-clop of the weary horses; to the schoolroom and the smell of polished wood and Miss Carson listing the significant dates of history; to the summer garden of 1914 and a photograph taken as a token to the survivors; to Joseph, young—how very, very young he seemed now!—and the room in Emily Sheppard's house where Bertie had proposed to her.

And all our yesterdays . . .

An almighty roar brought Liljana's world crashing down in a mist of shattered glass as a nearby blast caused the windows of her own home to explode. She was thrown to the ground and instinctively curled up on the rug, shielding her face from the many tiny shards that flew across the room. The pain of being flung down brought her back to earth and she staggered to her feet as quickly as she dared, bleeding and shaken to the core.

She was trapped.

Liljana knew that all around her in this corner of London she called her home, buildings that had stood unsuspectingly in their serried ranks for over a hundred years were tumbling down like children's sandcastles. Homes like Emily Sheppard's, like thousands and thousands of houses in England and Malta and Germany, were being obliterated along with their occupants. Homes like hers.

She skidded and stumbled down the narrow stairs and out into the garden where the Anderson shelter waited to welcome her. The ground rocked beneath her feet causing her to stumble again, but safety was so close that she jumped up immediately, telling herself there was no need to panic. Then as she took another step, a massive, invisible hand struck her with such force that she was thrown off balance and found herself lying flat on her back, winded and dazed from hitting the ground so hard. Liljana glanced up and was reminded of huge black insects circling and buzzing above her head across the grey square of sky. Then time began to slow down, and she saw the neighbouring house blasting open and starting to fall, the entire edifice—brick and wood and glass—bringing down with it the ten-foot garden wall by her side. Her last thought before she was knocked unconscious was that she was going to die, but she felt an eerie sense of calm descending on her simply because she knew she could not escape. In that split second, which seemed long enough to hold eternity, Liljana saw the short thread of her life unravelling before her eyes, before her body was engulfed by a torrent of crumbling stone.

***

So that was who he had meant, thought Kristjana, pressing one hand against Leo's shuddering head. He lay on his side, facing away from her, his head buried in his arms as though he could hide his distress from her that way. "The only woman you ever loved ... it was her, it was your mother."

"Of course ... of course it was, what did you imagine?"

She hurried round to the other side of the bed so that he would be able to see her when he opened his eyes, but Leo reached out and drew her towards him until all she could feel was the weight of his head resting on her arm. "I knew she was out there! I can't say how, but I knew she was alone out there in the middle of that raid! She was always so careful but that day I knew she was not in the shelter."

Before her eyes, Kristjana could see two men running, an older man and a young man, running after a boy who had been summoned to find them. She saw the fear on Bertie's face and almost wished she could intervene and stop their going any further. But Leo had told Kristjana that they ran all the way from the hospital to their home, where passersby were already pulling the survivors from the rubble. A housewife and her fifteen-year-old daughter, trapped but unhurt, were being freed from the cellar next door. In the Hamptons' ruined garden, an insubstantial figure, limp and unmoving, was being carefully lifted.

"Do not touch her!" shouted Bertie, but his throat was dry. She might have broken her neck or back, he thought, and those well-meaning men might be in the process of crippling her for life. "Leave her alone!" The two men who held her between them looked at him, realised immediately who he was and set her down on the grass in front of him.

"I'm so sorry, Dr Hampton," said one of them as they retreated, "is there anything we can do?"

"Fetch water!" he commanded, kneeling down. "Please. There's still a chance." If it had not been for the dust clinging to her, she might have been asleep. There were cuts and abrasions but no time yet for the extensive bruising she had no doubt suffered to become visible. Bertie placed a shaking hand to her neck and was surprised to feel a pulse beating defiantly under his fingers. He stooped forward and kissed her forehead. "Lily darling, can you hear me? It's Bertie. Squeeze my hand if you can hear me."

But her eyes creased with pain and opened. "I can hear you, my darling," she whispered, and he noticed at once how laboured her breathing sounded. "I'm so sorry."

"Why were you not in the shelter?" he asked desperately, as though it could possibly matter now. "What on earth were you doing out in the open in the middle of a raid?"

Liljana's eyes filled with tears. "I felt lost. Everyone's dead."

"It's all right," he promised, thinking that she was delirious. He took off his jacket to cover her as she had begun shivering. "It's all going to be all right. I'll take care of you." But even as he said the words, he saw a trickle of blood sliding out of the corner of her mouth, warning him of the devastating injuries he could not see. "Leo, call a priest."

"Don't!" she gasped, seizing Leo by the hand with unexpected force. "Please don't go! Send someone else. Don't ... don't leave."

Bertie slipped his arm under the small of her back and lifted her as gently as he could so that her head rested in the crook of his arm. "Don't be afraid, it's all right. You'll see."

"I can't feel my legs."

"It doesn't matter!" Bertie almost shouted, but his voice broke and he found it impossible to catch his breath. "It doesn't matter. I'll take care of you. I swore ... I swore I would. It's all I have ever wanted to do."

Liljana drew her hand away from Leo for a moment and stroked her husband's lined face. It was the first time she had ever seen him cry, and she was overwhelmed by the horror of having provoked him. "I meant to look after you," she said. "I'm so sorry. I never meant to leave you alone. I wanted to spare you that."

"Ma, don't talk like that," said Leo placing a hand on her head. "You're not going anywhere."

"Charlie will come home," she said, but her voice had dropped to little more than a whisper and they huddled closer. "He will live and come home. I knew it would be me who went away."

"No, no, Lily, please stop talking like this," protested Bertie. "You'll be all right, I have seen patients recover from worse than this."

He was lying and they all knew he was lying, Liljana most of all, who was shaking so violently that Bertie could barely hold her. "I don't want to go. I'm sorry…"

"Then don't go. Stay with us, my darling."

"I'm so sorry. I'm so very sorry."

Still murmuring her apologies she closed her eyes. Bertie and Leo felt her hands clenching with the final, invisible battle she seemed to be fighting, caught between pain and the fear of death reaching out to take her from the men she loved. Then quite suddenly it was all over. They waited for her to take another breath but she was silent and still, slipping away as quietly and discreetly as she had lived.

And Leo watched his father rocking back and forth, back and forth, his head buried in her hair, tortured by the knowledge that of all the many lives he had saved over the years—hundreds, perhaps thousands—the one life that had meant more to him than any other had slipped through his hands forever. Leo could hear him whispering the same words over and over again and moved a little closer, only to hear his father saying, "Come back, oh please come back. Come back."

Leo staggered to his feet and ran blindly down the street. He would spend his life running from that scene, but everywhere he turned, all he could see was his mother's face, her doll-like body wrapped in that vast man's coat and his father, sobbing and shaking, pleading with her not to abandon him.

31

The room had become a prison for both of them. Kristjana could feel the sterile walls and furnishings closing in on them as the light faded outside, and she had yet to find the energy to get up and turn on the electric light. Not that it mattered much, Leo could see so little and Kristjana was too distracted to be disturbed by the encroaching darkness.

Leo's box sat in her lap; Kristjana knew its contents very well by now: the handful of significant photographs; the letters including the one Emily wrote in her distress, little knowing the disaster it would indirectly cause; the small cross given to Liljana by the Burnett family cook nearly a hundred years ago.

"I want you to have it," said the gravelly voice of a man whose throat was dry with the effects of morphine. "The cross was found in her hand after she died. She hadn't touched it since her own mother's death, but she picked it up that day, almost as though she knew."

"It's too precious, Leo."

"It is worth nothing except for what it means to me, and there is no one else."

"You never married, did you?"

"No. I spent the rest of the war looking after my father. He went back to his work but needed care and attention. We spent the evenings listening to the wireless, or I would read to him. He never had much to say to anyone after she died. All the time Charlie was away, my father slept in my brother's bed, saying he preferred not to be alone."

"Charlie came home then?"

"Yes, I told you he did. Then Charlie and I took it in turns to look after him. After he died, we sold the house and shared a flat for a few years. After Charlie married I . . . I drifted somewhat."

"Like your mother."

"In a way. Being a doctor I could work almost anywhere. I travelled the world—Canada, Australia, New Zealand, Ghana, Zambia, even Malta for a while before Mintoff wrecked the medical system. It was the only country besides England where I felt at home—close to my mother, I suppose, and where the journey began. Then Jordan, Saudi Arabia, here."

"Did you ever go back to England?"

"Oh yes, I went back for holidays, Christmas mostly, to be with Charlie and his wife, but once he was gone there never seemed much point. When I became ill, I retired where I happened to be. By the time I had started making plans to go home, I was too ill to travel. It doesn't matter. I've met all kinds of interesting people—like you." It would have been a flirtatious remark if he had still had the strength to pull it off. Instead, he sounded wistful.

"Do you mind very much not being able to go back?"

Leo did not answer and stared at Kristjana so intently that she had to fight the urge to look away. "You should go back," he said slowly. "You should go home."

"I feel quite at home here," she said, which was an outrageous fib. She was not sure she had ever felt at home anywhere.

"You're a lost soul and you don't have to be. It's madness to run away from your own happiness."

"It didn't feel like that, I ..."

"Why are you so afraid of your future? Don't you know how many millions of people my age never had one? And the generation before?"

Kristjana felt too ashamed to answer; she had the sense that he had waited a long time to have this conversation with her. In the end, the best answer she could manage was, "Of course I know that, I'm sorry it happened that way."

"When I was a child, my father used to say that when the old are forced to bury their young, there is no hope because there is no future. He was thinking of all the young men who died in the first war, like my real father. He didn't know his generation would bury the young twice. Whenever I think of him, I see a grey-haired man weeping over the body of a young woman he never imagined he would lose, but that was the real tragedy. The young were lost and those of us who survived were too broken to build a future that was worthy of them. How old are you?"

"I'm twenty-three."

"A good age, I think. I can't remember. You should marry."

"Easy enough to say that."

"You pop the question then." To Kristjana's astonishment, Leo winked quite deliberately and the old, cheeky laugh she remembered, spluttered into life once again. "Since you're so independent, you propose. He won't dare refuse!"

"Now there's a thought." Leo closed his eyes, and Kristjana could almost feel the vitality he had experienced for the past half hour slipping away from him again. "Time for you to rest."

She reached across to pull the bedclothes over him as she had done so many times before, but he indicated that he wished her to stop. "Promise me you'll go home. You have made these weeks so much easier to bear. I would have given up by now if I had been left alone. But you must go home."

He was drifting off again. Kristjana folded his arms across his chest before arranging his bedclothes, because he seemed to have lost the strength to settle himself into his most comfortable position. "Good night. Sweet dreams."

"Good-bye."

She had reached the doorway before she realised what he had said and rushed back to him, pressing the alarm button before running out into the corridor to shout for the doctor over the sound of the shrieking alarm. Dr Nasser and two other figures in white rushed past her, almost knocking her down. "He's not breathing!" she managed to shout before crumpling up in a corner and covering her face so that she did not have to look at them making a last ditch attempt at restarting Leo's heart. She had seen it before—they were forcing a tube into his windpipe, applying electrodes to his chest—but she could not bear to look. Kristjana thought that she should have fled the room, but even at that moment, when she knew he was already gone, she could not quite bring herself to leave him and sat uselessly, unhearing, unseeing, whilst they worked on him with the tiniest possible hope of bringing him back.

At some point, she was aware of movement grinding to a halt and let her hands fall from her face. Silence. No talking or shouting, no crackling electricity. She opened her eyes and saw the medical team stepping back and leaving the room, except Dr Nasser, who had the task of pronouncing the patient dead. As he too turned to leave, he shook his head in Kristjana's direction. "I'm sorry, *Wardi*." He paused as though looking for something more profound to say, but nothing ever made sense in a death chamber and he patted her on the head instead. "You knew he was dying, didn't you? It's been ever such a long road for him. Sometimes it is better when it ends."

Only as he turned to leave did she realise he was speaking to her in Arabic. She managed to nod, but Dr Nasser had his back to her and could not see the acknowledgement. The door closed reverently behind him. Kristjana had been alone in that room with Leo for so many days now that it would have felt quite natural but for the silence. She had never noticed before how noisy human beings were, even when they were fast asleep. She found herself listening for Leo's laboured breathing or for the bleeps and murmurs of machines no longer running. She had never seen a dead body before, but she noted that they had covered his head with the bedclothes she had arranged so carefully and she was almost grateful.

The door opened again with a jarring squeak, causing her to jump. It was Bernadette. "Out you come," she said emphatically, "you shouldn't be here on your own."

"I was going to . . ." but she was not sure what she had planned to do. "I was going to pray, I suppose."

"Pray somewhere else, *habibti*, not here. You'll go crazy. There are plenty of churches in the Old City. Please leave him now."

"I'm coming." Kristjana picked up his box of letters and photographs, afraid that the cleaner might inadvertently throw them out when he came round. To her surprise, the cross was already around her neck. She had not registered the moment she had put it on. "I'm coming now."

She knew where she was going. Dressed in modest civvies—loose-fitting silk trousers and a long-sleeved tunic top—Kristjana stepped out of the front door of the hospital, stepping gingerly past the huddle of patients and doctors sitting on the steps smoking cigarettes. The ones with whom she made eye contact nodded in her direction as though acknowledging the death of a relative; some of the patients probably imagined he was. Out of the gate, she took the long, downhill Neblus Road that led to Damascus Gate and the mad, hot, busy world of the Arab Quarter, where she felt so at home among strangers.

It was unusually quiet at the Al-Arab hotel and Kristjana walked straight to a computer without having to wait. "Haven't seen you for a few days," said a voice behind her. "You okay?"

"Yes, sorry. A patient died."

There were four e-mails in her in-box from Benedict, but she clicked on the most recent, dated the previous day, and watched it slowly opening up on the screen.

I arrived home yesterday and found out from your landlady that you had still not returned, so I have booked a flight to Tel Aviv. However things are meant to work out between us, I can't bear for us to drift apart in silence. Please stop running. I am coming to find you.

Kristjana reached into her pocket and took out five shekels to cover the minutes she had spent staring at the computer screen, before signing out and walking towards the door. Two little boys fired toy guns at one another but politely stood aside to let her pass before carrying on with their game of imaginary warfare, whilst outside, two Israeli boys in khaki uniforms talked and joked together as they walked past, loaded guns pointing downwards.

As Bernadette had told Kristjana when she had commanded her to leave Leo's side, there were plenty of churches in Jerusalem, plenty of quiet, sacred places in which to mourn the dead. She could have gone somewhere significant like the Holy Sepulchre and commended Leo's soul to God in the cool and quiet of the empty tomb where death ought to lose all horror. Or she could have stood on the ramparts of the city and waited for the sun to set over those golden domes and spires, as though the sight of night falling might serve as reminder that time does not stop for the world because a few men and women have left it. Instead, Kristjana found herself walking past the site of an ancient pool where the gift of sight was given and the riddle of life unravelled.

She had sat in cold despair the last time she had hidden herself away in that crypt; now Kristjana knew that she could weep without feeling ashamed to make a scene because no one could see her as she struggled to put her thoughts in order. Leo was a man who had travelled the world and must have had so many adventures and encounters, but in his final weeks, when he had found a confidante with whom to share his life, he had only had the strength and the time to take her on one journey and to introduce her to one set of characters—Liljana, Emily, Joseph, Bertie.

Kristjana had come to know them and love them. When she thought of that terrible day in the Gaza cemetery, she realised that she knew something about them that Leo himself had never known, but he had died peacefully without going through the misery of learning that all was not as it seemed. Let him rest in peace. Let them all rest, all those millions of sad, frightened souls swept away by bloodshed only civilised man could have caused. *Dona nobis pacem* . . .

And if there was peace for the dead, could there not be peace for the living? Could there be peace for the survivors too, the children of the millennium who had come of age haunted by the ghosts of the most terrible century the world had ever known? Dare they pray to be granted peace?

Kristjana stood up and kissed the stone of her hiding place, thanking it for giving her shelter. There was nothing left for her to do. Someone was searching for her and she wanted to be found.